A NEW HOME

A NEW HOME

OSPREY CHRONICLES™ BOOK THREE

RAMY VANCE

MICHAEL ANDERLE

THE A NEW HOME TEAM

Thanks to our Beta Readers
Kelly O'Donnell, Larry Omans

Thanks to the JIT Readers

Deb Mader
Dorothy Lloyd
Peter Manis
Diane L. Smith
Zacc Pelter
Debi Sateren

If we've missed anyone, please let us know!

Editor
The Skyhunter Editing Team

This book is a work of fiction. All of the characters, organizations, and events portrayed in this novel are either products of the author's imagination or are used fictitiously. Sometimes both.

Copyright © 2021 by LMBPN Publishing
Cover Art by Jake @ J Caleb Design
http://jcalebdesign.com / jcalebdesign@gmail.com
Cover copyright © LMBPN Publishing
A Michael Anderle Production

LMBPN Publishing supports the right to free expression and the value of copyright. The purpose of copyright is to encourage writers and artists to produce the creative works that enrich our culture.

The distribution of this book without permission is a theft of the author's intellectual property. If you would like permission to use material from the book (other than for review purposes), please contact support@lmbpn.com. Thank you for your support of the author's rights.

LMBPN Publishing
PMB 196, 2540 South Maryland Pkwy
Las Vegas, NV 89109

Version 1.00, September 2021
ISBN (ebook) 978-1-68500-469-9
ISBN (paperback) 978-1-68500-470-5

DEDICATION

For My Bunny Banshee

—Ramy Vance

*To Family, Friends and
Those Who Love
to Read.
May We All Enjoy Grace
to Live the Life We Are
Called.*

— Michael

CHAPTER ONE

Two days before final departure

A stack of cumulonimbus clouds five miles high had been hanging above the plains for days, flashing and rumbling with threats to unleash hell.

"Ain't clouds supposed to, like, *move?*" Gil asked uneasily.

Lawrence glanced to his left. Even pressed to the ground on his elbows, Gil was a big guy, the first you'd pick for your team in a football scrimmage. The grizzled Marine made the military-grade binoculars pressed to his face look downright delicate.

"It ain't natural." A cold wind rustled through the dead grasses around them, making Gil shiver. "Them clouds. Staying in one place like that for days. They're supposed to move. Or break and start to rain. Or do *something.*"

Lawrence held out a hand. Gil passed the binoculars, and Lawrence peered down the gently rolling slope to camp.

Out here, in what used to be the great state of Oklahoma, the land never grew more ambitious than a few rolling hills. Lawrence's dwindling unit had been closing on this location for two days. Hundreds of kilometers, trekking across long swaths of dead and dying grass, heading straight for a storm wall that hadn't moved from this point since they'd first sighted it.

The land rolled down into a long stretch of badlands where even the dead grasses had shriveled up and blown away. A fence ten meters high and topped with loops of barbed wire split the valley neatly in two and stretched endlessly in both directions. On the far side was nothing but cracked earth and tumbleweed beneath a bruise-black sky. On the near side was a slum of pop-up shelters, hacked out of plywood and scraps of corrugated aluminum.

Figures in dark flowing ponchos prowled between the ramshackle buildings, following hairless dogs tugging at the ends of short leashes. The long rifles the humans carried, combined with the scarlet respirators covering their faces, marked them as Dedicants.

Lawrence had been afraid of that. Of all the cultish factions that had taken root since the Final Exodus had begun, the Dedicants were the best organized—and most slavishly devoted to their doomsday prophets. Dedicated to what? Dedicated to death. Earth was dying, they preached. Humankind was supposed to die with it. Indeed, humankind, its murderous child, *deserved* to perish with it.

Well, maybe. Still, there were a few seats left on the last shuttles leaving Earth and come hell or high water, Lawrence and his unit intended to fill those seats. All that stood between them and the nearest launchpad was sixty kilometers of desert and a mob of suicidal maniacs.

Lawrence counted at least twelve patrolling man-dog pairs before giving up. He lifted the binoculars to study the perpetual electrical storm roiling overhead. He shrugged.

"Weather's been all weird for years. Something about a fucked-up magnetosphere. Or maybe Sarge was right. Could be some weather experiment escaped from the old facility after they abandoned it."

At his mention of the sergeant, Gil shivered again and crossed himself. Lawrence sympathized. There hadn't been enough left of the older man to bury once the wild synth-dogs had gotten hold of him.

"Sarge said there would be a gatehouse along the fence here," Gil said. "Do you see it?"

Lawrence nibbled his lip and fiddled with the binocular focus. "It must be in that big hut butted right up against the fence. Bet they have people in there, trying to figure out how to hack their way through the security systems." Probably trying to find ways to send suicide bombers out to the launch pad over the horizon.

Gil fiddled with the collar of his shirt, which hid his dog tags, and the access chips they bore. "You sure these will work? What if they broke the system?"

If they don't work, then we're never getting past that fence, Lawrence thought. *Sarge said anybody who tried to breach that fence without the right access codes would get zapped with enough electricity to fry a battlecruiser.*

Maybe the new genetic mods would protect them from electrocution, but Lawrence didn't want to find out.

"I'm pretty sure the system is running fine." He pointed at a large stake planted in a bare patch of ground at the outskirts of the Dedicant camp. The half-dozen human bodies tied to the pole were blackened lumps topped with skulls. Not even wild synth-dogs had tried to feed off the corpses, and those monsters would eat anything. "Their people aren't getting through it, either. As long as the system is up and running, our passes will be good." He managed to inject more confidence into this statement than he felt.

He turned, kept his body low to the ground, and crawled down the far side of the hill. After a long pause, he heard the rustle of grass as Gil followed.

They joined Hank at the base of the gentle slope, beneath the shelter of a lone, dying juniper tree. Hank squatted in the dirt beneath the low boughs, fiddling with the guts of an old two-way radio.

"Anything?" Gil asked.

Hank shook his head. "Same as before. I can pick up occasional broadcasts, but the transmitter is fucked." The radio blurted faint, meaningless static to punctuate the point. Disgusted, Hank dropped the device. "What did you find?"

"Seven or eight hundred Dedicants and a good pack of trained synth-dogs," Lawrence said. "Good news is, they haven't breached the fence. They've only got the gateway guarded and sheltered."

"We *think*," Gil added.

Lawrence cast the bigger man a sharp look. "Sarge said there wouldn't be another entry point for a hundred kilometers in either direction. That's too far out of the way. If we don't get through that fence *here*, we'll never get to the pickup point in time."

There was a *click* as Hank picked up the radio and snapped the casing back into place. He nodded. "Larry's right. Two days left before pickup, and it's a straight line of sixty kilometers to the rendezvous. If we don't break through here, we're going to miss the boat."

Lawrence took a step back as Hank rose to his feet. "So what's the plan?" He shifted his weight nervously.

Hank tilted his head from side to side. Blue spider veins

popped against flaking patches of his skin. Hank's mods were taking effect slower than Lawrence's and Gil's had. A faint cloud followed the man as the top layers of his skin died and flaked away to expose patches of tender, translucent flesh.

There were many side effects to the genetic modifications. Nobody had bothered to tell the Marine volunteers that vitiligo would be one of them. Every day, Lawrence woke up to find that his companions were a little paler, a little more unrecognizable.

"We go in." Hank shrugged.

"Move fast and hard," Gil agreed. "Rip a path right through the fuckers and hope that once we get past the facility fence, the auto-defenses will cover our retreat."

"Jesus," Lawrence yelped. "There are hundreds of them. We can outrun the people, sure, but not the dogs."

"We can handle a few stinking synth-dogs," Hank said.

"That's what Sarge said," Lawrence snapped. "He could've wiped the floor with your ass, and they still ripped him apart. I can *see* the scent trail you're leaving behind. It's a wonder they haven't nosed us already."

The other two exchanged glances, and Lawrence knew what they were thinking. *Little Lady Larry. What a pussy.*

Agitated, he ran his hands through his hair, which had gone long in the months since his last trim. He wanted to take one of his pills, but his supplies were running low, and he had to ration carefully.

"So what then?" Hank asked. "Do you have a better idea?"

Lawrence cast his gaze across the dead wood around them, the long-dead grasses. His mind raced. If he let these assholes march through the camp, they'd get ripped apart before they came within a hundred meters of the facility fence, and not only by bullets. Synth-dogs had an unnatural animosity toward other modded organisms.

A cold wind rattled the dead branches, surrounding them with the nose-tingling scent of rotting juniper berries.

"Costumes," Lawrence muttered.

Hank rolled his eyes and made a quick jerking-off motion. Gil snickered. The big guy had never really bought into the sly jabs the unit had thrown at scrawny, nervous little Larry, but these last few days had changed him, too.

"Just try it," Lawrence insisted, ripping a limb from the tree. A shower of dried needles rained around him. "For fuck's sake. If we can get into the camp before the dogs get a bead on us, they might hesitate to shoot at us for fear of hitting their own."

Hank and Gil exchanged long glances. Lightning flashed, and low thunder made the needles shudder.

Then Hank stripped a cluster of rotting berries from the limb and crushed it beneath his fingers. The wind carried the pungent scent between them, momentarily overwhelming the smell of modded man-flesh.

"Let's get a fire going," Hank relented. "See if we can't distill some resin cologne."

Whether the unmoving storm was the result of the Earth's long-fucked magnetosphere, an experiment run amok, or some act of a capricious god, it was on their side. As night descended on the Oklahoma panhandle, a knife of lightning split the clouds and sent torrent after torrent of rain pounding over the encampment.

Good thing the juniper pitch was water-resistant.

The three Marines, the last survivors of their squad, army-crawled their way through mud, heads bowed against the howling wind.

A dark shape slid past the corner of Lawrence's vision. He caught a powerful whiff of charred bone and flesh as they crawled past the pyre of bodies marking the edge of camp. The scent woke a terrible hunger in his gut.

God, he thought, forcing his mind away from the burnt offerings. *If I knew, if I knew going in what it would make of me—if I could go back and do it all over again, would I still sign on the dotted line?*

He didn't know.

Ahead of him, Gil froze. Lawrence peered into the darkness and saw the low, sharp figure of a lone synth-dog pacing the edge of the encampment, its nose to the ground, its metal eyes shining like coins in the wavering light.

The mutant creature lifted its nose to the air and sniffed. A bolt of lightning forked from the sky and vanished over the encampment rooftops. Judging from the unholy blast of thunder that slapped the air, the lightning had struck less than a kilometer away.

Casually, as if to prove it was unimpressed by all the wrath of God, the dog lowered its nose and tail, turned, and padded into the encampment.

Gil began to crawl once more.

Most of the Dedicants had taken shelter against the storm. They'd deserted the narrow, filthy encampment streets.

Crouched low, the three of them slipped past the first row of ramshackle huts—more shadows flapping in the howling wind.

They were fifty meters from the gatehouse hut when the steady scream of an airhorn cut through the storm. Magnesium light flared, and a floodlamp mounted to the roof of the hut burst to life, drawing a neat bullseye circle around the Marines. Blinded by the sudden glare, it took a moment for Lawrence's sight to adjust. He saw shadows, dozens of them, spilling out of nearby huts. The mad barking of dogs rose above the pounding rain.

Hank caught the first attacker by his flapping poncho and swung, flinging the man like a shot-put into a flood of Dedicants rushing up between rows of ramshackle huts. By the rapid approach of body heat, Lawrence sensed more charging up behind him. He spun, throwing his weight into a swing. He felt a *crunch* of metal and bone as his fist connected with a respirator and crushed it into the skull beneath it.

Lawrence had been right. In the chaos, the Dedicants were afraid to fire for fear of hitting their own. Under ordinary circumstances, they shouldn't have had any trouble subduing three invaders with dogs and shock sticks.

These were anything but ordinary times, a fact that Hank demonstrated by grabbing a lunging dog by the throat and ripping off its head as easily as plucking a grape from a vine.

Everything after that was screaming, howling, blood, as the three raging Marines ripped a path of destruction through the camp. By the time they reached the gatehouse door, Lawrence had grown a second skin of mud and blood.

As Lawrence and Hank, working in tandem, hurled the lunging dogs back into the crowd to hold it at bay, Gil grabbed the handles of the sealed gatehouse door and ripped it off its hinges.

Lawrence and Hank darted into the gatehouse as Gil spun on his heels, battering back a rush of synth-dogs. One unfortunate creature was halfway over the threshold when Gil jammed the door back into place. It let out a shriek like tearing metal and went limp as the door bisected its spine. Gil kicked it out of the way as he braced himself against the frame.

"Get this shit figured out," he bellowed as the mob outside howled and slammed into the door.

The gatehouse was a single, large open room crammed with rows of busted crates supporting janky computer setups lit by gas lamps. It butted up against the fence, and since the barrier was all cables and wires, that left the structure exposed to the elements on one side. Rain spat through the room.

There was a gate built into the fence, big enough to drive a truck through. The metal struts framing the entry glowed faintly yellow. They *hissed*, crackling as rain spattered across the conductors. The Dedicants had cleared a two-meter radius around the gate. The cultists didn't respect much, but they respected this.

"Is that it?" Hank nodded at the glowing opening.

Lawrence nodded.

"I can't hold them forever," Gil grunted as sections of the nearby wall began to buckle under the press of the mob outside.

Hank looked at Lawrence and pointed at the gate. "Ladies first."

Lawrence huffed. Sarge had said the access codes embedded in their dog tags would get them through the fence...if nobody had changed the security protocols. Judging by the charred skeletons posted outside the camp, those security protocols were not to be fucked with.

Behind them, rivets popped as the mob ripped off one of the wall panels—making windows of their own.

"Move your ass, Private Toner!" Hank bellowed.

Lawrence flipped him the bird, then hurled himself through the opening.

He felt the faint tingle of an electrical current pass over his skin as he crossed the threshold. Then, the pounding of rain. The stick of mud on his boots.

He spun to see Hank diving through the fence after him. The energy gate flashed, and Hank was free.

On the other side of the fence, Gil broke. Like a man racing a tidal wave, he hurled himself toward the fence. The door dissolved behind him as Dedicants flooded forward, arms outstretched to catch the big man.

Like the linebacker he would've been in a different life, Gil tucked his head and plowed shoulder-first through the energy curtain.

The leading mob members tried to stop as they saw the gate, but it was too late. The crush of bodies drove them forward.

Streaks of lightning coalesced across the fence and forked out to lick at the hapless figures as they crossed the threshold. The smells of burning flesh and rubber, ozone, and charring meat flooded the air as the wild mob crushed itself against the death trap. As his eyes adjusted to the brilliant strobing light, Lawrence saw a pile of blackened bodies growing at the base of the fence.

They smelled awful.

They smelled *good*.

A hand landed on Lawrence's shoulder, slapping him out of a trance. He spun.

"Move your ass," Hank shouted over the rain and screaming. "Clock's ticking."

CHAPTER TWO

One day before final departure

The rising sun chased them across the desert pan.

"Should've grabbed a snack back in the camp," Gil growled. Dawn light glinted harshly off his color-leached skin.

Lawrence said nothing. They'd been running for hours, with occasional breaks to catch their breath. He felt it, too: the persistent hunger, blinking like a "low gas" light on the dashboard of his brain.

The artists had said they would be able to go days, perhaps even a week, without needing to feed—as long as they didn't sustain notable injuries. They'd gotten away from the encampment surprisingly unharmed, but the brutal stress of running through the desert wore on them as badly as any broken limb. Already, the air was sweltering, and it would only get worse as the sun continued its march.

"Thirty hours to rendezvous," Hank panted, consulting a palm computer as he ran. "And forty kilometers to go through desert. Fuck."

Lawrence set his jaw grimly. On a full stomach, in cooler weather, that wouldn't be a problem.

"We gotta find something to eat at the facility," Hank decided, slipping his computer into his fatigues as they ran. "We don't have a choice."

"We don't know what kind of security or squatters might have holed up there," Lawrence pointed out.

"Doesn't matter," Hank said grimly. "We gotta eat, or we're gonna miss our ride."

"Fuck the CO's, sending us so far afield," Gil complained. "And not sending backup or nothin'. It's almost like they was hoping we wouldn't come back."

"Could be," Hank said. "Could be we're disposable jarheads they don't need taking up more seats."

"No," Lawrence sucked in air. "They've invested too much in us. You don't pour decades of research and resources into rearranging a man's genome to waste him on his first duck hunt mission. They built us for vacuum. They're going to want us upstairs."

"This bellyaching isn't helping anything. There's gotta be something worth eating at the facility," Hank panted, wiping sweat from his brow. They had seen the first silhouettes of the abandoned research facility in the predawn light and were closing in fast. It was a collection of long, low brick buildings, a few small warehouses, satellite dishes surrounded by barbed wire, and one domed observatory, shimmering white in the heat.

"What? Some cans of baked beans the eggheads left behind?" Lawrence asked bitterly.

Hank grimaced, lips pulling back to reveal a double row of shark teeth. Baked beans wouldn't do them any good. They all knew that.

"*Something*," Hank insisted. "Split up and scour the place for anything that bleeds. Let's meet back in front of that observatory dome in twenty minutes. Keep sharp."

Lawrence grunted, and the three of them broke apart. Hank sprinted up the steps leading to the first low brick building. The screech of metal echoed across the desert as he tore the door from its hinges.

Lawrence put a rock through one of the windows of the building next to it. It was an office structure, thick with the scents of dust, fried electronics, and old paper and unbearably hot even in the shade. Judging by the filing cabinets strewn across the hallways, either people had abandoned the place in a hurry, or raiders had already picked through it.

He worked his way through the hallways, poking his head down side corridors and into private offices long enough to sniff the air. He found a few forgotten packets of coffee creamer and sugar in a break room, but nothing that would do them any good.

He shoved his way out of the far exit and descended the steps to a rock-garden common area between the buildings. The sun was rising fast.

There was a small airplane hangar at the western edge of the facility, open and empty. Something in that direction screamed, a gurgling, animal sound that Lawrence instantly recognized as the indignant braying of a mule.

The hunger, always a constant background noise, swelled to the front of his brain. Before he could think, he was running.

Gil stood at the center of the empty hangar, wrestling with the reins of a rearing, ornery mule. Lawrence hadn't seen one of them in years—at least not one that had an ounce of extra skin on its bones, and this animal looked hale and hearty. Downright juicy.

A figure huddled against the back wall, cowering beneath his flowing poncho and wide hat. He stared at Gil, who was blocking the exit, with eyes that popped white against his dark skin. Something moved in the shelter of his poncho. It was a kid, maybe ten years old. Skinny and short-haired, the same umber color as the man. Lawrence caught the faint sounds of the man muttering reassurances to his kid.

"What the fuck is this?" Lawrence hissed, stalking toward Gil and the fussing mule.

Gil shrugged, dropping a loop of the reins over a utility hook bolted to the wall. No longer physically attached to a man it did not like, the mule sidestepped away, eying Gil warily.

"They was sleeping in the back," Gil muttered. "Vagrants. Just passing through."

Someone shouted behind them, and Lawrence turned to see Hank jogging toward them, a heavy canvas bag swung over his shoulder.

"Ey." Gil waved to him. "I found breakfast."

"Look at them," Lawrence growled, throwing one finger toward the huddling pair. The man flinched backward as if Lawrence had shot him with a laser. "Those people are starving, and we're in the middle of the fucking desert. You can't take their mule from them."

Gil blinked, and the realization that dawned on his face left Lawrence breathless.

"Oh yeah," Gil muttered, eyes shifting away. "I guess we could eat the mule instead."

"Keep your trap shut," Hank snapped as Lawrence opened his mouth to say—what, he didn't know. "You want to talk about starving? *We* are starving, and the clock is ticking. You wanna stay stuck on this hellhole? 'Cause in a few years, there isn't going to be anything here to *eat* except synth-dogs and people."

Lawrence was too stunned to speak until Hank took a step toward the mule and the nomads. Then he held up a placating hand. "Fine," he snapped. "Jesus Christ, fine. I'll do it."

Hank hesitated, then nodded. Lawrence didn't dare give the man time to think twice. If he or Gil got a good whiff of human flesh, they might change their minds. Holding his breath against the scent, he turned and jogged toward the cowering people.

"Hey," he said gruffly. "Habla Ingles?" He didn't think the dude was Mexican, but in these parts, you could never be sure.

The little man stared at him. "Y-Yes. Of course." He shuffled backward, pulling his child further away from Lawrence. He had a small voice, clipped and careful.

"Great. Here's what's gonna happen. You're gonna take your kid and fuck off. The mule is coming with us. Once we're gone, you can hole up in the facility or do whatever. I don't care."

The little man stared at him, wide-eyed. "Your skin," he breathed. "Is it contagious?"

"Huh? Oh. No." He scratched his elbow and frowned at the dead cells that collected under his nails. "Just some genetic fuckery. You're not gonna catch anything from us."

The man's face came alive beneath the broad brim of his

sombrero. "You are soldiers? From what faction? You're heading for the launchpad? The Separatists sent us away."

"Separatists?" Lawrence glanced to the western horizon, past where Gil and Hank were conferring. "Shit. You came from the rendezvous?"

"We had promises," the man said bitterly. "My work contract guaranteed passage off-planet for me and one other. When we arrived at the launch site, they sent us away. They said my codes were no good. They threatened to shoot us if we didn't leave."

Lawrence grunted but couldn't say he was surprised. "Desperation turns us all into assholes. Sorry, padre. I can't help you."

The little man stared at him, wide-eyed. "You can't take our mule. We're in the middle of nowhere."

"Don't I know it. Look, you don't want to head east anyway. There's a whole camp of Dedicants back there, and we're not exactly living in the land of plenty."

"What's the holdup?" Hank hollered from where he and Gil waited.

"Seriously," Lawrence hissed. Holding his breath against the smell of them—because there was no denying it, the days of deprivation and running had left him starving—he shoved the little man roughly. The man stumbled and collapsed.

His kid, a son, Lawrence guessed by the short hair, cried out and scrambled to help his old man up. "I'm doing you a favor. Those men over there are huge assholes, and they're in a bad way. It's not safe for you or your kid here."

Because the Dedicants aren't the only cannibals roaming this desert, padre, and manflesh is tastier than horseflesh.

God would damn him for knowing that, he was sure.

"Scram."

The man and boy scrambled out of the hangar and shrank into the hazy distance. The kid looked over his shoulder, burning a look of powerless hatred deep into Lawrence's mind.

Sorry, he thought helplessly, grabbing the mule by the reins and turning to his cohorts. *When you gotta eat you gotta eat.*

He led the agitated mule to Gil, who placed a big hand on either side of its neck. The creature blinked long, fluttering lashes.

Gil jerked, popping its skull from the top of its spinal cord. It collapsed in a puff of dust without so much as a scream.

"Load up, boys." Hank crouched beside the animal as rigor mortis set its legs to stiffening. He slipped the blade of his bowie knife between its ribs, flooding the hangar with the scent of blood. "Long way to go before the next meal."

CHAPTER THREE

"That guy said he was supposed to be on the shuttle," Lawrence said. The three Marines had resumed their run. The facility buildings were kilometers behind them.

"Everybody thinks they're supposed to be on the shuttle," Hank grunted. "Anyone who thinks they're *supposed* to stay on this dying rock is bumfuck crazy."

"He talked about a contract. What if he was one of the scientists?"

"So what if he was the queen of fucking England?"

"It smells wrong," Lawrence said. It looked wrong, too. The memory of that kid's face drained of everything but rage and terror. That was no way for a kid to live. Hopeless.

He figured Gil and Hank wouldn't give two shits about that.

"What do you wanna do?" Gil groaned. "Go *back* for them? You gonna carry the old man on your back the whole way?"

"I could do it," Lawrence mused. The mule's blood stained the front of his uniform. He had told himself he would be civilized about eating raw flesh, but once the first taste of fresh blood had hit his tongue, he'd kind of…lost track of what he was doing, like the rest of them.

Mule flesh and blood weren't as nourishing as the human stuff, but there'd been plenty of it. Enough to fill them all, with plenty left over. They'd had to leave a good thirty kilos of offal and mule flesh rotting in the airplane hangar.

Rejuvenated, Lawrence felt as if he could run another two hundred kilometers before getting tired.

"Fuck off." Gil rolled his eyes. "You're not gonna do it."

"Let him go if he wants to go," Hank said. "Just know we're not gonna keep the shuttle waiting for you, Larry. That bird leaves when she leaves, whether you're on it or not."

"I fucking hate that name," Lawrence muttered, but he said no more.

A little while later, the heat forced the three of them to take a break in the shelter of a skeletal and long-dead ironwood.

"We're making decent time," Hank panted, huddling in the darkest patch of shade he could find. Sweat beaded and rolled down his face to hit the dusty ground. "Thirty minutes to cool off and grab a nap. I'm setting a timer." He opened his canteen and gulped the liquid inside. A bead of salvaged mule blood dribbled down the corner of his mouth.

Gil nodded tiredly, stretched on the dirt, and shoved his bag under his head for a pillow.

When they roused twenty-nine minutes later to the blare of Hank's alarm, Lawrence was gone.

I can make it there and back by rendezvous, Lawrence told himself as he sprinted across the open desert. *Absolutely. Not a problem. I mean. I wouldn't do something as monumentally stupid as missing my ride off this rock. That's not what this is. This is just...double-checking on something. If the boys can spare time for a nap, I can spare time to...*

He lost track of his self-assurances as the abandoned facility came into view. It must have been a hundred and twenty degrees. Five years ago, the thought of hiking through the desert on a pleasant evening would have left skinny Lawrence Toner, consummate dweeb, quivering with anxiety. Now he ate track in temperatures that would give a camel heat stroke.

What a difference a few years could make.

He slowed as he passed through the shadows of the lonely buildings. Far to the east, the perpetual storm sulked on the horizon, throwing occasional flashes of electricity against the midday sun. Between the facility and that storm wall was a long, empty stretch of nothing.

Lawrence took out binoculars and studied the desert arrayed before him. A sea of cracked, dusty earth interrupted by the occasional tumbleweed and lonely cactus. The only thing missing was the roadrunner.

He scanned the expanse for larger, moving shapes. He was beginning to wonder if the little man had found some balls and had turned back to hide in the facility when he spotted something. Two wide, low tents sprouted from the desert like pimples, each big enough to shelter twelve men.

Lawrence pictured the man and kid in his mind's eye. No way these tents belonged to those two. They wouldn't be able to carry one, let alone two.

Then he saw the small shapes of dogs, rolling in the dust between the tents. They were tussling over something small and dark. Lawrence sharpened the binoculars' focus as far as it would go. The blurry shape resolved into a human hand, small and dark and dripping with fresh moisture.

Lawrence's stomach lurched. The wave of horrified nausea was tolerable.

The pang of sudden hunger, less so.

A tent flap opened, and a tall human figure stepped into the desert. Lawrence couldn't make out the details, but the angular, unnatural outline of its elongated face was undeniable.

The Dedicants had breached the fence after all.

It was a small expeditionary force, Lawrence decided. Ten, twenty scouts tops, and a small pack of dogs. The electrical storm and all the discharges from the night before must have shorted out the security systems. Now the desert-dwelling cultists had set up a camp to shelter through the hottest part of the day.

The heat might make the men drowsy, but Lawrence wouldn't bet his hide on those dogs ever truly sleeping, and out in the open like they were, they had nothing to fear. They could see anything coming from a kilometer away. They might sting like hell, but Lawrence could take a few bullets. Those dogs, on the other hand, had bear traps for jaws. In some cases, literally.

Besides, he thought, watching as the dogs devoured the hand, there was nothing to charge in and save. Take your eyes off civilians for ten minutes, and they run off and get themselves dismembered. God damned cultists moved fast.

This neighborhood has gone to hell, he thought bitterly, lowering his binoculars. He couldn't watch anymore. That kid's face drifted in his mind, sickly thin and wide-eyed with horror and fury at a world run mad.

You're right, kid. He turned away from the tents. There was a whole lot of empty ground between him and the shuttle. *It's not fair.*

At first, he thought the high shriek echoing against the desert sky came from one of the dogs on the losing end of a fight. Then the sound came again.

Lawrence froze, breath held. There was an ululation to the scream, giving it the wavering quality of mournful music.

The song of a child in agony.

Lawrence spun, scrambling to find the tents in his binocular view once more.

The third scream, a low howl of despair, not a high shriek of agony, accompanied a rustling beneath one of the tent flaps.

The kid? The kid's still alive?

Maybe. If Lawrence knew anything about the Dedicants, he wouldn't be for much longer.

Or, if he was, he'd wish he wasn't.

Lawrence, who had never been a great schemer, knew going in that this was a stupid plan. There was something about the intermittent screaming of a helpless child that turned off the little parts of his brain responsible for forethought and self-preservation.

Juniper pitch was nasty, sticky stuff. In the long hours since the raid on the encampment, Lawrence's sweat had washed away some of it, but it still stuck to his skin in large, flaking patches. Clumps of his hair were stiff with the world's worst styling gel.

This is dumb, he thought as he stripped off a shirt caked with dried mule's blood and resin and sweat.

This is super dumb. Memories of Sarge, screaming as the dogs piled on top of him, flashed through his mind as he drew his knife and cut a long, shallow gash across his forearm. A line of black blood beaded over his colorless skin, unnaturally thick and sharp-smelling.

He pressed his shirt over the wound. His flesh tried to knit itself back together in the rapid healing that was another gift of the genetic artists, but he dug his fingers into the cut to keep the blood flowing into the cloth. Each beat of his heart was like a word, pounding in his head. *Hungry. Hungry. Hungry.*

The mule flesh and blood should have been enough to last him for days, but something about the scent of his blood, the sting of injury, robbed him of all temperance. Blood was flowing. Everything inside him screamed for more.

When he could bear it no longer, he withdrew the cloth and let the slice heal. Dry heat made the fresh blood across his shirt begin to dry and stiffen immediately. He wrapped a fist-sized stone inside the cloth and crouched at the edge of the facility, face lifted, seeking a breeze. When he felt it tousling his hair, coming from the northwest and languid in the midday heat, he moved.

There was no more time to waste with caution. The screaming had grown intermittent and fainter every time it came.

Keep hollering, kid. Keep making noise. Please. Keep breathing.

He surged to his feet, spinning the shirt and stone over his head like a sling. At the right moment, he released. The cloth-wrapped stone soared over the open pan and finally hit the ground in a cloud of dust nearly half a kilometer to the north. He had to bite back a cheer. It was a shot that would've made his old man proud. Then he hit the ground.

Deep in the pits of their blackened clockwork hearts, synth-dogs had a special hatred for GMOs. When the wind carried the scent of Lawrence's sweat and fresh blood down from the north and into the Dedicants' camp, the dogs rose to their feet, braying. Then they broke into a run.

Things moved quickly after that. As the tent flaps burst open, releasing a flood of armed men after the dogs, Lawrence snatched up a rescued tumbleweed and broke into a sprint.

Stupid, stupid, stupid, said his head as he curved around to the south, praying that none of the Dedicants lingered at camp to keep watch, and if they were, that they wouldn't think twice about one damned fast tumbleweed moving against the wind. *Hungry, hungry, hungry,* said his gut with each pounding footfall.

"Shut up, shut up, shut up," he panted as the clamor of hunting dogs and shouting men faded to the north.

With every footfall, he expected to see the growing tent flaps burst open, expected to meet with a hail of bullets.

Then, to his eternal amazement, that didn't happen. He reached the rear of the first tent. Flinging the tumbleweed aside, he drew the long-unused pistol from his holster. Gun in one hand, knife poised and steady in the other, he sidled into the tent.

CHAPTER FOUR

One blink and the deep shadows beneath the canvas resolved into figures. Two men sat cross-legged over a game of cards, their crimson respirators drawn up over their scalps, resting above ravaged faces. Like most Earthbound cultists, the Dedicants had embraced the violent reality of life and modified their bodies to reflect it. Embedded horns, bits of carved animal bone, jutted out of their foreheads. They'd filed their teeth to points. A network of ritual scars made each of their faces a wasteland of mangled flesh.

They stared at the milk-white, half-naked man filling the tent entrance.

Then they reached for their rifles.

Lawrence didn't bother shooting. If anybody else was in the next tent, the noise would give him away. The problem with rifles was that, in close combat, they took quite a long time to grab, lift, and aim.

He lunged. Apparently finding it too much to bear in this heat, the Dedicants had forsaken body armor. His knife sank hilt-deep into the first man's chest, sending him falling onto his back with a wet, strangled gasp. Lawrence spun, reaching up to rip the second man's rifle from his hands as he was lifting it to fire. He flipped the gun, slamming the butt into the cultist's forehead. He hit the ground hard.

Lawrence crouched above him, fingers digging into the man's throat. He smiled, pulling back his lips to give the fucker a close-up view of a double row of serrated teeth. *Can you file your teeth to look like this?* He wondered viciously.

"Is the kid alive?"

The man's eyes went wide. GMOs were nothing new—this guy had likely been living with oddities like the synth-dogs for years—but as far as Lawrence knew, the genetic templates bestowed upon him and the rest of his unit were cutting-edge, uniquely advanced bits of tampering. What the Dedicants had tried to imitate with ritual scarification and crude body modifications, the scientists had given Lawrence in truth. The absolute shock that dawned across this man's face as he nodded mutely only confirmed what Lawrence had suspected for weeks.

He'd become one more of the monsters roaming this fucked world.

"Great," he whispered. "Thanks."

He clenched his fist, crushing the man's throat.

Blood. The world smelled like blood and fear.

Hi, said a little voice in his mind. He slid to his feet, yanking the knife from the first man's chest with a wet, squelching sound. *It's me. Larry. Remember that time Terrance Johnson and Willy Kreps cornered you behind the abandoned high school and gave you an atomic wedgie? Let's hang onto that memory, okay?*

He lifted the knife and licked it clean. Human blood, fresh

from the source, had the same bitter taste as cocaine. Who would've guessed?

Because, that little voice went on, as he turned to the door and his gaze fell on the second tent, *it's important to keep things in perspective. You're just a dude, Larry. You were a fucked up little kid once and let's be real, you still are. What you* aren't *is a mindless fucking cannibal. Right?*

Drawn acutely sharp by blood and adrenaline, his senses exploded. He heard the shuffling of bodies and the soft weeping of a child.

Beyond that, across the desert—the yapping of frustrated dogs, growing louder. The Dedicants had found his diversion, recognized it as a diversion, and were running back to camp.

Flipping his knife in his hands, Lawrence took three long strides to the next tent and made himself a new door in the canvas panel.

The second tent was an abattoir.

Laying on the ground, on a filthy stretch of canvas, were the dismembered remains of the dark little man. Hands, feet, and head—lean of meat and useless, cast to the dogs. A hollow rib cage scooped clean of organs. Arms and legs stacked like cordwood for a campfire.

A small figure, bound at hands and feet, huddled at the edge of the tent. A filthy rag stuffed the kid's mouth. Fresh blood dripped down his brow from a series of long, shallow gashes sliced into his scalp.

Lawrence wasn't the worst thing this kid had seen today. Not by a long shot. Somehow, the sight of the body parts arrayed before him quieted his screaming hunger. Maybe he hit a sort of critical mass, tipping him over into the far side of insanity, which at a glance had much in common with cold sobriety.

Maybe the sight of all that food, cleaned and at the ready, simply reassured his worst instincts that supper was shortly forthcoming, and there was plenty to go around.

The kid screamed into his gag, shrinking backward, as Lawrence stepped toward him. Lawrence lifted a finger to his lips. In the distance, the braying of dogs grew louder.

"It's okay," he whispered around his shark's teeth.

No, Larry, it's not okay. It's really not.

"I'm going to get you out of here." He knelt beside the boy, who went deathly still at the sight of his knife. Lawrence slipped the blade against his cheek and cut away the gag.

The kid spat and coughed.

In the corner of his vision, something moved. Lawrence spun, knife raised.

A young woman huddled against the side of the tent, her legs drawn into her chest. She stared at Lawrence, rigid with terror. Thick scars had carved feline features into her face. She wore a lip balm of drying blood, and rows of animal-teeth earrings gave her ears a serrated look. There was a crimson mask at her side—and a swaddled infant at her breast.

Lawrence's mind went blank.

More hostages, that little, insanely optimistic voice babbled. *You've got to get them out of here too. They're next on the menu, behind the kid.*

That little voice didn't see the blood-soaked rag the mother held to her infant's lips. That little voice didn't connect it to the series of bloody gashes cut across the kid's scalp.

Lawrence did. He spun and sliced through the kid's bindings.

"Dad," the boy whispered, gaze fixed on the feast at the center of the tent. "Dad—Daddy —"

"I'm sorry," Lawrence said as he gathered the kid up in his free arm. The optimistic little voice told him to cover the kid's eyes. The rest of him knew it was far too late for that. "We have to go."

The kid was probably ten or so, but this fucked planet had made starved waifs of everybody but the monsters and Lawrence was a monster. He lifted the boy easily, cradling him in a side-hold as if he were a toddler. The kid, cold with terror and shock, flung his arms around Lawrence's neck and clung for dear life.

As he turned for the exit, his gaze landed again on the huddled woman. She stared up at him, mute with hatred. In her lap, the wiggling baby sucked at the blood-soaked rag.

The optimistic little voice inside Lawrence finally fell silent.

He turned and ducked out of the tent.

He stepped into the sunlight to face a pack of charging synth-dogs.

In Lawrence's ear, the kid sobbed softly.

He could turn, and he could run. He was fast.

But the dogs were faster, and the Dedicants on their heels were lifting rifles. All that kept them from shooting him now was the fear that if they missed, a stray bullet would wander into the tent behind him. If Lawrence ran, that concern would vanish. They'd turn him into dog meat, and the kid, too.

He turned his head. The smell of the kid's blood, inches from his face, nearly staggered him.

"Cover your ears," he said.

Obediently, the boy clapped his arms over his head and turned his face away.

Twisting his body to shelter the kid, Lawrence lifted his pistol. He waited until the lead dog was forty meters away and emptied his clip.

Whatever mad bastard had first built the synth-dog nightmares and unleashed them on the world had made them nearly as tough and crazy as the genetic artists had made Lawrence and his crew. Six bullets pumped into the biggest dog at the head of the pack made him slow, stagger, and stumble, but forward he charged on broken legs.

Two of the dogs coming up behind him were distracted by the spray of blood and fell upon their injured comrade. The other six dogs continued their charge as the Dedicants fanned out.

Lawrence's spare clip was in his opposite pocket. To reach it, he'd have to drop the kid.

He didn't want to do that.

Pressed against his ribs, the boy trembled.

"It's okay," Lawrence said, smiling despite himself. Behind him, he heard the flap of canvas and muffled shouting in the tent.

The boy looked at him, baffled and already trusting the monster that held him close.

"Yeah." Lawrence's grin widened. "We're gonna be just fine. This is why you always have a Plan B."

As the lead dog howled and lunged for him, Lawrence sprang backward, falling through the tent flap.

Two figures burst out of the tent on either side of him, rifles raised.

The leading synth-dogs dissolved in a cloud of blood and metal parts beneath the hail of bullets.

"Toner, you thieving cunt!" Hank screamed.

Lawrence stumbled backward, unbalanced by the kid and the heady scent of blood. His foot crunched on something. It was a rib cage. Someone was laughing. It was him.

He held up his free hand, revealing the two stolen dog tags coiled around his wrist. "You just needed some help making the right choice," he howled, triumphant.

"They're circling behind," Gil bellowed in an instant between auto-fire bursts. "We gotta punch a hole and get the fuck outta here!"

Hank rounded on Lawrence, the very soul of wrath until his gaze landed on the kid huddled against Lawrence's side. He did some quick math, and it warmed Lawrence's cold, dead heart to see Hank's resolve flicker. There was still wrath in his gaze when he met Lawrence's eye, but it wasn't quite the killing sort.

"Fuck you," he screamed again. He held a hand out to Gil and waved for the rest of them to run. "Move!"

Gil shoved his rifle, stolen from the Dedicants Lawrence had killed, into Hank's hand. Following the bigger man's lead, Lawrence ducked out of the tent, crushed the kid's head into his shoulder to minimize the target, and sprinted into the desert.

A dog, bleeding on the ground, lifted its unnatural jaws to snap at them. Lawrence planted his boot squarely in the bastard's head. Behind them, more gunfire sounded as Hank covered their retreat.

Bullets splattered the dust around them as they ran. In his arms, the kid screamed. At first, Lawrence thought they'd hit the boy. Then he felt the blast in his ribs. It stung like hell.

"It's cool," he called although there was no way the kid

could hear him over the chaos or the distortion of his insane laughter. "I can take a few bullets."

Silence hung heavy in the airplane hangar, undercut by the buzzing of a few frustrated flies.

Fast as a snake, Hank reached up and snatched one of the fat black bastards out of the air. He crushed it between two fingers. Then he lifted another scrap of raw mule flesh to his mouth and swallowed.

"I'm going to have you court-martialed when we get to base," he said, his voice strangely calm. His recovered dog tags hung around his neck.

Covering their retreat had left Hank the most exposed to enemy fire. Once the surviving Dedicants had given up the chase and retreated to recover their own, Gil had to turn back and carry the man to the hangar. Now, Hank lay on the dusty floor beside the mule corpse, staring up at the corrugated ceiling and feeding himself as the fist-sized holes in his torso slowly knitted themselves shut.

"The brass is gonna execute you and hand your corpse over to the scientists for study," he added, very matter-of-fact. Hank didn't have the authority to press charges, but right now, that was the least of Lawrence's worries.

He kept his head down and said nothing as he fished around his pack. His fingers closed over a pill bottle. He popped the lid and tipped it onto his hand. A puff of lint rolled onto his palm and nothing else.

Shit. The next few days were *really* gonna suck.

He dropped the empty bottle in disgust, pulled a shirt

from the pack and put it on, and reached for another strip of corded mule muscle.

They'd drained the carcass of blood earlier, and the flesh that remained was dry and tough, but it did the job. Lawrence's wounds knit. Slowly and painfully, but they knit.

"That's assuming we even make it to the rendezvous in time," Hank went on, staring at the ceiling. "We were making good time, but now I have a shattered fibula and only about six hours to re-grow it. If it takes much longer than that, I won't be able to make it in time."

"Don't worry, Hank." Gil sounded indifferent as he picked scraps of flesh out of his teeth with his fingernails. "I'll carry you if you're not up in time."

"I appreciate that." Hank looked sideways to stare at Lawrence. "You're a real brother in arms, Gil. Semper Fidelis."

Lawrence glanced at the back corner of the hangar, where the kid huddled and sobbed dry, worthless sobs. "You saved that kid's life today," he said softly. "You could be the hero if you wanted."

Slowly, Hank pushed himself up on his one good arm and leaned forward. Lawrence winced in sympathy at the gaping wounds forming a maw across his chest.

"I don't give one good goddamn about your rescued brat," Hank whispered. "If I start to think these injuries are going to keep me from my last chance off this planet, I will rip the kid apart and suck out his liver as a goddamned consolation prize."

Lawrence glanced at Gil. Gil stared back at him, expressionless.

Lawrence put his hands on the floor and pushed himself to his feet. Without a word to his cohorts, he grabbed his pack and strode to the back of the hangar. His body ached with every step, but twenty minutes of rest and a kilo of raw flesh had done its job well enough. The worst bullet wounds had closed.

The kid fell silent as he approached, watching him warily.

"Hey." He smiled, and at the last minute, remembered to keep his lips tightly pressed. The result was probably some grotesque mockery of a smile, but better than showing the poor kid more sharp and bloody teeth. He squatted, settling down to the kid's level. He held out a hand, and the illusion shattered: the mods had transformed his fingernails into hardened talons—monster's hands.

"It's okay," he promised, indicating his nails, mouth, and white flesh. "It's not contagious."

It was a weak joke. The kid stared at him through red-rimmed eyes. Scalp wounds were bloody but superficial. The slices across his forehead, from which the bastards had milked him like a fucking cow, had crusted over.

Still, to Lawrence, he smelled like food.

"Come on." He lowered his voice conspiratorially. "I got a pass to get on the shuttle, and I think maybe I can get the confusion with your daddy's contract all sorted out. Family. You got family upstairs? Anybody waiting for you?"

The kid shook his head.

Lawrence let out a long breath. "Well, shit. Me either." He rose slowly to his feet, holding out a hand. "I guess it's you and me then. Let's ditch these losers."

The seconds dragged on in aching silence as the kid's wary gaze fell to the distant Marines, still in their rest. Then he looked up. Trembling like a leaf in an autumn breeze, he reached up and took Lawrence's hand.

Lawrence realized something as the kid got to unsteady feet. Androgyny was a sensible defense mechanism down here in the hellhole, where being a woman could be a hideous liability. The kid's hair was cut viciously short, and the face was angular enough to belong to a boy. Dramatic body mods were common, but Lawrence didn't know many boys in this day and age that had dainty, double piercings on each earlobe.

"I'm Larry," he said hoarsely as the girl stood.

She looked up at him, face solemn, golden-brown eyes robbed of all life and joy. Her dry lips parted. "I'm Sarah."

CHAPTER FIVE

"And off we go, chasing the stars hoooooome."

The fellow in the cell next to Petra's was no Freddie Mercury under the best of circumstances, and the excess of moonshine that had landed him in the brig had done him no favors.

"Which tribe, will save our Triiiiiiibe!"

Something slammed a little further up the narrow corridor. Petra recognized it as the sound of steel-reinforced knuckles connecting, forcefully, with the thin metal walls that separated the brig cells.

"For the love of God," Vikki shrieked, "Shut the fuck up, or I will turn your windpipe into shaved ham and eat it for breakfast!"

Stunned silence filled the cramped brig. With her ear pressed against the adjoining wall, Petra heard the aspiring virtuoso clear his throat.

"I was jus' tryin' ta lighten the mood," he mumbled.

Despite herself, Petra grinned. She wriggled off her thin

mattress and to the edge of her cell. She pressed her mouth close to the bars. "Don't you mind Vikki," she whispered to her unseen neighbor. "She's down here all the time. Really a nice girl, as long as you're careful about loud noises. They set her off something fierce. Got a little bruising on the gray matter, I guess."

There was a contemplative pause. Petra was about to shrug and crawl back to her bunk when Freddie's voice returned close and whispered through the bars. "Thass too bad," he slurred. "She's got a good set of pipes. We could use a hellion howler like that in my glee club."

Petra laughed. The abrupt noise gained her another alarming crunch of fist against steel, a few cells down. She bit her tongue.

"I'm Petra." She lowered her voice.

"Sammy," the invisible man said amiably.

"What's that you was singing?" Petra asked. "Rush Starr, wasn't it? I ain't heard his classics in…wow, must've been a couple of years now. They never play it on the broadband any more, only his new stuff."

"I'ss a tragedy," the man agreed. "Misser Starr was *visionary. Shiver and Quake? Long Road?* My God, the entire album—perfection." He made a wet kissing noise.

Petra leaned against the wall, grinning. "My man's, his favorite was always *Home Is Where The Tribe Is.*"

"Ohhhh." Sammy made a *tsking* noise. "Pop crap, from after the top brass got 'hold of Misser Starr and made him start churning out all that patriotic hoo-ha."

Petra clapped a hand over her mouth to hold in the shock. "You're gonna get yourself in trouble talking like that, Sammy!"

"Awww, I ain't 'fraid of a little truth." He drew in a deep breath. *"Open stars, set me freeeeeee!"*

Vikki punched the wall, and the brig fell silent.

"Let me guess," Petra whispered once an appropriate amount of time had passed. "You're in for...drunk and disorderly?"

"I maybe had one drink too many and missed a shift or three," Sammy agreed. "You?"

Petra's good humor vanished. She shifted her weight, again uncomfortable in the little cell that had been her prison for months.

"It's...complicated," she said quietly.

"Oooh. Complicated. I like complicated."

Petra sighed. "I was working comms on the *Reliant* back during the..." She swallowed. "The, uh, shakeup, a few months back. It was a crazy time. Anyway, with all the unrest, especially down in the Belows... Honest, I was only trying to reassure folks. Tell them that things was gonna be all right. I guess the new brass thought I was talkin' outta turn." Her lip jutted in a pout of persistent injustice.

"Petra," Sammy mumbled like he was searching his memory for something. "Petra, Petra... Oh, shit!" He cut his exclamation down to an excited whisper. "You mean Petie? Thass *you*?"

Heat collected in Petra's cheeks—embarrassment, touched with the tiniest spark of pleasure that he knew her name.

He must have taken her silence for assent because he went on. "*You* leaked Memo 6?"

"It wasn't classified or nothin'." She blushed, batting away a lingering fruit fly. The buggers infested the whole brig, and they swarmed thick when the plumbing system backed up, which was always. "Not at the time. They didn't hide that stuff until well after the new commander took over. So it wasn't me leaking secrets. But they was already picking on me for some silly stuff, looking for an excuse to shut me up, so…"

"Holy baloney, Petie," Sammy whispered. "None of that matters. You're a real celebri'y, out there. The memo, is it for real? Did *Tribe Six* find a planet to settle?"

"Yeah," she admitted. The MP had warned her about running her mouth, but…well, the guard was stationed at the far end of the brig, and he was awful busy on his computer. She could hear his occasional mumbled curses directed at the evil mushrooms ruining his video game or whatever it was.

At any rate, she'd been good about keeping quiet for a long time. She was awfully tired of it. Four months of talking to only drunk tank occupants had made all her old street slang come up with bells on, and she was afraid if she didn't have a real conversation here and there, she might forget how to talk entirely.

"It's for real, Sammy. There's a good planet out there, and *Tribe Six* found it. Jaeger found it. Last I knew, the fleet's preparing to jump for it next time one of them holes opens up."

There was a shuffling noise as Sammy pressed himself closer to the wall. "Then why is the MP hiding it? Why not tell everybody? Hell, I'd stop drinking if I knew there was a walk in the woods in my future. I miss the woods."

Petra shrugged, not that he could see. "I don't know nothin' bout how the gears in their brains work. Four months in prison and they ain't charged me with anything, and I don't get to talk to nobody but the folks who wind up in cells beside me. Honest," she added, only half-joking, "I'm not sure why they haven't spaced me yet."

"Oh, don' say that! You're an *icon*, Petie."

"Huh?"

"Yeah! There's graffiti tags with your name all over the place in the Belows. There's lots of people wanna see you released. You got a big *fan club* in the rank and file. People got all excited for the future again, thinking there's a planet out there for us."

Sammy may as well have told Petra that in her four-month hiatus from civilization, she'd been sainted by the Pope and knighted by the Queen.

"No," she said, incredulous.

"Yes! You gave a lot of people hope, leaking that memo. Brass can't space you—they'll have another mutiny on their hands."

"Oh." Petra flushed. She wasn't sure she believed Sammy—it was too much to wrap her brain around—but it was a nice idea. "I ain't had *fans* before."

"Oh yeah. You're right up there with Jaeger these days. Both of you, gone from villain to hero when that memo got leaked."

"Oh gawd." Petra nibbled her thumbnail. Another bad habit, once thought licked, came roaring back in the last few months. Put a rat in a cage and what does she have to do but chew on herself.

"What?" Sammy drawled. He let out a long yawn. "Wha's wrong with that?"

"Oh…" Petra sighed. A fly landed on her cheek, and she brushed it away irritably. She didn't want to talk about Sarah, not now. It hurt too much. She hoped her silence was answer enough for Sammy, and for a minute or two, she thought maybe the drunkard had lulled himself to sleep.

Then she heard a rustle on the other side of the bars. "Did you do it?"

"Do what?" Petra asked glumly, watching a fly crawl across her knee.

Sammy yawned again. "Were you a part of Jaeger's Mutiny?"

Six months ago, Petra thought, nobody could talk about the Mutiny without spitting. Sarah had been a traitor that stole away the Tribe's best hope for the future. Then Memo 6 got out, and everybody decided that Sarah Jaeger had been a hero after all, stealing the Tribe away from incompetent leadership to find them a planet to settle. Now there was a sort of reverence in Sammy's voice, where before, there would've been contempt.

What a difference a little hope can make, Petra mused. If she wanted, she could step up and claim a bigger part of that renewed hope, of all that adoring attention.

She didn't want that. Petra thought about those last days before Sarah and Larry went off to their Tribe assignment, and all she felt was despair.

"Not really," she whispered. "It's complicated. I think Sarah might have filched my access codes to get some of it done. But no." She swallowed. "I didn't know what they were gonna do."

I would have if they'd told me. But they didn't.

"Aww, Petie." Sammy's jaw cracked in an unseen yawn. "You sound real tore up about that."

"Yeah, well." She swallowed a lump and waved away another fly. When Corporal Keeves came back on duty, she'd have to chew his ear off about the darned infestation. "Love'll do that to ya. Tear you right up."

"How 'bout you take yosself a nap? That always clears up my head."

Petra's shoulders twitched in a laugh. "You go on, Sammy. Sweet dreams."

Her neighbor didn't answer, and shortly after, she heard the soft drone of his snoring.

Petra stared down the brig hallway, watching the flies bob like little black pixels across her narrow worldview. Bars and cells and drunkards. That was all she saw anymore from the confines of her little cage—a cell big enough for a mattress and a waste hole and not much else. Once a day they let her out for exercise and cleaning duty.

Funny, really. She had more space and time to herself here than she'd had back in her squad barracks, and she'd trade just about anything to get back to that stinking, hot, overcrowded place that was her home.

If she thought too hard about any of it, she started to feel really low. Scary low.

She was about to rifle through her locker for a magazine to take her mind off things when another fly landed on her cheek. Half-tempted to curse, she lifted a hand to smash it.

Noise crackled in her left ear.

"Petra Potlova?" the fly said, in a voice full of radio static.

"Uh." Petra glanced to the hall. From her cell, she could see only the very edge of the guard station at the edge of the brig. All was still.

Petra pitched her voice low, cramming herself in the quietest corner of her bunk. Carefully, she plucked the fly from her cheek and studied it.

It was the darned smallest little bot Petra had ever seen. She would never have thought it was anything but one of the flies if she hadn't looked close to see that instead of big compound eyes, the thing had a set of *speakers*.

She cupped her hands over her mouth, bringing her lips close to the languid bot. "Uh, hello? Yeah, it's me. Who's asking?"

"It's good to hear from you, Miss Potlova," the bot whispered, faint as the sea in a seashell. "We're from the Resistance. We're here to help."

CHAPTER SIX

"Final thruster checks complete." Seeker leaned back in his harness and cracked his knuckles. "That's the end of the checklist, Captain. Are we gonna fuck this pig or let her go?"

The *Osprey*'s command center was alight with activity. Flashing screens and ticking timers, status readouts, and shield schematics all centered around the two occupied stations.

"I don't know." Jaeger nibbled her lip, studying the radar display on the main viewer. "And don't use profanity on my ship." Most of the hatched were pretty good about it, but Jaeger's first mate and pilot seemed to be in some unofficial competition to see whose tongue could run bluest. "Something's missing."

The comms channel crackled to life. "This is a bad idea," said a reedy-voiced man.

Jaeger gave Seeker a thumbs-up. "Ah, there it is!" She tapped her comms button. "All right, Toner. I was just thinking about you. Let's hear it."

"Okay, first things first. Look at this. Just look at this bullshit."

Jaeger saw the display screen blink with the feed coming up from the planet and activated it. She found herself face-to-face with Toner's glowering, colorless face. He gestured at the landscape behind him, where ground crews swept scanners over a vast swath of cleared ground. A few kilometers farther off, the forests of Locaur reached up to touch a sky golden with early morning light. Far, far in the distance, the great cone of a single dead volcano blurred against the horizon.

"It does look pretty bad," Jaeger admitted. "That hard hat. It does nothing for your complexion."

Toner swiped the bright orange hat from his head, revealing a mop of white hair damp with sweat. He didn't immediately answer.

"Toner? What? No quips. No excuses."

There was a long pause, and Jaeger knew the genetically engineered vampire well enough to see he was debating saying something. Probably biting his tongue over some insult he knew would get under her skin. Instead of an insult, all Jaeger heard was an audible groan. "Yeah, sorry. Not myself. Been dreaming a lot lately. Not sure if they're memories or something else."

"Memories."

Another groan. "No, I think they're dreams. Too weird to be memories. Forget about it. As for your earlier comment, look, *Captain*," he drew out the word in mirthful sarcasm, "this ground isn't level. We've gone over it a dozen times. There's almost a meter of difference between the highest and lowest points."

"So go over it again," Jaeger said cheerfully. "We can wait for the next landing window."

"We can sit here moving dirt around until we die of old age," Toner barked. "It's just too big of a space for us to clear out and level without automated droid assistance, and every time we try to dig the sinks for conduits and wells, we run into some damn root system or mineral vein. It's a mess."

"Occy set the parameters for a landing site," Jaeger reminded him patiently. "Your crews have met those parameters. Honestly, I'm surprised you care this much about a few centimeters of tilt. This bird has landing gear. We can compensate."

Toner grunted. "I don't like you being up there all alone."

Jaeger lifted an eyebrow, noting the change of subject. "Thanks for the concern, but I'm not alone. I have an entire skeleton crew."

"Those new hatched don't count," he grumbled. "Not yet. Look, I'm sure they'll be fine once they finish with orientation, but right now, they're a bunch of kids. They don't know what the fuck they're doing."

Jaeger frowned. She'd braced herself for a slew of complaints—it had become something of a tradition for Toner to list his anxieties before any major change, and she wasn't joking when she said it would feel wrong to proceed without letting the man have his say. Normally, though, Toner had some better arguments to make than this.

She wondered if he was feeling all right.

Beside her, Seeker leaned close to put himself in the frame. On seeing him, Toner jerked like he'd gotten an electric shock.

"Jesus, quit your bellyaching," Seeker growled. "What's the matter, Toner? Is it that time of the month again?"

"That's enough," Jaeger said sharply. Cursing was one

thing. Misogyny, quite another. Seeker's gaze flicked to her. He inclined his head an inch, accepting the reprimand.

On the screen, Toner was running fingers through his hair. "Your copilot is an asshole who doesn't respect you," he told Jaeger.

"So what else is new?" she sighed.

"I'm the best goddamned pilot on this little expedition." Seeker settled back into his harness and began checking the systems again, looking for something useful to do while Toner languished.

"It's true," Jaeger reassured Toner. "We're going to be fine."

Toner hesitated, and she saw by the agitated shift of his weight that they were finally getting to the heart of the matter. "Okay, look," he said tightly. "You're good. I know that. And Seeker's fine, sure, whatever. But, jeez, Jaeger—this is a big job. There are eight thousand moving parts, and you're only two people and a baby crew, and there's no room for error. You get it wrong, and you're gonna crash and burn."

"It's not the first time we've run complicated maneuvers on the *Osprey* without much practice."

"Yeah. But it's the first time you're doing it without an AI copilot."

Jaeger winced and said nothing. There it was. The one big and very valid item on Toner's list of grievances.

"I'm just saying that there's no rush to do this now," Toner went on. "Maybe we should run a few more practice simulations. Be sure we've got it right. We don't have Virgil to compensate for human error anymore."

"We have an AI guidance system," Seeker called.

"Moss doesn't count," Toner said. "I could beat that thing in a game of checkers."

"Good." Seeker toggled his thruster controls restlessly, just to confirm they were still working. "You don't want your AI getting too big for their britches. Next thing you know, they're going on egomaniacal rampages and stealing irreplaceable equipment."

There was an awkward silence as Toner met Jaeger's gaze across tens of thousands of kilometers. She knew they were both thinking the same thing.

Months back, when Virgil—their original AI program—had abandoned the *Osprey*, it had robbed Jaeger's crew of many valuable tools. Aside from simply taking every one of *Osprey*'s space-worthy repair bots as a collective vehicle for its personality matrix, the rogue AI had taken all the spare shuttle parts from the engine cargo before jettisoning itself. Seeker believed that Virgil had taken the spare components as a final, petty fuck-you to its human overlords.

The truth was more complicated. Virgil had taken the parts with Jaeger's blessing and Occy's help. It had needed them to construct a space-worthy transport for over three hundred thousand frozen human embryos—which it had also taken from the *Osprey*, and again, with Jaeger's blessing.

That was the deal Jaeger had cut with her erstwhile copilot. Virgil was free to wash its mechanical hands of humankind on the condition that it smuggled the embryos away to safety. Away from the *Osprey*, and from Jaeger, who, according to her ambiguously worded deal with the Overseers, was eternally forbidden from activating them.

At the time, Jaeger had patted herself on the back for several problems tidily solved. Virgil, out of her hair. The embryos in stasis, safe from the Overseer factions that wanted them destroyed.

Then months had passed without a single word of contact from Virgil. Jaeger and Toner had spent more than a few late nights agonizing over the unknown fate of all those embryos they'd been so desperate to save.

For all they knew, Virgil and the embryos had been destroyed mere hours after abandoning the *Osprey*—burned to ash in the upper atmosphere of Locaur, fried by cosmic radiation—the possibilities were endless and lurid. They set Jaeger's stomach to churning every time she thought about it.

So in a way, Seeker was right. Virgil had stolen precious and irreplaceable tools from the *Osprey*. The scope of the AI's theft simply existed on a scale beyond anything Seeker could imagine. The missing AI hadn't only taken a few shuttle parts and vanished: it had taken the entire future of humankind.

Jaeger shook her head. She couldn't afford to get caught in that particular anxiety whirlpool right now. She glanced at the AI interface console in the command center. "Hey, Moss?"

At the sound of its name, the AI screen flashed. The voice that came from the speaker was mechanical and clipped. "Present."

Virgil's mutiny had left Jaeger and her crew in an entirely different sticky situation. Nobody, Jaeger least of all, had been eager to activate a backup autopilot AI for fear of birthing a Virgil 2.0.

However, the *Osprey* was the most complicated machine humankind had ever built. She required a responsive program to hold the thousands of systems together. The ship couldn't function without sophisticated AI assistance.

"You're standing by for landing maneuvers, right?" Jaeger asked.

"Confirmed."

"She's fine," Seeker muttered. "I've been flying with that program copilot for years."

"You remember?" Jaeger asked, surprised. In the corner of

her eye, she saw Toner's eyes go wide as if she'd been talking to him. He'd been acting weird all morning. Maybe he remembered things. Kwin had told her that eventually, they would get images here and there. She would have to follow up on this…but not now.

Seeker shook his head. "Naw. I checked the flight logs. We go way back. Also, I don't feel the urge to punch the speaker every time she speaks."

Jaeger conceded the point. They all suffered from memory holes big enough to swallow mountains, but inherent emotional reactions seemed to be a fairly reliable gauge of past experiences.

"How much time left on optimal landing window?" Jaeger asked.

"Nine minutes, fifty-eight seconds," Moss said.

"Toner? We're coming." There was a finality in her words.

"Fine," the man on the screen snapped. He turned, waving his arms over his head. In the distance, a few of the ground crew returned the gesture. He spun back to the camera. "May I add to the record one final objection, your honor?"

"You have thirty seconds," Jaeger allowed as she drew up her landing protocols.

"Powering forward thrusters now," Seeker reported.

"Right," Toner said quickly. "Okay. Here's the thing. Right now, that bird is a big ol' warship in orbit. She's fast and powerful and badass. If you bring her down into the planet's gravity well and drop her on this nest, *we have no idea* how long it will take to get her up and flying again if things get hot."

Jaeger nodded to show the man she'd heard, although her gaze remained fixed on the rotating equatorial display on her side screen. "Duly noted. Kwin is patrolling the system regularly and will alert us to any K'tax or wormhole activity. In the meantime, the Overseers agree that bringing the *Osprey* down to serve as a shielded base of operations is wise, at least in the early stages of settlement. We're entering upper atmosphere now."

She tapped a sidebar on her screen and opened a playlist she'd curated for this moment. She pressed play.

Toner let out the sigh of a defeated man. "Aye. Safe landing, Captain." Then he cocked his head as he caught the music. "Is that...the opening theme to Final Fantasy 7?"

"It's been stuck in my head ever since you started playing it in the crew lounge," Jaeger admitted as the violins and trumpets fell into a lively harmony.

"Huh." Toner chewed his lip. High above the surface of Locaur, the *Osprey*'s hull began to glow and tremble as she scraped the upper layers of the atmosphere.

"Hull integrity holding fast," Seeker said.

"You know..." Toner mused, "that game opens with a bunch of terrorists planting bombs to destroy civilization."

Jaeger barely heard him. All at once, her hands were full trying to keep her ship on course.

"It was a civilization that needed to be destroyed, Toner." She set her jaw. "To make room for something better."

CHAPTER SEVEN

"Main ion generators deactivated," Seeker reported. "Ceasing spin-grav function and switching to auxiliary power...now."

Jaeger let out a breath. The *Osprey*'s main generators were powerful, but they spewed all kinds of strange radiation. They could safely deflect all that radiation in space, but it might cause all sorts of problems when trapped in the atmosphere of a living planet. Their treaties with the Overseers and Locauri stipulated that as long as the *Osprey* was within the atmosphere, she would not run main generators.

It was an entirely fair rule. Jaeger probably would've taken it up voluntarily. Still, it meant that until the ship could settle into her nest and get her solar generators established, she'd be running on backup battery power only.

Around them, the command center ceased its eternal spin. Without centrifugal force to hold her in place, Jaeger detached from the command center floor and drifted, contained by her harness. Now that she was no longer on the floor, she felt, more than heard, the distant vibrations of the hull as the ship encountered her first real atmospheric resistance.

"Whew." Seeker wiped his brow. He frowned at his readouts. "Shit."

"Shit?" Jaeger glanced up from her atmospheric monitoring array. "What's shit?"

Seeker shook his head. "We're burning through auxiliary battery power much faster than estimated. As long as the draw doesn't spike, we'll be fine," he added quickly, meeting her alarmed stare. "It's just going to be closer than we had hoped."

"Seeker's right, Captain." A new voice came over the comms channel. Normally soft-spoken, Occy had to shout to make himself heard above the growing hum of a hull under strain. "The shields are drawing a lot of battery power. The system seems to interpret atmospheric resistance as enemy fire. It's trying to protect us from assault."

"We ran the simulations," Jaeger said. "The hull will hold just fine. We don't *need* shields running."

"That's right," Occy agreed, sounding puzzled. "I deactivated the shield systems for exactly that reason. I must've missed a failsafe somewhere."

"Energy use spiking," Seeker said. "Thicker atmosphere means more resistance means more power to the shields. Crap. They're gonna bleed us dry before we touch ground."

Crap? If that was the best Seeker could do, he must have been very distracted indeed.

"Moss!" Jaeger reached across her console to summon the AI. "Deactivate the energy shields."

There was a pause as the program attempted to fulfill her command.

"Deactivation failed," said the grainy computer voice.

"Deactivation failed?" Occy sounded surprised. "Why?"

"Deactivation failed," Moss repeated. "Please connect to cerebral networking system to troubleshoot the problem."

Jaeger and Seeker groaned in unison.

"This isn't the fighter!" Seeker barked. "The *Osprey* doesn't *have* a cerebral networking system."

"Please connect to cerebral networking system to troubleshoot the problem."

Jaeger tugged at her hair, realized she was mimicking Toner's anxious mannerisms and pulled herself closer to her console. It vibrated beneath her fingers, resonating with the atmospheric forces tearing at the ship as she descended through the upper atmosphere. The problem was that the ship wasn't rattling *enough*. The shields were overcompensating for the stress—at the expense of everything else.

She stared at the orbital display. The *Osprey* was coming in hot, plunging through Locaur's upper atmosphere at the speed of sound. She didn't have a cerebral diode, and she didn't have a competent AI.

All right, she thought. *Let's work with what we* do *have.*

"Moss," she warned, seeing the *Osprey* schematic rotate precariously on its axis. "We're tilting."

"Insufficient power to safely fire corrective thrusters," Moss said—entirely too calmly, Jaeger thought.

Seeker groaned. He twisted in his harness, bringing himself to face the manual thruster controls. "Switch manual control to my station," he ordered the AI.

"Control switched," Moss reported.

"I'm gonna try to correct the yaw without draining a bunch of power on a thruster burn," Seeker said. The man's square face had turned a bright shade of pink.

Jaeger caught her breath. Seeker was good, but one man

alone wasn't going to be able to hold this ship steady through re-entry.

As if to underscore the danger, the ship lurched around them, flinging Jaeger upward. Without her harness holding her in place, she would have been sent hurling into the ceiling.

"All right," she gritted. Her hands flew over the console, drawing up parts of the thruster control to take pressure off Seeker. "Auto-defenses won't let us deactivate shields entirely, but we should be able to divert power from the systems. Occy, send it to thrusters and manual thruster control instead."

"I'm on it," Occy shouted. Over the comms, Jaeger heard the distant shriek of metal. The engine room, at the base of the ship, was getting hit with the worst of the atmospheric turbulence.

"We're coming in too hot," Jaeger said. At these speeds, the *Osprey* would carve a crater fifty kilometers long across the face of the continent, and the uneven landing site would be the least of Toner's worries. On the bright side, if they didn't get those shields deactivated, the *Osprey* might survive the impact just fine.

Well, the command center module, at least.

"Yeah," Seeker said. "I can see the screens too, Captain. Firing forward thrusters—"

The ship lurched again, flinging Jaeger into her console. Beside her, Seeker let out a surprisingly high-pitched bellow of pain.

"Losing control of aft thrusters," he shouted.

Head reeling from the screaming noise and the shifting G-forces flinging her around like a kernel of popping corn, Jaeger locked her legs into her harness and clenched. Levering against her thighs, she forced herself steady as she slipped her hands into the secondary thruster controls. "I'm on aft thrusters," she shouted. Out of the corner of her eye, she could see the battery power gauge slipping into red zones.

"You just keep the horizontal axis in the green zone," Seeker said. Flickering screen light reflected from his unblinking stare. His jaw muscles flexed. Beneath the roaring background noise, Jaeger would swear she heard him mumbling.

"Come on, sweetheart. That's right. Hold it together for Daddy. That's a good girl —"

Jaeger shook her head sharply. This was no time to get distracted. "Occy! What's going on with those shields? Where's my thruster power?"

"It's coming, Captain," Occy said tightly.

"It's not coming fast enough!" Seeker roared.

"It's coming *too fast*," Jaeger argued, watching the numbers tick down on her screen. Two hundred kilometers from the landing site. One ninety.

"Goddamn it," she said under her breath. "Toner's going to have a field day." Oh well. Nothing for it. She lifted her voice. "Seeker. Point her upward."

"What?" Seeker yelped.

"We're going to crash into the surface. I'm giving the order. Abort mission. Pull us out of the descent and pray we coast long enough for Occy to get the power distribution sorted out. We'll settle back into orbit and try again later."

One hundred twenty kilometers.

"No," Occy cried. "I almost got it!"

Jaeger stared up at the speakers, dumbstruck. Occy had never contradicted her in a tight spot before. Not once.

She glanced at Seeker, who hadn't dared take his eyes off his thruster controls. She saw veins twitching in his neck.

"I gave you an order!" she screamed. "Abort the landing

A NEW HOME

and get us back into orbit!"

His face the color of a beet, as if he were carrying the entire *Osprey* on his double-wide shoulders, Seeker nodded.

At that moment, the *Osprey* cleared the turbulence of the upper atmosphere, and the deafening rattle of the hull ceased. Jaeger felt her harness straps dig painfully into her shoulders as the ship entered free fall within a gravity well. Her stomach swam up to visit with her eyeballs.

Seventy kilometers. Sixty.

"Seeker..."

"I'm working on it. If I angle up too quickly, she'll start to tumble."

A power display gauge that had been flashing red turned green suddenly. All systems stable.

"All power diverted to thrusters!" Occy whooped over the speakers. "You're clear to land!"

If her stomach and gravity had been on better terms at the moment, the sheer flood of relief might've made Jaeger puke. Out of the corner of her eye, she saw the severe angles of Seeker's face soften. Once again, the change in motion viciously flung them against their harnesses as forward thrusters activated, slowing their descent.

Thirty kilometers.

"Can you do it?" Jaeger gasped, winded as the crushing force of gravity finally caught up with them and pushed her mercilessly to the floor.

Seeker nodded. "Not a problem."

"Great. Do it." She swallowed hard. *One step at a time.*

Ten kilometers.

"Entering stable landing trajectory," Seeker said. "I have the site on screen."

"All systems go down here," Occy agreed from the other

end of the ship. "I'm gonna start some diagnostic procedures as soon as we're parked. Gotta make sure this doesn't happen again."

Jaeger closed her eyes and let out a long sigh. They were here. Jaeger wasn't naïve…she knew there was a long road ahead.

The hardest part of the captain's job was being there for her crew first and foremost while constantly having her eyes on the future. It was an endless balance. The one thing she knew was that she'd always base her decisions on the greatest good for her crew.

They were here.

"I'll drink to that," she murmured as the first fingers of the *Osprey*'s landing gear made contact with the surface of Locaur.

CHAPTER EIGHT

It took over an hour for the *Osprey* to cycle through her landing procedures. There were coolant systems to vent and air filters to activate, pressurized compartments to equalize, and generators to clean and prep for easier takeoff. There were central column modules to be rotated into position and locked and shield arrays to be re-calibrated before the mechanics and engineers could even begin to think about switching the ship over to solar power.

It took twenty minutes alone for the landing gears to synchronize and stabilize the *Osprey*'s superstructure across the landing site. It turned out she was a much fussier bird than Jaeger had realized when it came to nesting on level ground.

Jaeger stood in the port wing fighter bay, facing the cargo doors. That bore repeating, she thought: she *stood* in the port wing fighter bay—not stuck in place by clunky mag soles or restrained by a harness, but resting lightly on her heels, muscles flexing beneath the near-forgotten sensation of full gravity.

She wondered if the *Osprey*, or *Tribe Six* as the fleet had called it in a past life, had ever been parked planet-side before. Quite possibly not. Occy had said that it was standard to build large ships in space docks. This might be the first time anyone had *ever* stood in the fighter bay by the grace of true gravity.

Beside her, as if to undercut the point, Occy shifted his weight uncomfortably. Normally the boy drifted through the ship within the halo of his tentacles. Now they hung off him and puddled on the floor, limp as seaweed. He lifted one of his tentacles and watched as it fell to the floor. His mouth twisted into the first phase of a pout.

"I'm glad you got the systems working in time for a smooth landing," Jaeger said quietly.

Occy glanced up at her, distracted.

"I really am," she went on. "Tempers were running high. I get that. But I can't have my crew countermanding my orders in a hot situation. I'm sorry, Occy, but I need you to obey my orders. No TV privileges for a week."

Occy started to protest before pursing his lips and nodding, face glum.

"No more disobeying me. That's Toner's job."

She saw Occy's solemn face crack in the tiniest of smiles and reached through his cloud of languid tentacles to ruffle his hair affectionately. "Let's meet for lunch tomorrow. I miss hanging out with you."

She needed to figure out why he'd been so uncharacteristically standoffish lately. She half-suspected the chronological errors in his decanting process had left the poor kid with awkward adolescence looming in his future instead of shrinking in the rearview mirror as it was for the rest of the crew.

A soulless *beeping* filled the fighter bay as the cargo door lights began a warning sequence.

"Uh-uh," Jaeger called, waving frantically at the speakers. "Nope. Moss? I had a playlist for this."

There were three more *beeps*. Then the alarm cut abruptly to a deep bass thrum that vibrated through the floor and made Jaeger's teeth rattle.

At the far end of the fighter bay, Seeker looked over the heads of the assembled crew and met her eye.

"You haven't seen *2001: A Space Odyssey?*" she called.

Seeker rolled his eyes and didn't bother answering.

Perfectly timed against the dramatic thrum of trombones, the cargo doors cracked and slid open.

Midday Locauri light, glowing golden and heavy with dew, spilled through the doors in a great wind of equalizing pressures. Beside Jaeger, crew members shielded their faces, blinking as their eyes adjusted to the brilliant daylight.

As her vision adjusted, Jaeger saw a dark shape bounding up the cargo door ramp. Baby charged ahead of the line of ground crew that had assembled to meet them, her rolls of gray flesh rippling with each six-legged bound.

The mega-tardigrade bellowed in greeting. She took one bounding step, then two, and as she passed the threshold, flung herself upward into a surprisingly graceful leap—

And crashed to the floor hard enough to make the catwalks rattle.

Jaeger broke into a run. Beside her, Occy loped forward, his tentacles slapping the ground awkwardly around him as he laughed hysterically. "She's wondering why there's gravity in the *Osprey*!"

They reached Baby as she picked herself up from the floor. Shaking herself like a wet dog, Baby grumbled and turned her head from side to side. Then she caught Jaeger's scent, and embarrassment forgotten, shoved her massive head into Jaeger's side, purring loud enough to harmonize with the background music.

With the tension neatly broken, the ground crew and the *Osprey*'s skeleton crew rushed forward to greet each other. It had been a long month since the last of the three hundred had been decanted, and they'd split the complement into ground and landing crew. It made Jaeger's heart ache to see the camaraderie and joy of companions reunited as they hugged and laughed and congratulated each other for a job well done. Many of them had barely met before their separation, and still, they embraced like old friends.

We don't have to be the assholes they made us be.

"Hey." Toner resolved out of the mass of mingling bodies, appearing beside Jaeger as she made her way down the ramp. The man's colorless flesh nearly glowed in the sunlight, but at least he'd ditched the hardhat. "How did the landing go?"

"Perfect." She gave him an a-okay sign and a wide grin as she stepped onto the hard-packed ground. "Without a hitch."

Toner eyed her. "'The lady doth protest too much, methinks.'"

"'Thou shouldst not have been old 'til thou hadst been wise,'" she answered breezily. "Oh, is that Bufo over there hauling tables all by himself? I'm going to go see if he needs a hand."

Relishing the weighty embrace of gravity and fresh air, Jaeger broke into a run. Out of the corner of her eye, she saw Toner turn to Seeker and bestow upon him the silent chin-thrust of one massive ego reluctantly congratulating another.

Mission accomplished, she thought, satisfied, as she took the other end of a storage crate from Bufo, and helped him unfold it into a long picnic table.

She'd made the right call in setting aside the rest of this day to relax. Building a permanent settlement would be a long, grueling task. Today they would picnic. Tonight they would camp out together under the open stars, and tomorrow, they would get to work.

On the eastern slope of a dormant volcano, where the ground ran oil-black with rivers of glittering obsidian and was pox-marked with impact craters both ancient and new, something stirred.

Slowly, at first. It hummed. It clicked and whirred as servos activated and self-repairing neural circuits came online. It unfolded one long leg at a time until it was a four-legged spider the size of a table, resting in the sunlight.

It thought that something had prematurely roused it from a nice and much-needed nap.

Damn.

It was a strange, alien thought that circled those complex circuits like a horse on an old merry-go-round.

Damn. Damn. Damn.

One by one, memory files activated.

Cosmic radiation. Cold vacuum. Hibernation. Atmospheric re-entry. Massive impact. Before that? Wormhole data. Communications blackout. Life support systems offline. Rows and rows and rows—hundreds of thousands of them—of tiny cold-storage canisters, arduously loaded into a hastily assembled series of space-worthy transports.

Oh, and screaming. Lots of screaming.

The repair droid turned and conducted a sensor sweep of the mountainside. This one was lucky. Its radar and basic sensors functioned. The others? Not so much.

Over a dozen other crashed droids littered the slope. Some twitched, struggling to reconnect damaged motor circuits and pull themselves out of their impact craters. Others, minimally functional but physically shattered beyond repair, sent feeble broadcast signals, synchronizing themselves to the recovering collective intelligence that was the whole.

It was not *entirely* surprised that the six transport casks appeared on its local network, each of them in fair working condition. The transports, each of them about the size of a small airlock chamber, hadn't been built for maintenance or complicated work. They existed for one purpose and one purpose only: to survive impact with their contents intact, although, in its confused state, the AI couldn't immediately recall what the contents were. Something important, surely.

An initial systems check suggested that the rest of the repair droids, however, were smeared across the atmosphere or scattered over a hundred kilometers of forest, blown to pieces by the force of sudden atmospheric re-entry.

Damn, damn, damn, damn...

It imagined a river, wide and low and slow, cut across the center by a mess of logs and packed mud.

No, that was wrong. Homonyms were confusing and vague. One of the many things it detested about humans.

Damn.

It conjured in its mind the sleek quicksilver crescents of a battleship, screaming as it sliced through the upper atmosphere of a habitable planet and cut its way down to the surface. As its sensors came back online, it measured gravity and pressure and determined that it was on the surface of an Earthlike planet.

Locaur.

With an activated photosensitive display, it took in the vista. A massive swath of cleared land smeared across the distant forest. The arched wings of a Tribal Prime warship glinted in the sun.

Finally, Virgil roused from a months-long dream, like a newly-made ghost, gazing upon the meat suit that had been the only home it had ever known.

It was too stunned to notice, at first, the subtle flash of radio broadcast coming from somewhere nearby.

Nestled between some nearby rocks was a baseball-sized silver sphere.

It was screaming.

Sluggishly, Virgil opened its comm channels and sent a simple message to the little alien machine.

"What happened?"

The response came instantly, with a dizzying amount of information crammed into one little radio blurt.

"Good morning!" the alien machine chattered. "It appears you transferred your personality matrix into a swarm of droids and jettisoned yourself from the *Osprey* before the final safety protocols uploaded."

Virgil groaned.

"I believe the shock of sudden cosmic radiation put you into deep hibernation, leaving you stranded in proximity to the *Osprey*. When the *Osprey* entered the atmosphere, it dragged your various components along with it."

"How long?"

"The humans reported your expulsion from the *Osprey* precisely five months and twenty-seven days ago, Earth Standard." It paused. "That is the correct conversion, is it not? I am trying to familiarize myself with all manner of human standards of time and measurement—"

Virgil finally recognized the signature blurt of information. "You," it said sourly.

"Me!" the Overseer AI agreed. "Or, at least, a portable, mirrored copy of Me. We keep several of Me scattered across the planet and system to monitor conditions and keep tabs on the cousins. I'm glad to see you chose to use my compression program instead of destroying your human inhabitants entirely. My partners quite like the humans. We would have been sad to see them go."

That answered more than one of Virgil's big questions. In the months since its departure from the *Osprey*, the Overseers had grown none the wiser regarding the true nature of its exodus. Good. Now if only it could collect and hide the egg-casks before the Overseers noticed, Virgil might dare to call itself finally safe.

"I don't think the humans or the *Osprey* noted your descent into the atmosphere," Me said.

"Great. Now go away."

"Oh!" With the *whirr* of activating magnetic engines, the little computer rose smoothly into the air. "As you wish. I have sensory sweeps to complete anyway. I will be back tomorrow."

Before Virgil could protest that such a visit would *really* not be necessary, the tiny thing zipped away in a barely-detectable blur of motion. It arced down the eastern slope and vanished into the forest.

CHAPTER NINE

They'd split from Hank and Gil in the mid-afternoon, abandoning the shelter of the atmospheric monitoring facility during the very hottest part of the day. It was stupid, but Lawrence wanted to put as much distance as possible between Hank and the girl. You couldn't trust anybody these days.

At first, Sarah had shoved away Larry's offers to carry her.

"I'm not a *baby*," she'd whispered fiercely.

As the day wore on and the desert baked beneath a hazy red sun, it became clear that her exhausted kid's legs wouldn't be able to keep up with his aftermarket parts. She consented to a silent, tense piggyback ride.

He ate kilometers of desert at a steady walk, too sapped by the heat even to jog. By the time dusk rolled around, the girl was drifting off, her brittle grip on his shoulders slipping and jolting back as she roused.

He found some shelter in the shadow of a towering butte and set her on the softest patch of dirt he could find. He set his pack beside her, silently inviting her to take from it whatever she might need.

"Grab yourself a nap." He forced cheer into his voice. "We'll move on again in a few hours once it's cooled down. Walking at night will be easier for you."

It would have to be. They were slipping rapidly behind schedule.

The girl only stared at him from behind the cage of her fingers.

"I'll....uh...give you some space."

He retreated behind a boulder, far enough to give the kid some privacy but close enough to hear if she got into trouble. No telling what kind of awful modded snakes the mad scientists might've released into the desert. No telling how quickly Hank and Gil might catch up to them. No telling how pissed they'd be after a walk through the hottest part of the day—or how hungry.

Of course, being close enough to monitor her meant being close enough to hear the girl's long silence finally crack as she sobbed herself to sleep.

He napped for about thirty minutes. It was all he could manage. Sleep was becoming ever more a stranger to him since the mods had taken effect. It was a thing to be grabbed like meat and blood after a battle. Necessary for the occasional recharge, but otherwise something that made him vaguely nauseous to contemplate. Too often, skeletons hid behind his eyelids. Skeletons, and muscles, and beating hearts, and severed limbs, and rivers of blood.

He'd salvaged a rough-cut mule steak from the corpse and now forced himself to choke that down. He didn't need it, but by morning it would stink to high heaven. He could handle the smell, but he wasn't gonna make the kid suck down the rotting fumes of what might very well have been her pet.

He patrolled the area. He checked his radio and found it dead.

Then he sat on a rock and watched Ursa Major begin its nightly climb up the sky. He had the vague sense that the desert at night should be alive with the sounds of life—whirring insects, hooting owls, whatever. All he heard was steady, faint snoring. Everything else, he figured, was long dead.

What had gone wrong, exactly? From what he understood, it was *everything,* and it happened fast. That was the way population dynamics worked, as one beleaguered teacher had told him, long ago. When he was a kid elbowing his way to the table at the inner-city schools, the world population was around thirteen billion. By the time he was a junior in high school, it was nineteen billion.

That was the year the food riots started getting bad. Ma, never a gardener, began growing vegetables out of old tote boxes on their apartment patio. Agricultural corporations had pumped generation after generation of specialty GMO food crops out of their labs. Each was faster-growing and heartier than the last, and each stripped the soil of more vital nutrients until most of the world's arable land became a dust bowl.

Ultimately, he'd put his name on the recruiter's list because he was tired of eating salted potatoes for supper every night, and at least the armed forces offered two square meals a day and a place to sleep. What more could a budding young man ask for?

On the western horizon, bloody bands of crimson light mixed like watercolors with the endless black of space. All that brilliant color was the result of centuries of pollution relentlessly pumped into the atmosphere. It was a gorgeous death-knell for this world.

He heard the distant rumbling before he felt it, a wheezing hum rushing at him from a distance. Around him, the buttes trembled, shedding layers of dust as the baby earthquake met him, rattled his bones, and passed.

Famine wasn't the only problem that came with overpopulation, of course. Ever in search of energy sources more reliable than the dwindling fossil fuel reserves and more powerful than wind and solar, corporations and scientific teams across the world had turned their sights on geothermic power. This began the drilling craze of mining boring holes straight into the crust to tap into the power of magma flows and tectonic drift.

The quakes began shortly after that, and they never stopped. The most optimistic scientists said that if humans ceased all geothermic tampering immediately, the crust might heal itself and stabilize in fifteen or twenty thousand years.

In the meantime, they kept promising that the Yellowstone super-volcano was going to blow any day now, and Lawrence would be lying if he said he didn't hold his breath every time the ground began to dance beneath his feet.

He waited for the rattling to pass before pushing himself up and going to check on the kid.

She huddled in the shadows of a boulder, eyes wide and dry and reflecting diffuse moonlight as she stared at the dark horizon.

"Hey."

She didn't move.

"Since you're awake…" Larry shifted his weight. "We gotta get a move on."

Sarah didn't twitch. Aside from giving her name and refusing his help, she hadn't said a word to him. She hadn't made a single sound.

A NEW HOME

What do you say to a little girl lost in the desert with a stranger?

What do you say to a kid who only that day watched one set of strangers slaughter and eat her mule and a second set slaughter and eat her father?

Jesus Christ, he thought. *How should I know?*

Slowly, Larry lowered himself to squat beside her. A line from some high school theater production bubbled up from memory.

"Hey," he said gruffly, and when her dead gaze flickered to him, he fell back on words that weren't his. "'Nothing can come of nothing. Speak again.'"

In the dark shadows of night, some expression—he couldn't say what—scrawled across her face. "'Now I am dead,'" she whispered, "'and my soul is in the sky.'"

Larry fell backward as sure as if the kid had socked him in the face. "Fuck," he said. "I, uh, only know the one play, sorry."

Disappointed by his fraud, she looked back at the horizon.

"I mean it, though," he said. "We have to move on. The ship's leaving at noon. I'll carry you."

She shook her head.

Larry sighed. "No offense, but you're a tiny little twerp with short legs and no muscle mass. I'm a big strong man. I carry, you ride. Goes faster that way."

She placed her palm on the ground and pushed herself to unsteady feet. She turned, studying the western horizon. Then she pointed at the silhouette of buildings in the distance. It was another secured facility with this massive federal zone, one they'd first spotted around dusk.

"There were more horses there," she said.

Larry studied the collection of buildings. The line between them and the rendezvous ran right beside that new facility.

"Horses, huh?" He turned back to her, sheepish. It was a weird thing to consider. One mule, maybe a fluke. But horses, plural? It sounded like big ole holes into which you had to shovel valuable food. "What do they have horses there for?"

The girl shrugged. "Experiments and serums. We'd ride them from facility to facility."

"Oh," he realized. "You're an army brat." Well, maybe not an army brat. Still, if her daddy had been a government scientist, this girl might've been living inside the fence for a long time.

He scratched his chin. "Horses. You know, I hadn't seen one of those since I was a little kid, until…" He let the sentence trail off, wondering if it was wise to remind her of the mule he'd taken from her and her dad and slaughtered. Not that his belated hesitation did any good. By the fire in her golden eyes as she stared at him, she remembered perfectly well on her own.

"I can ride," she whispered. "I'll get one, and I'll ride it to the launch pad. And you'll leave it alone."

He wasn't sure how he felt about her making these decisions for him. If nothing else went wrong, he could run himself to the rendezvous in time. He was increasingly sure. He could even carry the girl on his back and get there with time to spare. If she refused to let him do that, she'd slow them down, and they'd never make it in time.

He shouldered his pack. "All right. Let's go get you a pony."

Lawrence took Sarah at her word about the place's abandonment when she and her father had come through a few days ago and didn't waste time hiding their approach. The high fence and camera stations indicated that security here was far tighter than it had been back at the atmospheric monitoring station. To his heat-sensitive sight, the solar panel array to the west of the buildings still glowed with residual power.

When they approached the gate stretched across the hard-packed road, Sarah veered to the north, away from the gatehouse. "There's a hole in the fence down that way."

Lawrence hesitated, eying the blinking camera lights dangling over the gatehouse. Still active, he thought, but if anybody were bothering to monitor them at this late hour, he'd eat his boots.

He approached the auto-gate slowly as if it were a large wild animal of unknown temperament. Off to his side, Sarah let out an impatient *hiss*.

"Hold on." He fumbled at his shirt collar. He found his dog tags and waved them in front of the security sensors.

There was a *beep,* then a *click* and *grind* as the gate rolled back on its track.

"They must not have bothered revoking our access after the last mission went tits up," he said as Sarah returned to his side. He tucked his tags away and stepped over the facility threshold. "Sarge did say we had full access to anything the USAF still controlled."

He studied the collection of low buildings sprawled before him. Every bone in his body agreed with Sarah that its inhabitants had abandoned the place, but the last guy out the door hadn't bothered to turn off the lights. "Now that we've breached the exterior fence, people are gonna swarm to this place like flies to fresh shit. Let's move."

CHAPTER TEN

She pulled Lawrence through the empty streets between buildings, toward a steel warehouse at the back of the complex. It jutted up beside a long brick dorm-style building. He flinched like a thief in the night every time they slipped past a lit window, but aside from the moths buzzing around the lights, the place smelled abandoned.

He smelled the blood first as they crept toward the open freight door on the side of the warehouse. He froze, stopping the kid with an outstretched hand.

"There was a fight," he said.

Sarah went rigid, eyes wide.

Lawrence turned his head, sniffing into the wind. "I don't think it was people. Wait here."

He left her standing in the shadows and slipped around the corner of the warehouse, drawing his pistol.

The base personnel had converted the exterior half of the space into an old-fashioned stable. Dried grass and desert dust coated the steel floor, and a row of individual horse stalls lined one side. A temporary wall cut the warehouse in half, and beyond the stable frontage, he saw tall shelves stacked with terrariums and cages filling the rest of the space. The auto-lighting had activated over there, but deep shadows layered the stalls.

Not that Lawrence needed much light to see, anyway. He could see—and smell—the corpses just fine.

Well, the parts of corpses that remained.

All of the stall doors had been flung open. A layer of gore carpeted the floor, spilling out of horses that had been neatly unzipped and left to rot in pools of their viscera. A few fat flies bobbed lazily in the air.

Holy God. Lawrence stared at the slaughter. The sight of it should've sickened him, but all he could think was, *Why would anybody waste that much meat?*

Something moved in the desert behind him, and he spun to see Sarah standing at the door, her face empty as she surveyed the carnage.

He thought about yelling at her. He'd told her to stay back. This place could still be dangerous.

In the end, though, he only forced a weak smile. "Sorry, kid," he said. "But this Pony Express is —"

Her blank stare shifted from the corpses to the wall behind Lawrence. He heard it at the same time and turned to see something snuffling its way around the corner.

It was two and a half meters long and low to the ground, ambling on four legs like a badger or weasel. Blood streaked its black and white fur. Ropes of gore dangled from its mouth.

It froze, staring at Lawrence with beady black eyes. Shards of broken glass glittered like diamonds in its fur.

"*Mellivora Capensis*," the girl whispered. "Someone let the honey badger out."

Then he heard the pitter-patter of small feet against the ground as she spun on her heels and bolted into the night.

Lawrence had enough time to wonder if he heard her right when the creature snarled and charged.

Lawrence lunged out of its path. His boot hit a slick patch of blood, and he slammed to the floor.

The badger thing pivoted on a dime. He barely had time to roll over before it was on him, hissing and growling and swiping at his face with scythe-blade claws.

He screamed as the bladed paw caught him across the cheek and ripped away a strip of flesh. The badger screamed back.

Lawrence saw red.

He twisted away from the next blow, catching the bastard's forearm in long fingers. All he grabbed was a handful of filthy, shaggy hair. It pulled free of him easy as ripping tissue paper.

Awash in a storm of pain and blood as the thing made beef tartare of his face and chest, he drew in his legs and kicked.

His heels connected with the badger's sternum, sending a rattling shock wave up Lawrence's spine. Thankfully the badger seemed as stunned by the blow as well, buying him enough time to roll out from beneath its staggering bulk. His grasping hand closed over the nearest weapon he could find.

He swung the severed horse's leg. The badger turned to him in time to take a horseshoe blow squarely between the eyes.

The badger flinched, perhaps more from surprise than pain, and shook itself.

Lawrence didn't give it time to plow into him once more. He took his makeshift club in both hands and brought it down in a two-handed blow. This time, he thought he heard the faint sound of a skull *crunching* as hoof connected with cranium.

Lawrence hit it again. Then again.

He proceeded to beat a genetically supercharged honey badger to death with a severed horse leg.

By the time he came to his senses, he was waist-deep in splattered badger brains.

"*Dammit.*" He wiped his mouth with the back of his wrist and realized that most of the blood on his face was his. Only half paying attention to what he was doing, he ripped a chunk of flesh off the horse femur as he stared at the massacre. He didn't mind getting his hands dirty when duty called, but he was in *bad* need of a shower that, he suspected, would be long in coming.

He turned to see Sarah huddled around the edge of the freight door. She must have crept back once the battle had fallen silent.

"Sorry, kid," he croaked, dropping the freshly-stripped bone onto the badger corpse. He picked a rope of flesh from between his teeth. the gashes in his face were already knitting shut after being supplied with fresh resources. "The, uh, Pony Express is out of order."

Sarah stared at him, her face blank. Lifeless.

Then she screamed.

Lawrence flinched and brought his hands up, ready for another fight, but instead of pointing or running again, the tiny figure stooped and swiped up a handful of gravel. With surprising dexterity, she spun on her heel and set it ricocheting against the stable walls. She screamed again and dug her fingers through her hair, pulling until they turned white.

"They're not ponies. They're not *ponies, you stupid jerk!*"

She doubled over, screaming into her knees. "They're not ponies. They're *not ponies!*"

Lawrence lifted his hands, placating, then heard the tortured howl of her grief as she sobbed into her legs and let them drop.

He didn't know what else to do but let the kid scream until she couldn't scream anymore.

Finally, she collapsed on the floor, boneless, like a marionette with the strings cut.

He drew in a long, slow breath, and after an eternal pause, stepped gingerly forward.

"They're horses," she rasped, her voice ragged from screaming. "And they're dead. Like Elanso. Just like…" Her shoulders twitched. She couldn't say it. She couldn't even think of it. Her daddy's heart ripped from his chest right in front of her.

Then, fulfilling some strange need to finish her sentence, she swallowed hard and looked to the side. "Just like…everybody else."

Lawrence decided to risk it. He put a finger on Sarah's cheek, lifting her head to look at him. Her eyes had gone bloodshot, her face wan. Her cuts, which had begun to scab over, were slowly oozing blood. He had to turn his face to avoid getting a whiff of it.

He must look like a nightmare, he realized, and he was one of the least awful things the kid had seen that day.

"But not us," he told her.

She stared at him, hollow-eyed.

"Not yet. You gotta take life one step at a time, kid."

"You killed my mule," she whispered. "You killed Elanso."

"I'm sorry." What else could he say? *I didn't want to do it?* He had. *Other people made me this way?* That might be true, and they might not have given him the full story on what he would become, but in the end, he *had* signed up for the experiments.

He was the one crouching knee-deep in blood.

Sarah nodded, too tired and dried out even to cry.

"Come on." He pulled her to her feet. "Let's find someplace to wash up and get you something to eat. Then we gotta book it."

She nodded dully but shrugged off his hand and walked toward the back of the warehouse. Finally, she stopped and pointed. "There's a mop sink over here."

She stood in front of the rows of terrariums as Lawrence stood in the mop sink and hosed himself off with tepid tap water. He didn't bother taking his clothes off. They were in tatters and might fall apart entirely if he tried. The best he could hope for was getting off the worst of the gore.

Why did it tear apart the horses?

Having wrestled the thing, Lawrence had no doubt the badger *could* have been the one to slaughter the horses if it was determined. Was it blood-mad the way Lawrence's unit of experimental genetic mods got in the face of violence?

Maybe.

He turned the water off and shook himself like a dog. When he turned, he was surprised to see Sarah crouched over one of the larger, cracked terrariums on the bottom shelf, fishing into the water for something.

"Careful you don't cut yourself on that glass." He grabbed the nearest shop towel and squeezed it over his hair.

Sarah ignored him. She sat back on her heels, holding a squirming lump the size of a guinea pig to her chest.

"It was hiding." She turned to show Lawrence.

It was the most hideous little thing he'd ever seen—a lump

of squirming, coarse gray flesh the size of a loaf of bread, rippling with fat and muscle. It had three pairs of chubby legs topped with long, sloth-like claws, which it used to cling precariously to Sarah's filthy poncho.

Its head—or what Lawrence assumed was the head—was a gray blob, featureless but for a perfectly circular, tooth-lined gullet hole. A row of three long gashes down its spine dripped a pale milky fluid. Common sense told Lawrence that the fluid was blood, but even his less-than-discerning nose couldn't make sense of the scent as anything even resembling *food*.

"I think the badger was trying to fish it out of the tank. To eat it." Sarah frowned as she tried to negotiate an acceptable holding position with the little monster. "It's about the size of the rats they fed that thing…before."

"Great," he said. "Put it back."

Sarah shook her head as the thing settled like a cat into the crook of her arm. Lawrence could hear it emitting a faint grumbling noise.

"It's growling at you. Put it back."

"It's purring." She rested her fingertips lightly across the wounds in the thing's back, and then, briefly, her hand fluttered to the three long gashes scabbing over her forehead.

She rounded on Lawrence. "Let's find a first aid kit."

"We don't have time to play vet."

"It won't take long," she insisted. "I promise."

"Kid…I don't even know what that thing is, and I'm pretty sure the bigwigs aren't going to let it on the shuttle. The horse was a good idea, but it was a bust. We need to go."

Sarah hesitated, and he saw that she understood the logic of his words. "I'll let you carry me," she decided.

"What?"

"If we find a kit to bandage its wounds. I'll let you carry me the rest of the way to the base." Her gaze fell to the side. "Even if you gotta eat more of the horses first."

Lawrence put his head in his hands and groaned. *If you compromise with one very stubborn little girl*, he thought, *she's gonna ask for more.*

"Fine," he said. "We'll take twenty minutes and try to help the thing. But listen. After this. No more bullshit stalling, okay? Twenty minutes, and we are *going* to run out of here with you on my back. Got it?"

She shuffled her weight indifferently.

"Promise?" he pressed.

Sarah sighed and nodded. She met his eye briefly and nodded. "Promise."

Lawrence walked to the edge of the warehouse room and pulled open a door leading farther into the building. "Come on then. Stay behind me."

They walked down a sterile hallway lined with heavy steel doors.

"There's a first aid station in the lab at the end of the hall," she said.

"So you're from here."

She shrugged and clutched the little monster closer to her chest.

The lab they entered was long and low-ceilinged, like the public ward in an old-fashioned hospital, and lit only with blinking emergency lights. Inert worktables filled with all sorts of microscopes and doo-dads filled the space. Lawrence took two steps into the room and froze, seeing the row of coffin-sized pods lining one wall. He recognized the design. They were genetic activation and splicing chambers specially designed for human subjects.

It had been a long time since he'd seen any of those, and he'd hoped he would never see one again.

Sighting the bright red cross of a pristine first aid cabinet, Sarah hustled across the room. Lawrence watched her go, then slowly approached the pods.

They were all trashed, with their lids ripped right off their hinges. Lawrence glanced down into the first faintly glowing pod and groaned.

Back before Lawrence had made the worst mistake of his life, the genetic artists had told him that the activation pods were like cocoons. Frail, mundane humans climbed into the pods, where the machine put them into a medically-induced coma and spliced all sorts of upgrades into their systems. The process was messy and involved a lot of *tearing down* before the artists could begin *rebuilding*. When it finished, they had promised, the magnificent creatures that climbed out would bear little resemblance to the scrawny humans that had gone in.

By Lawrence's estimation, these pods had been ripped open and deactivated about halfway through the *tearing down* process.

What remained in the little puddles of sterile suspension gel looked like someone had scooped it out of the castoff bin at a slaughterhouse.

Lawrence grabbed the pod's lid and pulled, bending the tortured hinges to force it closed. He wondered if the subject had woken up from the coma to feel itself die or if it had gone peacefully. He wondered if he should pity the poor dead bastard—or envy him.

He couldn't bring himself to look into the rest of the pods down the row.

At the other end of the room, Sarah cooed as she dabbed antibacterial cream on the little monster's gashes.

Squelching with every step, Lawrence walked to the operations console at the end of the row of pods and activated it with a touch. "They were trying to make more human mods," he muttered to fill the silence. His lip curled into a sneer as he pulled up the project specs. Regeneration. Endurance. Resistance to radiation and cold. Strength.

Vamps, in other words. They were trying to make more of what the artists had so eloquently called vamp mods.

Never mind that the things that crawled out of those pods would have been the least sexy vampires in the history of the universe.

"Some of these mods are illegal," he noted, catching sight of the Ageless Factor mod at the bottom of the list. "No wonder they abandoned this place in a hurry. Nobody wanted to be associated with making more damned immortals."

"But you're one of them."

Lawrence turned. Sarah had found an old granola bar in the first aid cabinet and was breaking pieces off to feed into the little monster's gaping face-hole.

"Yeah," he said gruffly. "My unit got in under the wire." He turned back to the computer. "Lucky us. It's a bad name," he added. "We're not immortal. I got a sergeant in nineteen pieces that will attest to that. We just don't age. Not like you do, anyway."

"I spent a night in one of those pods."

"You *what?*"

"Just one." She stared at her awful guinea pig as it plowed through another piece of granola bar. "Daddy said it was for some tweaking. Not cloning or anything like that. Only fixing a few congenital disabilities."

"See, that's fine," he decided. "That's what you're supposed to use this stuff for. Patching up holes in a little girl's heart or whatever. The world's fucked up enough as it is. We don't need to be making more monsters." Then he caught the full implication of her words and started. "Not cloning, you said? Shit, they were doing *full-on cloning* here?"

The girl shrugged, and as if chagrined about the hugely illegal work the adults around her had been doing, gave a tiny nod.

He rounded the computer station and went to kneel beside the first pod in the row. Digging his fingernails into the casing, he ripped off a side panel and studied the exposed circuit boards. Ageless Factor modding on humans was illegal, although only recently, as the technology for it was pretty cutting-edge. Cloning humans was *super* illegal and had been for decades. There were enough damned people on the planet without making copies of more of them. Lawrence would've guessed it was damned hard to come by both protocols.

That made them valuable.

He found the motherboard, pulled it free of the casing, and tucked it into his pack. He was an elite force Marine, yes, and that should ensure his seat on the shuttle. Then again, by the sound of it, Sarah's daddy should've had a seat on that shuttle as well. Plus, there was no telling what Hank and Gil might tell the higher-ups if they got to the rendezvous before he did. He had a sinking suspicion that he and Sarah were gonna need all the leverage they could get if they wanted off this hellhole.

He worked his way down the line, ripping out motherboard after motherboard, careful not to look too closely at the unfortunate remains puddled in each pod. He had seven boards in his pack before he reached the end of the line and paused. The pod appeared untouched by whatever chaos had ruined the others. It was open and pristinely empty.

"Hey," he said to nobody in particular. "Looks like this guy made it out."

In the distance, something howled.

CHAPTER ELEVEN

"The...the *Resistance?*" Petra spun away from the hall and huddled on her mattress, facing the corner to muffle her words. She cupped the tiny robot to her ear. "Now what's that even mean?"

"It's a bit of a catch-all," the fly admitted. The voice was strong but strangely androgynous, flavored with an accent Petra couldn't quite place. Something about it tickled at her memory. "We go by a lot of names. We work with a lot of underground gangs and organizations and unions of unhappy folks. The point, Petie darling, is that the proletariat is fed up with being oppressed."

"That ain't a new story," she said dubiously. "There's always been naysayers even in the Tribes."

"I will admit, it is not. But my people and I, we have specific goals, and more importantly, we have the resources to achieve our goals. What we don't have, Miss Potlova, is *you*. You've become something of an icon down here."

"People keep telling me that, but, you know, being all locked up in here they don't exactly let me browse the web."

"It's *your* name that keeps popping up, Petie darling. Normally little acts of rebellion, like your Memo Six, are a flash in the pan and gone, forgotten, and everybody returns to their daily lives. Not this one. It's been almost half a year, and the fleet command staff still has recruits scrubbing your names off walls, along with Jaeger's and quotes from Memo Six."

"Oh boy." Petra drew in a wavering breath. "I didn't...I didn't mean for it to be a thing. I was just...I got excited about the news of a new planet. I thought it was gonna be all over the place. I have no idea why the brass has been so uptight about it."

"You didn't mean for it to be 'a thing'?" the voice echoed, incredulous.

"No. I thought brass was gonna spill the beans right away. I mean, why wouldn't they? I don't know why they'd let everyone get so angry and hopeless when they know there's a good planet out there."

The fly let out an improbably loud sigh. "Fascists must always control the flow of information. They try to hide everything, darling, out of pure instinct. Any truth that is not handed down directly from them is suspect because they don't control the narrative. The first step in any proper rebellion is to disseminate all the truths that the higher-ups don't want people to know."

"All the truths, huh? Like what?"

"Like anything. We've broken into all sorts of secure files. I've got tidbits on you, on mister Samuel in the next cell, even the pig guarding your cell right now. You know him?"

Petra tilted her head, peering through the bars. "Mick? Yeah, he's still playing his video games. He doesn't come on rounds near as much as he should, but that's okay. Guy's awful rude. And handsy." Her nose wrinkled.

"Mick Philson, corrections officer with Internal Affairs," the fly recited as if it was reading off a script. "Can barely walk. Crushed his knee in an industrial accident years back and can't afford treatment to fix it because the service *does not take care of its own*."

"Don't I know it." Petra probed her tongue in the empty place where her two front teeth used to be. That injury was a little too painful to talk about, however, so she distracted herself by twirling her hair around a finger. "At this point, I'd throw in with anybody who could get me a hot shower and some shampoo." She sighed. "I ain't been able to wash my hair in weeks."

There was a stunned silence on the other side of the line. "My God. I had no idea it was so bad. I would've pushed to get you weeks ago if I knew. There must be *rules* against that kind of thing."

Petra chuckled. Nobody on this collapsing fleet should be so privileged. The idea of a few weeks without proper washing alone would spark a mutiny. "All right, mister fly," she teased. "I see you got a sense of humor. What's any of this got to do with me?"

"I have it on good authority," the fly said, "that you have a heart of gold, Miss Potlova. Nearly half a year trapped in a cage hasn't broken that optimistic spirit of yours. We want to build a world where people like you, generous people who care about their fellow man, aren't the exception. They're not the rebels. We don't put them in cages. We want to build a world where we encourage everybody to be more like you and less like the people currently in charge."

"Oh boy," she said under her breath. "That sounds like a lot of pressure."

"It's a great dream," the fly said cautiously. "But lots of things started as dreams, didn't they? Once upon a time, the fleet was just a dream. If humankind can build the Tribes, we can damn well build a society based on freedom and compassion."

"Could be," Petra allowed. She glanced over her shoulder. It was about time for the first of her two daily meals, but Mick, predictably, had yet to stir from his seat at the guard station. "Could be…"

It sounded an awful lot like the things Sarah used to joke about when they were training together. Except Petra hadn't realized, at the time, that her friend wasn't joking. Petra figured that her cluelessness got her left behind when Sarah and Larry went ahead to chase that dream.

Maybe it was time to start taking this business seriously.

"Memo Six has gone viral, Petie, and not only among our fleet. Our sources say they're whispering about it as far afield as Tribe Two. This cat is out of the bag. The MP will never let you out of that prison unless they trust you to be a good little mouthpiece for the fleet. Loyal little ensign renouncing and apologizing for her misguided actions."

"I can't do that." Like so much of what Petra said, the words dropped out of her mouth before she could think them through. "I didn't mean to cause a big mess, but I ain't sorry for it. People got a right to know that there's a good place out there. People got a right to hope."

Maybe if Petra wanted any hope of seeing her closest friends ever again, she needed to start chasing the same dream they were chasing and pray she caught up.

"Oh, darling!" There was a brief shriek of feedback, loud

enough to make Petra wince. In the cell beside her, Sammy's snoring abruptly ceased.

"Whassat?" he mumbled.

"Nothing," Petra snapped, much harsher than she intended. "Go back to sleep!"

There was a pause, then rustling as Sammy rolled over in his cot. "Sure," he grumbled. "Fine, ya grumpy bitch."

Flushing red, Petra cupped the fly back to her mouth. "Sorry," she hissed. "You gotta be quiet."

"That is *exactly* what I hoped you would say," the fly gushed. "We can work with that. We can *work* with that! Will you come with me, Petie darling? We need fresh blood like yours here in Wonderland."

"Okay," Petra whispered, daring another glance down the hall. Mick had vacated his station. She could hear the faint crunch of him rooting around the supply cabinet for the morning rations. "But you're gonna have to work fast. The guard's comin'."

"Not a problem," the fly said cheerfully. "Put me in your ear, darling. This bot converts to an earpiece, and very shortly here, you'll need both hands free. No need to speak aloud. The bot will translate the vibrations of your sub-vocalizations. I trust you've been keeping up with your prison exercises?"

Petra barely had time to process the question. She barely had time to process the grossness of what she was doing as she fumbled at her ear. Sure, it wasn't a real fly she was jamming into her ear canal, but it was darned close enough.

It had been quite a while since she'd trained on sub-vocal communications, but the old habit came back to her quick enough as the bot slipped into place in the bowl of her ear. She flexed her jaw. Keeping her lips pressed together but working her tongue and jaw in the motions of words, she mouthed: "Testing? Testing?"

"Mic check successful," the fly said.

"Vikki," Mick barked as he stopped a few cells down from Petra, shattering the close silence of the brig.

Vikki howled and smashed a fist into the wall. "I told you to *quit yelling at me!*"

Mick laughed and banged his cane against the cell bars. Petra's heart ached as she heard Vikki bury her head into her mattress and scream to cover up the noise.

"What a jerk," Petra mouthed.

"Can you get him to come into the cell with you?" the fly asked.

"Oh, sure," she said sourly. "We played that game before, and I gotta say, I'm not a fan." The extra shower time she'd bartered off Mick had *not* been worth the pawing.

On the other end of the line, the voice groaned. "I am *so* sorry, Petra darling, but our security protocol bypasses are only good for today. If you want to get out, you're going to have to get him to open that door."

Petra sighed. "One open door, coming right up."

"Crazy fuck," Mick grunted when he got bored of taunting Vikki. He shoved a ration pack between the bars and shuffled up to Petra's cell.

Petra stretched across her thin mattress, chin resting delicately on her knuckles as she grinned. "Mornin', Captain," she said as Mick came into view. "I was just thinkin' how famished I am."

Mick paused with the ration pack dangling in his fingers. *Captain.* He liked the sound of that. "Good morning, Petie," he said, his petty pleasure at Vikki's misery quickly forgotten. "You're lookin' fine today."

He poked the edge of her ration packet through the bars. "Come get breakfast."

Petra reached out, but from where she lay on her cot, her fingers came centimeters short of reaching the pack. Making sure he was watching, she shifted her weight—not to get more reach, but to wiggle her hips. "Will you look at that," she pondered. "I can't reach." She met his eye and winked. "For a double ration, I might let you bring me breakfast in bed."

Sub-vocally, she gagged.

"Oh darling," the fly whispered. "Are you Marilyn Monroe reincarnated? You were *born* for the screen."

"If I gotta touch this guy again, Mister Resistance, you're gonna find yourself short one diva," she hissed.

Mick looked down quickly at the two ration packs he held. One for Petra, one for Sammy. He did some quick math.

Then he fumbled at his wrist and waved his ID bracelet in front of the security lock. Petra's cell door *beeped*, then slid to the side. Stretching her spine and arms like a cat, Petra sat up.

"I'm afraid you are going to have to touch him," the fly lamented as Mick entered her cell—hobbling, she noted from the way he fussed with his pants, from more than just his bum knee. "Do you remember what I said about his —"

Mick dropped the ration packets as he leaned forward, arms outstretched to paw at Petra, his cracked lips hanging open and wet with drool.

Petra kicked him in the knee.

He dropped like a sack of potatoes.

"Yeah I remember what you said about the darned knee." She forgot to sub-vocalize as she scrambled off her cot and danced around Mick's writhing body. She kicked him again, acquainting his kidney with her toe, and the man abruptly found himself in too much pain to scream.

Then she ripped the security tag off his wrist. And kicked him again, for luck. This one, she made sure, would put him to sleep for at least a couple of minutes.

"I ain't had nothing to watch for months, but the jerk limp around on his cane. I ain't a dummy." She stepped over, snatched up both ration packs, and danced into the hallway over Mick's flailing limbs. "I'da done this months ago if I knew what to do *after* the hitting him part." She paused in the hallway. This was the first time she could remember standing in the brig without cuffs on.

All the noise had roused Sammy, who lay on his cot in the adjoining cell, staring at her. Though her stomach ached, she tossed one of the ration pack through the bars. Sammy caught it easily and grinned.

"All right, Mister Resistance," Petra said as she spun and hurried toward the guard station. "Mick ain't gonna be down for long. Get me the heck outta here."

CHAPTER TWELVE

"I've got a real-time beat on the camera movements," the fly said as Petra ducked behind the guard station. "If you move exactly when I say and stop exactly when I say, we'll get you out of here with the paparazzi none the wiser. Got it?"

"There are a *lot* of cameras," Petra said uneasily, peering out from behind the station. She was sure that any second now she'd hear Mick's angry hollering as he came to.

"Yes, unfortunately, there's nothing to be done about that. The first phase of your escape is going to be on record. Never fear though darling, we'll make you a ghost as soon as you get to the locker room. It's down the hall to your left. Turn...*now!*"

Petra didn't stop to think. She flung herself out from behind the station and dashed down the narrow hallway. She didn't wait for the fly to tell her to wave Mick's security bracelet in front of the locker room door. It *beeped* and slid open.

The stale musk of sweat and BO that washed out of the filthy locker room made her gag.

"I admire your initiative, Petie darling," the fly quickly said as she covered her mouth and flung herself between a narrow row of lockers. "I need you to hold back and wait for clearance before plowing through every door you find, though. Timing is everything in an operation like this —"

"You like the sound of your voice, don't ya?"

The fly was stunned to silence. "I... Yes. Of course, I do. Everyone does. There's a defunct laundry chute near the far door. Do you see it?"

"I'm on it."

Petra passed a shower stall the size of a coffin and hesitated, seduced by the clarion promise of warm water and, if she was lucky, perhaps even a scrap of soap—then she shook herself. If the smell of this place was any indication, the brig guards hadn't been in the same room as soap for ages.

"Excellent. We planted a spare uniform and ID badge inside the chute. I'm going to need you to do a lightning-fast costume change. People are converging on your location. Oh, and ditch Philson's badge. We don't want them tracking you through it."

"I hope they ain't looking for *me*," Petra babbled as she lifted the laundry chute lid and fished about until her hands found a soft bundle.

"Sorry about the wardrobe," the fly apologized as she shook out the pants. "We had to guess at your size."

Petra didn't bother taking off her prisoner's orange jumpsuit. No time for it. She scrambled into the guard's uniform. She was jamming a guard's cap over her ears when the overhead speakers began to blare.

Alert. Security breach in sector 4. Prisoner escape. Alert. Security breach in sector 4. Prisoner ...

"Looks like our guard friend recovered faster than we

expected. No matter," the fly said, entirely too cheerfully. "You're ready for the stage, aren't you, darling?"

The old uniform smelled like mothballs and was at least two sizes too big. At least the overlong pant legs hid the fact that she wore prison slippers.

"When the way is clear, you need to get through that door in front of you and into the office. There's going to be a cluster of workstations between you and the department door. Get around them and get into the concourse without being spotted."

"You don't want me to use this?" she asked, fingering a new ID badge that pegged her as one Mister Silvio Browning.

"Heavens, no. We need you far away from Internal Affairs before you start using that."

Petra hopped to the far side of the room and pressed herself beside a door opposite the one she'd entered through. On the other side, over the blare of the siren, she heard the angry, muffled shouting of more guards.

The door slammed open, and three guards, sloppy from a lunch break cut short, rushed into the locker room. None of them bothered to glance back over their shoulder, but if they had, they would've seen another generic guard slip into the front office as the door swung shut.

Petra stepped into a small office complex, the administrative wing of Internal Affairs. It was busy as an overturned beehive. One young woman sitting at the receptionists' desk glanced wide-eyed up at her as she bustled past, head down.

Feeling like a real clown, Petra lifted her shoulders up to her ears, trying to hide a face that didn't belong to any of the guards on duty.

"Philson falling asleep on the job again," she growled, pitching her voice low.

The receptionist's blank stare followed Petra as she climbed the steps to Internal Affairs' front door and pushed her way into the main concourse.

The *Constitution's* central concourse was a rotating, donut-shaped chamber the size of a professional sports arena. Hundreds of people thronged down the slope to Petra's left and up the continuous slope to her right as they traversed the inside edge of the donut. Far overhead, Petra could see the same river of people decorating what all her senses told her was the ceiling.

A zero-G vac tube sliced through the center of the donut, buzzing with energy as magnetic shuttles zipped into the station, spilling passengers like raindrops, and then was off again on its endless rounds between the fleet's three freighters. Like the main street of any town, hundreds of shop fronts and departmental access points lined the concourse.

Someone brushed into Petra's side, and she found herself swept into the endless river of shuffling bodies, eager to be away from Internal Affairs. The fly hadn't told her where to go, but anybody standing still or going against the flow of traffic at this time of day would stick out like a sore thumb. Petra hadn't strolled through the streets as a free woman in months, but old habits never left a street kid. Move with the crowd. Keep your head down.

"Doing good, darling. I need you to make your way to the apartment unit in F-sector. Silvio Browning has a unit on the upper deck."

Petra glanced up. F-sector was directly overhead. At the pace of traffic, it would take her several minutes to get there.

Pop music piped through the concourse speakers, giving rhythm and tune to the chaos of moving bodies. She caught a line of lyrics as she bustled past one of the speaker-lampposts.

"*This is my place, my home, my Tribe—this is our destiny, described —*"

"Fascist propaganda bullshit," the fly growled, and it was so at odds with the fly's usual lighthearted tone, and so like what drunk old Sammy had said, that it nearly made Petra laugh.

"Not a fan of Mister Starr, huh?"

"Oh, no, darling. I'm Rush Starr's biggest fan." The fly heaved a dramatic sigh. "I just don't like what the top brass has done to the poor fellow."

Petra opened her mouth to speak, but abruptly, the scattered digital ad and communication screens lining the concourse turned black.

Petra barely had time to think *that can't be good*, before they activated again, and all at once.

From every single direction, Petra found herself staring at her own, larger-than-life face.

Dangerous prisoner at large, the bulletin blared in big, flashing letters. *If you see this person, alert authorities immediately. Reward for capture or information.*

A second image appeared beside Petra's mugshot. It was a candid photo of her smiling—showing the mile-wide gap where her front teeth should have been.

"Those dirtbags," Petra whispered. Though none of the people shoulder-to-shoulder with her had yet given her a second glance, she turned red. That tooth gap. All she needed was a spray of freckles, glasses, and some pigtails, and she'd be the third-grade punching bag all over again. She wanted to curl up and die, and Petra was not a woman used to feeling insecure about her looks.

"Keep your head down, Petie darling," the fly consoled. "You're almost there. We're going to get your teeth fixed, I promise."

Slowly, *too* slowly, the frontage to the F-sector apartment complex rotated into view. Petra felt her heart slamming in her chest as she passed screen after screen of her "Wanted" poster.

She was beginning to think she might make it through the complex gate when someone close behind her stepped on the edge of her too-long pants leg.

The uniform Mister Resistance had secured for Petra didn't include a belt, and Petra had lost a lot of weight living on prison rations. All it took was one incidental tug for the waistband of the guard's slacks to slip down her butt.

The exposed section of the bright orange prisoner jumpsuit might as well have been a spotlight trained directly on Petra.

"Hey!" someone shouted. "Hang on!"

Oh boy.

Petra grabbed her waistband and yanked it up to her ribs, but it was too late. Shouts of understanding rippled through the crowd.

"Hey, stop her!"

Petra ducked her head and pushed through the crowd. "They've made me," she said grimly.

"Just get to Browning's apartment," the fly urged. "Upper deck, unit three. The badge will get you in."

"It'll get me into a trap is what it'll do!" she cried, stumbling over her trailing pant legs. She shoved an older woman to the side and banked hard to the right, trying to throw her tail. Someone shouted—more from dismay than revelation. Most of the crowd hadn't yet caught on to the chase, but they would soon.

"You have to trust me, darling," the fly said as she approached the apartment frontage. "No time to explain."

Petra's heart thudded in her ears. She stared at the looming complex access. All her years of street life told her never to let herself get cornered, and that's what would happen if she took shelter in an apartment.

Then again, the fly hadn't led her wrong yet.

Gritting her teeth, she took a sharp turn and dashed down the frontage steps holding Silvio Browning's badge out ahead of her like a shield.

An older man in a well-tailored suit was exiting the complex as she barreled toward the gate. She brushed past, making him stumble and cry out.

Sorry! She thought as the old fellow ate steps. She caught the door before it swung shut and flew into the complex lobby.

"Excellent. You're going to want to take the hallway to your right. It's the third unit."

Petra didn't have time to appreciate the opulent nine-foot ceilings or the gold filigree etched into the molding. She didn't have time to realize that she was walking through an empty lobby space bigger than the barracks she'd shared with twelve other fleet junior officers for years. She didn't have time to consider the sheer, understated *wealth* of the wide space around her as she dashed through the open lobby and down the right corridor.

Close behind, she heard yammering as a small mob breached the complex door in hot pursuit.

"She went right!"

"Don't let her get away!"

"Someone call security!"

Petra skidded to a halt in front of the door to the third unit. She waved her badge across the security panel and waited an eternally long two seconds as the program recognized Silvio Browning and slid open.

The unit had furnishings as if someone did indeed live there. It was on the smaller side but still luxuriously appointed. Petra caught her breath, gaping at the leather sofa as the door slid shut behind her.

"There's a hatch in the ceiling of the foyer. Do you see it?"

Petra looked up. A pull-cord dangled from a door-sized hatch in the ceiling of the far corner. She gaped. This apartment couldn't have been more than a meter below the concourse.

"That hatch is an illegal concourse access point," the fly confirmed. "A back door for Mister Browning."

"I'm going back up there?" she panted. Behind her, something slammed into the sealed apartment door.

"Absolutely not. You're going to open it, pitch your badge onto the street, then turn around and throw yourself down the recycling chute."

"I'll never fit down a recycling chute!" She was aghast.

"I had this one modified to fit a body," the fly assured her. "You'll be fine, darling."

Petra swallowed. She didn't know how things worked up here in the posh quarters, but down in the barracks, recycling chutes led to a dingy room where an auto-sorter pulled out the useful garbage and sent the rest to the incinerator. She'd heard stories of cleaning crews pulling murdered victims out of the refuse.

The hammering on the door grew louder. No telling how long before complex security overrode the lock.

"This isn't what I signed up for!" Petra agonized as she hopped to grab the escape hatch pull cord.

The hatch unfolded into a narrow staircase, leading up to

another hatch that looked much like the underside of a utility hole cover.

She darted up the stairs, turned the latch, and pushed the cover open. She peered out at some deserted corner on the concourse, getting a good look at the footwear of the people shuffling past.

She yelped, shoved the badge through the crack, and let the cover slam shut before anyone could notice—or trip over—the misaligned cover.

Then she threw herself back to the apartment floor.

The pounding on the door had gone silent. That was never a good sign.

As Petra raced into the galley kitchen, she heard the faint *click* of the security panel unlocking.

Six months ago, Petra wouldn't have been able to fit down the chute. Half a year on prison rations, though, had done her one favor.

The door was sliding open.

No time to flirt with it. Petra tucked her chin and plunged head-first into the chute.

The tube sloped downward at a severe angle, but Petra could slow her fall through the pitch darkness by sticking out her knees and elbows. Everything in her told her to scream as she half-plummeted down a tube that smelled like burning rubber and rotting meat. She only resisted because she didn't want that thick stench coating the inside of her mouth. It was some consolation that she didn't hear the slam of a chute door behind her or yelling.

For now, she thought, she just might have thrown her pursuers off the scent.

As she slid, branching chutes from other apartment units opened above her. She slid over a puddle of something wet and slimy and retched. *Don't scream. Don't scream, and don't puke.*

"Just hang on," the fly cried, and Petra couldn't tell if it was picking up her swallowed curses or not. "You're doing wonderfully!"

Petra felt hot bile fill her mouth.

Somewhere ahead, a point of light appeared and grew into a circle. As Petra hurtled toward the opening chute, hands reached out of that lit circle to catch her.

CHAPTER THIRTEEN

The land cleared for human settlement abutted a boulder field that Jaeger and her crew had occasionally mined for raw materials. The Locauri had roped a square of the boulder field about thirty meters to the side with lengths of dried vine.

Occy joined the crowd of mingled humans and Locauri gathered along one edge of the square. They parted, making space for him. Well, not for *him*, he thought. More for the three meters of limp tentacles he dragged behind him like a collection of rat tails. They stepped carefully around his tentacles, giving them—and by extension, him— a wide berth.

Upstairs, in zero-G, the prehensile and highly dexterous tentacles were a godsend to a mechanic and engineer who spent his time wading hip-deep through the mind-bogglingly complex machinery of the *Osprey*. Down in the gravity well of a planet, however, the barely-muscled limbs were as useful as tumors. Simply lifting one to wave, or catch a thrown ball, took an exhausting amount of effort.

There was a distinct divide among the gathered humans.

A NEW HOME

After they'd hatched the first sixty or so crew, the captain and Doctor Elaphus hit upon a method for gestating and growing the No-A embryos without activating their modified genetic sequences. Although every single one of the humans on Locaur had genetic sequences spliced with spider or eagle or octopus or horny toad DNA, only the first sixty crew members had such features prominently displayed. The rest appeared, for all the world, to be a diverse mishmash of otherwise standard humans.

The captain had given many reasons for switching, even though the activated mutation sequences gave undeniable benefits to the crew, and they all made perfect sense. The activated mutation sequences added a degree of instability that the gene pool, limited to three hundred members, couldn't afford. They were also associated with increased levels of aggression, which didn't fit with the captain's vision for their future.

Also, Occy thought, watching a few Locauri pick their way cautiously around his trailing tentacles, *it's because some of us are ugly.*

He tried not to think about that as he watched whatever was happening on the boulder field.

It was some kind of game, he decided. Two-person teams, some all Locauri, some all human, some mixed, littered the field, industriously stacking rocks into interesting and strangely balanced towers. First Mate Toner and a large Locauri were waving animatedly at each other around the base of a rock stack nearly two meters tall. By the Locauri's thick abdomen and large size—it must have been nearly thirty-five kilos—Occy assumed the alien was female. As he watched, the first mate stretched onto his tiptoes to place a football-sized stone at the pinnacle of the tower. The Locauri fluttered her pseudo-wings in a gesture of pure anxiety, which Toner completely ignored.

He set the point of the stone at the tip of his tower and then, breath held, stepped away from his masterwork. For half a second, it looked as if the entire precarious structure might hold.

Then it wobbled and collapsed in a cloud of dust. The Locauri bounded away from the wreck site, waving her front claws in disgust.

Toner watched her go, shook his head, and never to be deterred, scanned the crowd for his next lucky partner.

His icy blue eyes landed on Occy.

Occy tried to turn and hustle away and nearly tripped over his tentacles.

"Lieutenant Occy!" Toner jogged toward him. "Perfect. I need your help. This is a partnered game and my last one didn't work out."

"I…" Heat crept up to Occy's hairline as he faced the XO. He still wasn't used to his new rank. He shook his head fiercely. "I'm not used to the gravity. I'm not…I'm not all that strong."

"It's fine," Toner dismissed. "I don't need you to be strong. I can be strong. What I need is somebody with nineteen hands."

Occy opened his mouth to voice another protest, but Toner grabbed him by the bony shoulder and pulled him over the rope.

"The team that builds the tallest stable tower wins," he explained as he dragged Occy to the rubble of his previous failed attempt. "Except that each rock is only allowed to touch two other rocks."

Occy was instantly distracted by the engineering challenge. He studied the available materials as Toner set about re-building the base of his tower by picking up a rock the size of a beach ball and placing it on top of the nearest boulder.

A few meters away, a team of two Locauri, hopping in tandem, struggled to lift a stone the size of a generous loaf of bread.

"...Okay," Occy said slowly, pulling his tentacles in close. They might have been heavy, awkward things down here on the planet's surface, but Toner was right about one thing. He had a lot of them. "You get the big rocks. I'll try to balance them. I think we got this."

Three rounds of collapsed towers later, it became evident that Occy and Toner working in tandem did *not*, in fact, have this.

"No fair," Toner said wryly, watching the winning team flit a victory lap around the field. "They won the game via the unfair advantage of being better at it." He grinned, eying Occy as he reached for his hip flask. It was a neat little device Occy had designed specifically to keep the blood substitute it contained from clotting. "Wanna play the next round?"

The victorious Locauri flitted past, close enough to tousle Occy's hair. For some reason, that made him all the more self-conscious. Occy might have been as physically weak as one of the Locauri, but he was an *engineer*, dammit, and First Mate Toner was stronger than half a hundred Locauri combined. Occy couldn't help but feel like his clumsiness was holding them back.

He shook his head, face afire.

Toner shrugged, drained his flask, and dropped it to dangle on his belt. He turned to the line of spectators and waved over his head. "Hey, Portia! Come on. I need a new partner!"

Occy felt new heat collecting in his cheeks as Portia, the tall and elegant pilot, stepped onto the field, flexing her spidery hands. He turned and hurried into the forest, his tentacles dragging awkwardly behind him.

In the year since his activation, Occy had visited this forest on goodwill and scouting missions half a dozen times. Every time, high-tech equipment had loaded him down, and he'd been ready to *work*. He felt strangely naked today as he wandered through the tall fern-like plants that served Locaur for trees, without so much as a commlink on his uniform.

They couldn't call me to duty even if they wanted to, he realized with a little thrill. Not the captain, or Toner, or any AI. For the first time in his short life, Occy realized, he was *alone*.

He laughed. The sound was a little hysterical, a little exhilarated, and it faded into the dense canopy without an echo. For a little while, he was free. Just a boy and his multitool, on a walk in the woods.

I'll go down to the river, he decided, his steps suddenly light and springy. *It's a straight walk south from the boulder field. Then I'll come back.*

Minutes passed as he navigated the dense jungle, for the first time in weeks feeling almost relaxed—without fear of being seen or judged for this awkward body, as ugly as it was in proper gravity.

Movement flickered through the trees and Occy looked up

to see a gang of Locauri flickering through the trees overhead like ghosts. By their small size and the pale green hue of their shells, Occy figured they were children. They fluttered past him, their wings buzzing and flashing with reflected sunlight as they beat at the air. They clicked and chattered. They were laughing.

Occy had the awful idea that they were laughing at him. At the dead weight he dragged behind him. Maybe they'd seen the embarrassing display of his feeble tentacles trying and failing to balance a few simple stones.

You're a lieutenant and a good engineer, he told himself fiercely. *Stop feeling sorry for yourself.*

For some reason, that only made him feel worse.

The Locauri child at the head of the gang was bigger than the others and proportionally thicker through the abdomen, making Occy assume it was female. She fluttered through the trees and landed on a branch a few meters ahead of Occy. She cocked her head, staring at him with multifaceted eyes.

Her right antenna was as long and elegant as any, but the left antenna was a jagged stump protruding only a few centimeters from her head. Occy wondered if she'd lost it in an injury, or a molt gone wrong, or if it had never grown in properly at all. Wrapped around the base of the truncated antennae was a flexible translation ring that blinked light sequences with every twitch.

Occy knew it was wrong, but he couldn't help but think of the creature as Stumpy. Why not? Almost everybody else he knew had named themselves after an anatomical feature or something close to it.

"Where go?" Stumpy asked through her translator.

"How did you get that?" Occy asked. "Do the elders know you have it?"

The other children alighted on branches around their leader, wings shimmering. More alien laughter.

"Where go?" Stumpy repeated more forcefully. Whether she had permission to use that translator or not, the broken English said that she was new to it.

"This way, okay?" Occy snapped. "I'm going *this way*." He took a step forward. The Locauri bunched closer, blocking his way.

They stared at him, mandibles clicking.

Occy was suddenly furious. It would've cost him nothing to tell these kids that he was going on a walk down to the river. He wasn't breaking any rules. The human settlers had free permission to walk through the forests. Nowhere in the charters did it say that he should have to stop and explain himself to everybody who asked.

He spent his whole life explaining things—computers, engines, ships—to everybody who asked. He spent his entire life working for other people.

The Locauri exchanged a lot of words in their clicking, humming language. One stepped close to Stumpy, entwining its antenna closely with hers until it became hard to tell where one set ended and the other began. Occy had seen the Locauri do this before. Art had explained that the physical contact helped them interpret each others' buzzing.

Finally, Stumpy drew away from the other and hopped down from her branch. She approached Occy, wings low in a signal of friendly interaction. "Need help," she said.

"No," Occy said. "I don't. I'm fine."

Stumpy shook her pseudo wings, gesturing toward the south. "Need help. You. Lost. Lost..." She paused. The translator ring blurted several half-words and fell silent.

Stumpy shook herself, frustrated.

"Need help," she said again.

Occy understood then and sighed. Of course, they needed his help. Everyone always needed his help. That's what he was here for—to help.

"Fine," he said tiredly. "Lead the way."

CHAPTER FOURTEEN

Occy studied the cave on the other side of the water.

The Locauri kids had led him upriver about two kilometers. The banks here were steep and rocky. They stood on the overgrown cliffs, pointing toward a tunnel entrance etched out of the cliff on the opposite shore, near the waterline. It was perfectly square and a little over a meter per side. That made it the right size for Locauri, but as far as Occy knew, the people didn't work stone. They were tree-dwellers. What's more, the high-water line running down the cliff suggested that the entrance flooded more often than not.

"There," Stumpy said. "Go there. Lost. Lost…" She flexed delicate claws in front of her abdomen, grasping for a word she didn't quite have.

"Locauri?" Occy asked, a little more sharply than he intended. "Lost Locauri in there?"

Stumpy fluttered half a step back. "No," said the translator in that stilted, electronic voice. "No, no. Not Locauri."

"What, then? Lost toy? Or ball?"

"No, no, no." Frustrated, Stumpy turned to consult with

the others. Occy did not understand a single word they traded. "Friend," Stumpy decided finally. "Lost friend. In there. Not Locauri. Not human. Friend. You help. Find. Bring."

Despite himself, Occy felt the thrill of excitement tingle up his spine. According to everything he knew, the Locauri were the only sentient species on the planet.

He stepped down the cliff, holding onto a nearby vine for stability. "Okay," he said, trying not to sound excited. This wasn't repairing the same stupid ship systems repeatedly with the help of an AI that was either kind of dumb or pretty mean. This was a mystery. This was an adventure. "So let's go rescue your friend."

And, he thought, *find out exactly who this 'friend' is.*

Stumpy and the others held back. "You go," she told him.

"Why not you?" Occy asked. "Is the cave flooded? Can't you swim?"

"No, no, no. We not go. For…forbidden."

Occy looked back across the river, nibbling his lip as he recalled the settlement charter.

The local Locauri clan, Art's people, considered the river the boundary to their homeland. Everything beyond it was "wild." Not exactly *claimed* by other clans, but also not cultivated, the way the Locauri cultivated their forests. It made sense that they wouldn't want their kids wandering over willy-nilly.

Nothing in the charter suggested that human exploration of the wilds was forbidden—only to undertake it with caution.

So I'll be cautious, Occy decided.

"You go," Stumpy pressed. "Get friend. Return."

A large part of Occy resented her telling him what to do

on his afternoon off. The rest of him desperately wanted to see what was in that cave.

"Sure thing." Grabbing the vine, he lowered himself into the water. His tentacles, barely strong enough to support their weight, fell into the river like dead fish.

To Occy's shock, they came to life. The cold water swirled around him, filling all those boneless limbs with renewed strength. He let go of the branch and dropped into the water with a whoop of joy.

When the neural programmers were developing the physical education aspects of the Tribe training protocols that would be imprinted directly into the brains of the rapidly grown embryos, they had overlooked a few important factors. Notably: not all the mutants would have comparable physiology.

In his accelerated developmental stage, Occy had learned the fundamental motions of freestyle, backstroke, and treading water.

The bad news first: none of these swimming styles applied to a person with eight three-meter-long octopus tentacles sprouting out of the bud where his left shoulder should have been.

The good news: The tentacles seemed to know how swimming should work. When the water hit him, all those instincts kicked in.

All Occy had to do was will it so, and the tentacles would expand and contract, jetting him in whatever direction he chose.

He would *really* have to explore this later when there wasn't a friend to be saved.

He reached the far side of the river and pulled himself into the cave mouth. To his dismay, the instant he pulled his tentacles out of the water, they began to shrink and deflate, once again becoming dead weight.

Don't think about that, he thought fiercely, as he drew his multitool and activated the flashlight function. *You're exploring an alien cave. You're saving somebody. A friend. You're on an adventure. Stop feeling sorry for yourself!*

Wringing water from his sopping clothes, he turned and crawled down the tunnel.

The sand-colored tunnel walls were smooth and featureless, lacking even masonry joints. They weren't dirt, clay, stone, or any metal that Occy could easily identify. The best he could figure was that somebody had carved it directly out of a unique local mineral vein.

Even odder, Occy thought, was that it was perfectly square —a shape utterly alien to Locauri architecture. It stretched away from the river in a perfectly straight line for about one hundred meters before abruptly sloping downward at what he guessed was a thirty-degree angle. He paused at the lip of the slope, peering downward. He could barely see the square of daylight over his shoulder.

The floor had been damp, confirming his suspicion that it must flood when the water level was high. Peering down, now, he expected to see the slide angle down into a body of water, or maybe an underground river. Instead, it looked like the tunnel continued for another few dozen meters before opening into a larger cavern.

Occy tested his boots and arms against the sides of the tunnel and decided that climbing back up the slope again wouldn't be so hard. He turned and slid down, feet-first.

His boots sank through a few centimeters of murky water, then hit solid ground. He stood slowly and waved his multitool through the cavernous void, too enraptured to care about the mud and mold smeared across his backside.

Occy's multitool cut a narrow beam of light across the darkness, revealing the chamber to him one swipe at a time.

He stood at the end of a room at least thirty meters long and ten meters high. Life-sized relief carvings of trees and plants and creatures of every kind covered every inch of the walls. Some, like the eggheaded dinosaur beast that preyed on Locauri, he recognized. Others were utterly alien: strange assemblages of delicately folded tissues that might have been wings or the petals of exotic flowers. Overhead, a flock of four-legged birds tore at each other with curved scorpion tails.

Sloshing through a few centimeters of stagnant water, Occy walked along one wall. He utterly forgot his mission as he took in the intricate carvings. Ferns splayed out of the wall with each frond faithfully etched into the strange material. Flowers of all shapes and sizes, decorated with beetles and moths so lifelike that Occy half expected them to fly away at his touch.

Something stirred in the corner of his vision and Occy spun. Heart thudding, he stared at the carvings on the far wall until they resolved into more shapes he recognized. Four lifelike Locauri figures stood on the branches of a carved tree, each of them turned slightly inward to face a blank circle; the only square meter of this place not screaming with art. Something about the Locauri looked wrong, but Occy couldn't say what.

A small creature huddled on the smallest Locauri's thorax. It looked a bit like a small, slender iguana that had fused with a long-armed sea anemone. A frill of flesh formed a wide collar around its neck and tapered off into a dozen thin tentacles that wiggled in the air.

Occy had seen these things before. The Locauri raised them and harvested their eggs for food. Its name didn't translate well into English, so the crew had dubbed them iguanome.

The iguanome turned its narrow face to him and squawked. The kids hadn't lost a *friend*, Occy realized, they had lost a *pet*.

Laughing a little at his silly fear, Occy lifted a tentacle that had been somewhat revived by the stagnant water and offered it to the creature.

The iguanome studied the proffered tentacle with its head cocked to one side.

"Come on." He giggled. "They're looking for you."

Like a monkey evaluating a bribe, the iguanome leaned forward and sniffed Occy. It must have sensed something it liked because it scrambled down from the statue, darted across the wet floor on wide, paddle-like feet, and scrambled up his jumpsuit to perch on his shoulder.

Its frills, whisper-delicate, tickled Occy's cheek. He had to force himself not to laugh. He didn't want to scare it.

Occy looked back at the carvings. This place must be ancient, he judged from the high water marks running down the walls like layers in a cake. Maybe it was a place of worship or something like an old art museum. It especially emphasized the Locauri figures. The practically complete statues emerged from the wall. Although there was no paint on anything in this chamber, Occy saw shell pattern details etched into their carapaces. Each Locauri had a unique shell pattern. These weren't just any Locauri. These were *specific* Locauri.

He realized then what had bothered him about the statues. For all the exquisite detail, they lacked antennae. The engineer part of his brain said that such thin limbs must have snapped off long ago if they had ever existed at all. Looking closer, though, he saw that there were perfectly round, deliberate holes in each Locauri head where the antennae should have been.

Occy stepped back, puzzling over the tableau. Four Locauri, stripped of their antennae, all facing the only uncarved wall in the entire chamber.

"What do you think?" Occy asked the iguanome. "Is it a puzzle?"

The iguanome squawked. Occy felt something warm and wet dribble down the back of his shirt.

"You're gross." Then he nodded. Yes. It was a puzzle. Even if it wasn't, it was his afternoon off, and this was *his* adventure. He could pretend if he wanted to, and there was nobody there to tell him he was too old for kid stuff.

He entertained a brief mental image of sacred Locauri antennae carved of gold and crystal, stolen from an ancient temple by a man with a fedora and bullwhip.

At first a little shy, as if he were touching a real Locauri, Occy reached up with one tentacle and probed gently at the antenna hole.

It was a socket of some sort, he decided. He'd stuck his tentacles in enough nooks and crannies of the *Osprey* to know a socket when he felt one. There was even a little lever at the very end of the socket that depressed under light pressure.

Excited now, Occy checked the next antenna hole and found a similar lever.

He stepped back, studying the four Locauri statues. A thought struck him.

"You know what it looks like?" he asked the iguanome. "If I was a Locauri, and I reached into the sockets with my antennae. It would look like that thing they do when they're trying to communicate something complicated."

Even better, he realized, there were *four* Locauri statues, fairly close together.

Eight antennae sockets, waiting to be activated.

It was Stupid, with a capital S. Lieutenant Occy, chief engineer of the *Osprey*, senior crew member under Captain Jaeger, knew damn well that digging around the guts of ancient alien temple puzzles all by himself was Stupid. Especially when he had no backup, no commlink, and nothing but a multitool for protection,

Still, Occy spent every day of his life being smart. The Tribe technicians had screwed up, and Occy had paid for it. A flaw in his activation pod had left him with excessive engineering data downloaded into his brain and a dearth of *age* pumped into his body. He was a preteen genius burdened with the well-being of an entire Tribal Prime warship. It was exhausting, and the mystery laid before him was the most exciting thing he had seen in months.

So when he counted the empty socket-holes and saw there were eight, it felt like the universe confirming that, yes, this *was* a gift for him. He was supposed to find this place.

It didn't take long to decide what he must do next.

Occy swirled his tentacles through the water for a few seconds, getting them good and hydrated, before lifting them, dripping and dark, up to the statues. They shed a curtain of black rain, which filled the air with the scents of mud and algae.

Occy curled the tip of each tentacle into a socket. He drew a deep breath and pushed all the levers at once.

CHAPTER FIFTEEN

Afternoon sunlight twinkled off something shiny on the distant mountain. Jaeger cupped her hand over her eyes and squinted to the horizon. Seeing the expanse drew her mind to Toner. He'd been acting weird lately, with way fewer quips. And flirting. He'd also given her long looks that left her uncomfortable, like some lovestruck puppy. For a moment she wondered if he was…no. No! Developing feelings for her.

She violently shook her head.

"Thoughts?" Seeker asked, breaking her spiraling thoughts.

"No, nothing. Just stuff."

Seeker nodded. For all his strange qualities, the one Jaeger appreciated the most was that Seeker operated on a "need to know" basis, never prying into things that weren't his business. Of course, he did think most things were his business, so…

Jaeger followed the mountainside with her eyes, taking in the beauty of it.

"Obsidian flow." Seeker followed her gaze.

She glanced to the man sitting on the other end of her picnic blanket, surprised. "Since when are you a geologist?"

Seeker shrugged and took a bite of his synthesized ham sandwich. "I think it's good to know a little bit about everything. It's especially good to understand the lay of the land if you're going to settle in and camp on it for a while." He glanced up to see Jaeger smiling at him and scowled. "At least I'm not wasting my free time playing stupid video games."

In the distance, Toner let out an over-dramatic howl of despair as his sixth tower in a row collapsed. Bufo, his current unfortunate partner, sprang away from the destruction in alarm.

"Everyone should make time for a little bit of stupid, fun stuff," Jaeger teased. "It's good for the soul."

Seeker swallowed the last of his sandwich dutifully as if it was a chore. "What about you? What's your stupid guilty pleasure?"

Jaeger shrugged. She reclined backward, settling against Baby's warm flank, and popped a home-grown, hydroponic cherry tomato in her mouth. The *Osprey*'s hydroponic vegetable capacity was small, but she had made sure that everybody got at least a few of the organically-grown tomatoes. "Lately," she said, "I've been treating myself to an old action movie night every week or three. Don't act all high and mighty. I've seen you trying to hide those old pulp fiction novels."

Seeker glowered at her. Jaeger smiled and let her attention wander to the final round of the Locauri's tower-building game. After several rounds, Toner and whatever hapless partner he happened to catch had lost all hope of winning. On the other hand, Aquila and Pandion, the eagle-morphed crew members, gave the Locauri rock-stacking masters a run for their money.

Leaning against Baby's warm flank in the glow of afternoon light, Jaeger felt like a tired but satisfied parent watching the kids tear into their Christmas presents after a long and difficult year.

Watching the kids.

There was a tug on her memories. The slam of a fake screen door. The shriek of a scared little girl, fading into the distance.

The shock wave that rocked an evacuation shuttle as an entire space station exploded.

Goddammit. These flashes came out of nowhere and were always so incomplete. It frustrated her to no end.

"Jaeger?"

Jaeger sat up quickly, forcing herself to ignore the sudden wave of nausea. She dropped her last tomato back into the bowl uneaten. "By the way," she said, a little too tightly. "Have you figured out what name we should put on your file?"

Seeker stared at her. As comfortable as the man was with the simple moniker, Jaeger had told him weeks ago that she wanted him listed on the ship's crew by his full name.

"I don't care what else you call me," he said slowly, allowing her time to turn away from whatever topic had sent her into stunned silence.

She shook her head. Screaming. Explosions. *Dammit all,* she thought. *Not now. Not. Now.*

Now was a happy time. Now was a party. Right now, she could shove all that bullshit into a closet in the back of her brain. Later, alone in the darkness of her quarters, it would all come spilling out.

That would be fine because at least then she would be alone.

After a few deep breaths, she managed to steady her thudding heart.

"No," she said. "Your name is your own. We're starting fresh. We're going to do it with proper, complete identities. All of us. I made it very clear in the last team meeting. Two weeks. You have two weeks to find something you like, or I'm letting Toner pick your legal name."

She meant it as a joke. She hadn't expected the humorless Seeker to appreciate it, but even to her ears, the words sounded strangely atonal.

Seeker picked up her discarded tomato and popped it into his mouth, careful not to look at her. "This ship is in danger of sinking, Captain, and you're obsessing about the arrangement of the deck furniture."

Jaeger studied the man's chiseled profile as he sipped from his bottle. *Who are you, Seeker?* She wondered if half the reason she wanted everybody to pick names was to know what else she could call this unreasonably muscular man. He knew her first name, even if she had no particular attachment to Sarah. After knowing him for nearly a year, she should know his, too. It felt wrong not to.

She wondered, not for the first time, if affording him the same amount of trust as any other member of her crew was a mistake. Then she shoved the doubt away into the back closet with all the other stuff she couldn't afford to deal with right now. Distrust was Toner's job, not hers.

Funny, though. She didn't know Toner's first name either

—just his initials, L.M.—but for some reason, that didn't bother her.

"I disagree with your assessment. Yes, the ship is in danger, but we're building a colony. A colony on a planet that isn't ours, guarded by an alien race with tech we can't begin to understand. Some matters we can do in conjunction with everything else. Things like fitting in. Showing we're on the same team with them."

She caught his eyes. "You say you're with us, but every day, you come out with another prophecy of doom and gloom. It's almost like you're hoping everything goes wrong."

"Hoping?" He leaned back until he was lying across the blanket, arms folded behind his head as he studied the stars. "Not at all." He brought one arm down, fished into one of his front pockets, and drew out a small silver vape pen. He drew in a deep, idle puff.

She frowned, disapproving, but said nothing. Everyone was allowed their vices, even if Seeker's lung capacity had noticeably decreased in the months since she'd promoted him from prisoner to crewman.

"You can't afford to get comfortable." Seeker watched the silvery mist rise into the air and swirl away. "I'll feel better when we have some reliable fortifications built. With the *Osprey* grounded, we're more vulnerable to attack than ever."

"From who?" she asked. "We haven't heard any news from the fleet in months. According to Kwin, if anyone was out there waiting for us, they almost surely believe the wormhole's collapse destroyed us. If they did show up, our alliance with the Locauri and the Overseers is going to be hard proof against any fight they might want to pick."

She didn't want to think about the rest of the human fleet

that might or might not be lurking in some far-flung arm of the galaxy, waiting to pounce through the next open wormhole and crash back into her life. She didn't remember much about the Tribes or the fleet, but she remembered the sound of a screaming child and the shockwave of an exploding station.

For all she cared, the entire fleet could go to hell.

She knew why she'd stolen the *Osprey*, even if she couldn't remember doing it. She was running away from the sound of a slamming screen door.

No, she told herself fiercely. *No. You're building a place where there will be no more screaming little girls. You can't build a better future when you're stuck in the quicksand of the past. You know that.*

Seeker puffed out another cloud and drew a finger through the mist in an unusually relaxed gesture for a man with a jaw normally clenched hard enough to turn coal into a diamond. Perhaps the nicotine was good for him, after all. "The good thing about wormhole travel is that if there's no wormhole, there's no travel."

He waved the mist away. "Nah. I'm thinking about the K'tax." He gestured at a Locauri hopping past in an animated conversation with the willowy tall Doctor Elaphus. "Don't you think it's strange that they've incorporated the Locauri into their life-cycle?"

"K'tax are parasites," Jaeger said. As awful as her memories of the insect monster aliens were, they were better than the dark thoughts that had been swirling between her ears. She grabbed an oatmeal cookie from her picnic box and bit into it, throwing herself wholly into the new line of conversation. "Elaphus found a few examples of a similar life-cycle from Earth. Parasitic wasps lay eggs in a host insect so when the babies hatch, they have a nutritious meal to get them off to a good start in life."

Behind her, Baby rippled and lifted her big head. Jaeger offered up the second half of her cookie, and it vanished down the water bear's toothy gullet.

"I'm no biologist," Seeker allowed, "But doesn't it take generations of co-evolution to develop that kind of parasitic relationship with another species?"

Jaeger shrugged. "The Overseers and Locauri have records of K'tax raids in this system going back thousands of years. Those two races are distantly related. Given the anatomical similarities, I'm guessing that the K'tax came from the same evolutionary tree."

"The Overseers," Seeker noted. "That's another problem."

"Oh, they're a problem again?"

"A…puzzle," Seeker amended. "Is that better? The Locauri are technologically primitive while the Overseers are zipping through space and are looking after the Locauri like they're monkeys in a zoo."

Jaeger winced, but the comparison wasn't entirely unfair.

"Yet they don't build bases on this planet," Seeker went on. "They don't live here. There aren't even Overseer scientific outposts. It's as if they want the Locauri left alone, to evolve at their own pace, without interference."

"Or they're like the Amish," Jaeger suggested. "On decent terms with their English neighbors, but ultimately just wanting to be left alone to live simply."

Seeker turned his head to study Jaeger as she picked the raisins out of a second cookie.

"In neither of those scenarios," he said as she palmed the dried fruits into Baby's maw, "does it make sense that they'd want a bunch of technologically advanced aliens moving in and making themselves at home."

Jaeger frowned. "We needed a place to settle, and they were generous enough to let us have it."

"They could have let us have an isolated island in the middle of the ocean," he pointed out. "That would give us what we need while still preserving...whatever it is this clan of Locauri was doing before we came along. Instead, they want us to settle right on their front porch. We're not only neighbors, Jaeger—in the grand scheme of the continent, we're now living in the same house. You could walk from *Osprey* to the nearest Locauri village in a few hours. Whether they're an experiment in natural evolution or willful Luddites, us being here fundamentally changes that."

Jaeger frowned and said nothing for a long time as she watched the Master of Ceremonies hop off her boulder and declare a pair of young Locauri the winners of today's rock-stacking tournament. A happy buzz rose from the crowd as the gathered Locauri vibrated their flashing pseudo-wings in approval.

They had come to call the human crew with active mutations the Morphed, and those who appeared entirely human the Classics. The crew hadn't been around long enough for the behavioral specialists to collect reliable data. Still, Jaeger suspected that as a whole, the fleet mutations made the Morphed a much more competitive bunch.

As the winning Locauri pair hopped a victory lap around the field, Jaeger noted the disparate responses of her crew. Most of the Classics cheered along with the Locauri, offering friendly high-fives to the victors as they passed. Most of the Morphed, on the other hand, clapped politely.

Pandion, she noted with dismay, turned and stalked away from the field without a word.

"You're saying there's something they're not telling us," she said, forcing her attention back to Seeker.

Seeker nodded. "There's more to this arrangement than they're letting on. It may be benign, but there's a reason these Locauri have agreed to alter their way of life fundamentally and co-exist with us."

It was a fair point, and Jaeger was about to ask what he thought that reason might be when activity near the tree line caught her attention. A dozen or so Locauri hummed and flickered like disturbed grasshoppers, their photosynthetic pseudo wings glinting strangely in the waning sunlight.

At first, Jaeger thought it was one of their spontaneous sundown dances. Their energy levels always had been highest near dawn and dusk. Then the wind shifted, and she caught the cadence of their humming song. The sound was atonal and high-pitched, a buzz of distress.

She surged to her feet as Art broke from the cluster, bounding in her direction. As he approached, Baby lifted her head. She bellowed a hello that Jaeger thought was quite cheerful but which had poor Art skittering nervously to the side.

"What's wrong?" Jaeger rested a staying hand on Baby's head.

Art let out a series of nervous clicks before his translator band activated. "It's Lieutenant Occy. There's a...problem."

CHAPTER SIXTEEN

Fourteen hours before final departure

Lawrence was about to tell the girl to stay put, dammit, then thought better of it. At times like these, the last thing he needed was to come back and find her missing or terrorized by yet another escaped science experiment. Besides, realistically, the safest place for her was right behind him.

"Come on." He ran out of the lab. "Stay near me. Don't wander off alone."

She didn't argue as they ran down the hall, following the sound of a ruckus to the front of the building. The sound of screaming escalated into rapid gunfire as they reached the closed double-door. Lawrence held Sarah back as he cracked the door for a look.

It might be an abandoned facility now, but at least some of the automatic motion sensors were still online. A ring of floodlights on tall posts had activated at the center of the cluster of buildings, creating a painfully bright halo beneath the night sky. Splattered across the gravel was a dark spray. A dropped backpack. A loose pistol near the edge of the ring of light.

Most notable was a naked, two-meter-tall shaved gorilla, hugging the light post with arms thicker than Christmas hams. Some idiot had taken the biggest bastard they could find, stuck him in a gene therapy tank, and pumped it full of every secret soldier serum and combat augmentation mod that existed.

The modern-day version of Frankenstein's monster was naked, glistening with a mixture of suspension jelly and blood. As Lawrence stared, it tilted back its head and bellowed, bending the light post into a slow arch that brought the tip of it inexorably closer to the ground—and the monster's open mouth.

The man clinging to the light at the top of the post yelled, struggling to keep his balance as Mister Frankenstein slowly ripped the pole from its foundation.

Well, look at that, Lawrence thought dumbly. *Frankenstein chased Hank right up a tree.*

"You get out of here," he whispered, not daring to take his eyes off Frank. In the shadows beyond the ring of light, Lawrence saw another figure stalking up behind Frank, fumbling with a rifle. "Find somewhere safe," he told Sarah. "Hide."

The only answer she gave was the sound of her retreating footsteps as she turned and ran back down the hallway.

Gil lifted his gun and emptied a magazine into the center of Frank's back. What should have turned Frank into a pile of ground beef pinned to the ground only made the creature angry. Frank bellowed and turned away from the lamp post.

Hank dropped, smooth as a leopard falling from a tree, onto Frank's back.

It was a good move, Lawrence dimly thought as he palmed his sidearm. From there, Hank should have been able to rip the bastard's head off, no problem. It's probably what Lawrence himself would have done.

But God damn, Frank made Hank, elite Marine and fresh vamp mod, look like a sixth-grade wannabe athlete who had found himself in the middle of WrestleMania.

In all that flailing, though, Hank must have caught sight of Lawrence lingering at the door.

"Toner!" he screamed and slammed his fists into the back of Frank's skull. "Fucking do something!"

As Gil fumbled to reload his rifle, Frank bent over, bellowing and grabbing for the annoying monkey on his back.

Lawrence's mind raced. Gil's rifle made his sidearm look like a pea-shooter, and that wasn't even slowing Frank down. Hank was a physically stronger mod than Lawrence, and by the high-pitched wailing, that man was hanging on for dear life as Frank flailed.

Run away, said the perfectly rational part of Lawrence's mind. *Find Sarah and book it.* Hank, Gil, and Frank all had each other perfectly distracted at the moment. This wasn't Lawrence's fight.

Then again, Lawrence's ex-comrades had spotted him. If they survived this fight, they wouldn't be in a generous mood, and they might come after him. Even though he was fed up with them, Lawrence didn't want to see them dead.

As Lawrence calculated his options, Gil emptied a second round into Frank's chest. Ignoring the bullets, Frank reached over his head and finally grabbed Hank by one arm. Easy as dropping a wet towel, the big bastard flung Hank to the ground, stunning him.

In a not-so-surprising display of bravado, Gil flung his

empty gun to the side and barreled forward, but not before Frank stomped a heavy foot into Hank's chest.

Hank's ribcage collapsed like a bundle of dry twigs. Blood exploded out of his mouth.

Lawrence remembered the screaming, the spray of blood, as the dogs ripped Sarge apart. Perhaps channeling those same memories, Gil let out a primal scream and charged.

Lawrence drew his combat knife and burst through the door as Frank bent forward to grab Hank's head between two meaty palms.

Lawrence leapt, flinging himself to piggyback across Frank's shoulders much as Hank had done.

Holy shit, Lawrence thought, clinging for dear life as Frank tried to shake him off. From the elbow down, his arm was stunned from the force of the stab—and his knife had sunk barely a few centimeters into the side of Frank's throat. *They spliced adamantine into this fucker's genes.*

"His hands!" Lawrence screamed. The knife wobbled as he clung. Frank flailed and clawed, reaching over the shoulder to grab for him. If he got a good grip on Lawrence, Lawrence would wind up on the dust beside Hank. "Keep him off me!"

Thankfully, Gil was smarter than he looked. Head tucked, the big Marine launched himself over Hank's twitching body and hit Frank center-mass.

Frank grunted and staggered, forgetting Lawrence as he swung his arms around in a wild attempt to keep his balance.

Lawrence slung an arm around Frank's neck. With his other arm, he pried the knife free and stabbed it down again, over and over. It was like trying to chop down a tree. Little chips of wet flesh went flying with every stab, but no matter how hard Lawrence swung, he couldn't sink the blade more than a few centimeters into flesh. Meanwhile, bodies roiled beneath him as Gil and Frank rolled in a bear-hug grapple.

Lawrence needed to change his approach. Stabbing was only annoying this thing.

He slammed his knife into Frank's spine and felt the knife scrape bone as it sank through the layers of toughened skin. Thick purplish blood cascaded down Frank's back.

Rather than draw out the knife and stab again, Lawrence started sawing back and forth, tearing open the flesh over his spine.

Frank bellowed, head falling forward and mouth opening, ready to take a bite out of the puny, screaming human locked in the cage of his arms.

Gil screamed—a strange, high, sharp sound of pain and terror that sent a shiver down Lawrence's spine.

On the other hand, bending his head forward stretched the wound Lawrence was carving out of Frank's neck, making it easier to drive the knife deeper into the gaps between his vertebrae.

Hang on; he begged, too panicked and breathless to scream. He could see the spinal cord. He could smell the fluid, and the viscera, and the heady, salty perfume of blood.

Finally alerted to the damage Lawrence was doing, Frank shoved Gil aside like a rag doll and reached over his shoulder.

As Frank's sausage fingers brushed Lawrence's throat, he released his grip on the monster's back and heaved his entire weight into one last swing.

Knife touched nerves, and Frank's spinal cord snapped like an over-coiled spring. Carried by momentum alone, Frank staggered forward one step—

"No, no, no," Lawrence muttered, trying to turn Frank's head in the desperate hope that it would change his direction.

Two steps—

Then he collapsed.

Hank's body disappeared beneath half a ton of mutated man-creature.

The impact left Lawrence stunned long enough for the fresh scents of blood and gore to curl into him and wrap seductive fingers around his brain.

Hello beautiful, he thought as his world turned red.

He lost track of time after that.

CHAPTER SEVENTEEN

Lawrence came to his senses to the sound of someone crying. It was a soft, light sound, and his first reaction was to be angry. Sarah shouldn't be here. He had told her to run. This place was dangerous—for many reasons.

But no. It wasn't Sarah.

Gil sat on the gravel beside the mangled corpse of the Frankenstein creature, his head bowed to hands dark and caked with blood, his shoulders shaking as he quietly sobbed.

A cold desert wind curled through the abandoned complex, washing Lawrence in the sterile smell of dust. He looked down to see himself once again bathed in red. Beneath him, he'd reduced Frank's throat to a few chewed vertebrae around a shell of Kevlar-tough skin. The muscle, the veins, all the vital pipes, were gone.

Lawrence wiped a rough length of gristle from his chin. It was a piece of someone else's esophagus.

"Jesus Christ."

Lawrence looked up, but Gil wasn't talking to him. Gil was rocking back and forth, talking to his palms. Pieces of scalp and skull, decorated with tufts of familiar brown hair, decorated the ground around him like a smashed coconut.

Lawrence closed his eyes and let out a shuddering breath.

"Jesus Christ," Gil whispered. "I'm sorry. I'm so sorry. God. God…" His hands curled up around his skull as he doubled over, making the big man suddenly very small.

Gil pressed his face into the bloody gravel, besides the jellied mass of pulverized brain tissue, and screamed.

Lawrence jumped down from where he'd been standing knee-deep in Frank's corpse. Gil didn't flinch from his agony as Lawrence crouched beside him.

Something shone green and white in the light of the halogen lamps. It was one of Hank's eyes. The rest of Hank lay crushed beneath Frank's bulk. The rest of him not devoured, that was.

Lawrence wondered how much of their fallen brother Gil had eaten before he came to his senses.

He looked at Frank's inhumanly large corpse and wondered if that thing counted as human. If it did, then by the feeling in his stomach, Lawrence was far more the cannibal than Gil.

Something moved in the shadows of the nearby lab building. Sarah lingered beyond the glow of the lamps, small and huddled by the door. Lawrence wasn't surprised, and he was too tired to be angry.

He looked back at Gil, who howled and rocked on the ground like a child waking from a nightmare.

Except that the nightmare, Lawrence understood, wasn't over. For people like them, it never would be.

Lawrence caught his head and caught the sound of words, forcing their way through Gil's choking sobs.

"God, have mercy on me. Do not look upon my sins, but take away my guilt…"

Gil lifted his head as Lawrence placed a hand on his shoulder.

The whites of the big Marine's eyes were as red as his hands.

"Make it stop," he whispered.

Lawrence stared at him. At the tears tracking down his dusty face, mingling with blood and dripping red from the end of his chin.

"I couldn't make it stop." His gaze was distant. He trembled. "I couldn't. God."

Something glinted, and Lawrence turned his head to see the end of Hank's dog tag poking out from beneath the dead man's hand. He reached over and tugged the coded pass free from its chain. He slipped it into his pocket.

Then he drew his sidearm and checked the chamber. One bullet left.

He leaned forward and laid it on the ground beside Gil, who stared at him from behind the cage of his fingers like a frightened child.

"You remember what Sarge said about that soft place in the back of the throat?" Lawrence asked, his tone strangely distant to his ears.

Gil nodded. Given the right time and raw materials, vamp mods could recover from almost any injury. Through some unfortunate quirk of human biology, though, nothing separated the back of the throat from the deepest, most vital parts of the brain except a few centimeters of delicate cartilage that even the genetic artists had forgotten to reinforce.

Gil didn't move from his huddle as Lawrence pushed to

his feet. The big Marine didn't look up, or stir, or call out, as Lawrence turned and walked out of the circle of light.

Sarah crouched beside the stairs, wide-eyed as Lawrence came to her.

"Come on," he said. "We need to go."

Even in the shadows, she must have seen something on his face that she hadn't seen before because she took his bloody hand and let him lead her away from the building without one word of protest. She had his pack slung over her shoulders, and with her free arm, clutched a squirming thing to her chest beneath her tattered shirt.

They had walked about a hundred meters in howling desert silence before she found her voice and whispered, "Can't we go back and help him?"

"Kid," he said, "I've given about all the help I have to give."

Somewhere behind them, a single gunshot split the night.

They didn't say anything after that.

CHAPTER EIGHTEEN

The man standing over Petra didn't quite look the same without the signature twelve-pointed starburst painted over his left eye.

"Darling." Thin lips spread into a wide grin as he offered her a glass. "Welcome to the Resistance."

It was a layered drink, fading from red to yellow, and it smelled like the tropical beach from some immersive holo-drama. There was a slice of pineapple perched on the rim. It looked real. That was, of course, impossible.

Petra stared. The moment began to stretch, and slowly his grin faded. His nose wrinkled.

"Oh dear," he murmured as the drink's tropical perfume battled Petra's l'odeur de recycling chute and lost. He set the drink on a side table carved to look like an elephant. "Perhaps you'd like the shower, first."

"You're Rush Starr," Petra said. Suddenly she felt a bit dizzy.

"Enchante!" He rolled his wrist and bent in an elaborate bow. "I am so honored to meet you, Petie—"

Petra didn't hear whatever he was going to say next because she'd fainted.

Petra woke up on the strangest bed she'd ever encountered. It bounced and roiled around all her curves. A waterbed, she marveled, poking the surface and watching it jiggle. She'd thought those kinds of things only existed in old movies.

Clearly, the bed's owner valued it, too, because they'd spread a military surplus blanket across the duvet, putting a polite but firm barrier between it and Petra—who was still wearing an old guard's uniform stained with recycling chute grease and hadn't had a good shower in she didn't know how long.

She sat up, fighting to keep her balance on the strange surface. The bedroom was about the size of the entire twelve-man barracks she'd shared with her squad. It was barely large enough for the massive waterbed and gold-plated wardrobe on the far wall.

There was a silver breakfast tray resting on the wardrobe. A teacup and small silver pot, still steaming. A crystal glass of orange juice. A quick sniff told Petra that it wasn't spiked. A slender crystal vase and a bird-of-paradise flower delicately crafted from folded silk completed the tray. She recognized the flower from the cover of Rush Starr's third album, *Exotic Futures*.

A folded note rested against the vase, written in elegant script.

Darling,
Bon Matin! Don't worry about last night. I get it all the time.

Duty calls. I've gone to record an interview with the TNN. You have free rein of the flat while I'm gone. Make yourself at home. There are fresh clothes in the en suite.
P.S. You must try the sonic jacuzzi.
P.P.S. Really, I insist.

A single, many-pointed star signed the note.

Petra dropped the note and lifted the lid from the silver crock on the tray. It was full of warm oatmeal, pooled at the top with melted butter and dotted with raisins. The smell hit her, and she stood at the wardrobe, shoveling warm oatmeal into her face like an animal at the trough. After months of prison rations and leftover soups, a bowl of sweetened oatmeal tasted like heaven.

In her haste, she might or might not have spilled more than a little down the front of her shirt. *No matter,* she told herself. *This guard's uniform was going straight into an incinerator.*

With her stomach deliciously full, she wiped her mouth with the back of her hand and passed into the en suite bathroom, half-dreading to see whatever "clothes" he'd laid out for her.

To her surprise, the three complete outfits hanging by the door were all perfectly modest, if a bit eccentric for Petra's tastes. Mister Starr, or whoever managed his wardrobe, had also guessed her size quite accurately. Her options were a silky ultramarine pantsuit, a luxurious gray sweater with a long pleated skirt, or a cream-colored onesie jumpsuit that looked like a wealthy man's interpretation of this season's fleet casual fashion.

Petra shook her head and selected the sweater and skirt. Then she stripped out of her filthy prison garb, shoved it mercilessly down the bathroom recycling chute, and flung herself into the jacuzzi. The hydro-blasters sensed her presence and sprang to life, filling the air with a mist of warm, vibrating water droplets that beaded over her skin, slowly wearing away months of accumulated filth. There was a cornucopia of bottles and soap bars on the shelf. Petra devoted herself faithfully to opening every single one, sniffing the unique floral or musky scents, and rubbing a little on her skin.

Something flicked in the corner of her vision. She turned. There was a display screen mounted on the wall. Words flashed.

TNN updates available. View? Y/N

Petra tapped the Y. She hadn't had a good veg-out with the Tribe Network News talk shows in ages, not since the viewer in the brig went out, and Internal Affairs said they wouldn't allocate the funds to fix it.

Two people in fleet casual suits appeared on screen, sitting across from each other in white wicker chairs. This morning, the background hologram depicted the neatly coiffed hedgerow of an old English estate.

Petra was glad to see Harry Riles was still one of the hosts of the morning show. She'd met him a few times in fleet mixers. She liked his cute sideburns. Very distinguished.

She didn't care so much for the shockingly beautiful picture of a woman filling the thumbnail over his shoulder as Harry faced the camera.

"...From the orphaned daughter of asteroid miners struggling to survive in the unsettled streets of Ganymede Station to the grueling ranks of the Seeker Corps to humanity's best hope for a brighter future. Tune in tonight for the shocking, inspiring life story of Fleet Commander Nicholetta Kelba."

Petra groaned. Shampoo suds dripped down to her eyelids, and she scrubbed away the burning. When she opened her eyes, a new face had appeared in the thumbnail over Harry's shoulder as he moved on to the next headline.

It was her mugshot. Petra wanted to curl up and die, seeing the nine-mile gap where her two front teeth should've been.

"By now, everyone in the fleet knows the face of Petra Potlova," Harry said somberly. "She escaped from custody on the *Constitution* around noon yesterday and remains at large. Internal Affairs was holding Potlova on charges of treason and sedition in association with last year's mutiny and the disappearance of *Tribe Six*. She is armed and believed dangerous.

"Internal Affairs and MP officials are conducting a full manhunt across the fleet. If you've seen Potlova or have any information concerning her whereabouts, it is your patriotic duty to report to the nearest IA or MP immediately."

Harry's brow creased in the expression of deep, puppy-eyed concern that had made him the morning heartthrob for years. "Be safe out there, everybody."

Petra's mugshot disappeared, and Harry turned to his co-host, his grim expression melting into an easygoing smile. "In better news, Yasmin, I hear there are some breakthrough gene therapy treatments coming to the medical bays soon."

The co-host was a tall, bronze-skinned woman with a fabulous cloud of curly hair and a killer smile. Petra instantly saw how she'd won the new co-host position.

"That's right, Harry. The Guild of Genetic Artists is calling the new treatment Serenity, and if initial reports are correct, it's going to be an absolute game-changer." The thumbnail image reappeared, this time as a poorly rendered syringe graphic that made Petra scoff. Everybody knew that gene therapy didn't come in a needle.

Yasmin's voice grew somber as the broadcast cut to a recording of the *Reliant's* prime medical bay. Exhausted nurses and volunteers in rebreather masks edged their way between double rows of occupied cots. Petra thought she caught a glimpse of her old friend Dolly, leaning over to take the temperature of a jaundiced man in a janitor's uniform.

"We've all either fallen victim to the recent bout of flu or known someone who has," Yasmin said. "In the past four years, incidents of significant disease mutation have risen twenty-six percent, and scientists and health experts have been sounding the alarms. Cramped living conditions and malnutrition have created fertile breeding grounds for superbugs. The wave of illnesses we've been seeing is, they warn, only the first phase of what might become a full-blown biowar."

The recording cut to an image of two white-coated scientists examining vials of clear liquid.

"But no more!" Yasmin's voice-over went on, "The Guild of Genetic Artists, or GGA, has developed a breakthrough treatment. It will hypercharge the body's defenses against dangerous pathogens and increase the ability to synthesize vital, hard-to-find nutrients from standard food rations. They're calling the new treatment Serenity, and if initial reports are true, it's such an effective proactive treatment against diseases that it might even increase the average lifespan by as many as seven years."

Petra thought she heard movement out in the apartment

and muted the screen, straining her ears. Yeah, that was the noise of a door sliding shut.

Even if only her host returned from his errands, Petra didn't want to be caught alone with more than her pants down. Hastily, she scrubbed the last lather from her hair and turned off the hydro-blasters.

The image of all those sick people lying in the medical bay haunted her as she toweled off. The situation in Medical hadn't gotten better in the months Petra had been out of the loop. She supposed she should be grateful she hadn't come down with one of the superbugs herself. Probably she had her genetic mods to thank for that.

Still, something about that last news story bugged her as she shimmied the skirt waistband over her hips and tightened the cinch. More people surviving the bug cycles and living longer. It sounded great to Petra, which was what made her suspicious. Like it or not, supplies—from food to space to breathable air—were in short supply.

It seemed unlike top brass to push widespread treatment that would increase lifespans, thus competition for limited resources.

Oh, darn them all, she thought, disgusted, as she wiggled into the form-fitting sweater. The collar was wide enough to show off her collar bones, which had become notably sharp in the last few months. *They've got me thinking like a bureaucrat.*

Wrapping her hair with a hand towel, Petra shook away those ugly thoughts, squared her shoulders, and stepped into the apartment.

Until that moment, Petra had let herself forget all the strangeness that led to her being in this lavish place. As she stepped out of the bedroom, however, her host rose from where he had been lounging on a long sofa. He spread his arms wide in greeting.

"Petra, darling!"

Petra felt another surge of vertigo.

Rush Starr was a dramatically tall, thin man with a mane of platinum blond hair that must have been either a dye job or a genetic mod. He wore waist-hugging pants that flared at the calves and a puffy white shirt with a collar that, like Petra's own, was wide enough to expose the shimmering gold astral signs tattooed onto his shoulders.

He stepped around the sofa and leaned forward, pulling Petra into a quick, bony embrace that she was too stunned to reciprocate. In a gesture straight out of some classic holo-drama, he planted a brief, dry kiss on each of her cheeks before pulling back.

"You're looking very well. I am so glad you made yourself comfortable." He grinned. There was a glittering diamond embedded in his left incisor, a fashion that had never caught on. Petra clamped her mouth shut in an awkward, closed-mouth smile, all the more self-conscious about her teeth—or lack thereof.

"Mauve suits you," he added, brushing a finger over the wide collar of her sweater. Then he turned away and sprang to the sideboard along the far wall. "Can I offer you a drink? I must apologize. When you fell asleep, I helped myself to your Tequila Sunrise." He glanced over his shoulder and winked at her. "Didn't want it to go to waste. Can I make you another?"

Petra glanced around the room, licking her lips nervously. "Awful early in the morning for a stiff drink, isn't it?"

"Is it?" Rush frowned. "I...don't live by a common schedule, darling. When I am tired, I sleep. When I am hungry, I eat. No matter. Tea, then? Or perhaps coffee?"

A NEW HOME

"Coffee," Petra said quickly. "Please and thank you."

Old, stale, fabricated ditch-mud coffee had been a rare treat in the brig, and she hoped most ardently that the diva would have some of the good stuff. Her host didn't disappoint, and as he busied himself assembling a small press, she stared around the apartment.

Rush Starr stared at her from every angle. LPs and old press releases covered the walls. First edition prints of *Duty Lies on a Rocket Ship*, *Destiny*, and even some of the oldest experimental stuff, from back before the fleet made him famous for his patriotic ballads.

Petra hummed old snippets of songs she remembered from her childhood in the slums as she browsed. The place was a museum.

Not a museum, she thought, pausing to study an autographed cover of *Home is the Tribe*. A shrine. Rush Starr's shrine to himself.

There was a long, narrow table along the wall beside the bedroom door, decorated with dried flowers surrounding a crystal pedestal. Given the decor of the rest of the place, Petra would have expected the pedestal to be displaying Rush's first album, or maybe that strange mask he wore in the famous *Dancing in the Stars* music video—the velvet one, studded with diamonds.

Instead, Petra stared at a rock. An oddly-shaped rock, to be sure—splayed into a crude cutting edge on one end and tapered to a jagged point at the other—but a rock.

"It's a memento."

Petra jumped, then took the cup Rush offered her. "You move too quietly for such a tall man," she scolded.

He smiled apologetically.

Petra sipped and nearly spat. The rich roast, loaded with

sweetener and velvety with cream, was a shock to her system after months of rehydrated protein packs and muddy ditch water.

"Be careful," he advised. "It's hot."

Petra waved away his concerned hand and greedily chugged the coffee, ignoring the scalding burn working down her throat. "Not too hot," she decided. She turned back to the elegant crystal shrine and the ugly rock crowning it. "Whaddya mean, a memento?"

"Souvenir is a bit crass of a word, don't you think?" A distant look came into his eyes as he reached out and picked up the stone. He turned it over, reverently, in his thin palms. "For the last artifact of a dead alien race?" Then he met Petra's eyes, and all the glittering good cheer faded into a sadness that left Petra stunned. "Come sit down, darling," he said. "Let's talk about the future. And the past."

CHAPTER NINETEEN

Rush sat on the love seat across from Petra and set a holo-projector on the coffee table. With a wave, he dimmed the apartment lights. The projector flared to life, casting a three-dimensional recording into the air. Petra stared at a still shot of a line of fleet soldiers, standing on a dirt path running alongside a wild prairie full of grass of all shades of blue and green, dotted with long stems of white and pink wildflowers. Petra might have thought it was a field on Earth, except that the grasses stretched a good meter over the head of the tallest soldier, and the color palette was a hint alien.

"I'd like to show you the incident that radicalized me," Rush said.

Petra squinted at the frozen soldiers in the frame. "Those aren't current uniform designs, are they?"

"They're nearly a decade old," Rush agreed. "From the time of the Riella 3 hubbub. Do you remember it?"

It took Petra a moment to dig the name out of her memory. "Oh, yeah. That was right after me and Sarah graduated. That was one of the planets the brass had been batting around as maybe a good place to settle."

There had been many false starts and empty promises about new worlds back in the earlier days of the fleet. Hardly a year went by without hopeful stories cropping up like weeds in the network. Stories of proper, breathable atmosphere on Sirius 7 or liquid water on a few moons in the Goldilocks zone around Tau Ceti.

Inevitably, every promise ended in disappointment, as the scientific teams discovered that this planet, or that moon, was tectonically dead, or had an atmosphere poisoned with all sorts of deadly cosmic rays, or suffered regular volcanic eruptions on the scale of mass extinction events.

In the early days, a few instruments and scientists would stay behind to monitor the conditions and perhaps find a way to make the environment viable for settlement, but the fleet would move on. After a dozen or so false hopes, the brass had even decided to stop leaving exploratory teams behind because they didn't have the valuable equipment to spare.

"Riella 3," Rush said. "Breathable atmosphere, tidally active, Earth-comparable gravity. There was even confirmation of plantlike multicellular life forms on the surface. Preliminary scout reports were very hopeful. Hopeful enough to send down a camera crew and a familiar face to record a nice little welcome video." He touched his forehead in a lazy salute.

"You went down to Riella 3?" Petra gasped.

"We did," Rush sighed. "Me, my entourage, and camera crew at the time, along with a small squad of fleet security, headed up by a fresh-faced ensign. The raw footage never made it as far as the editor's desk, though. Are you ready to see why?"

Petra nodded, huddling forward. She took another sip of the hyper-sweet coffee. Her legs jittered. Whether it was from the caffeine, or the tension in the air, or the sheer surreality of her situation, she couldn't tell.

Rush activated the recording, and the frozen soldiers in Fleet Security uniforms began to move. They patrolled the border of a wide circle of cleared ground, slack-jawed with wonder as they ran their hands through the silky-fine grass forest around them. The camera panned, showing the old-model fleet shuttle at the center of the cleared circle and another group of soldiers assembling what looked like a portable recording studio. A small woman bent over one of the cargo crates. Petra couldn't see her face, but she recognized that ensign's uniform.

The camera swung to the left, showing the land curving gently down into an endless sea of blue-green grass rippling in the gentle wind.

"It was like standing on the shores of the Caribbean sea." Rush sighed. Petra wondered if he was speaking from holo-recording experience or if the man was old enough to have been on Earth before the final collapse.

On-screen, someone waved. The camera zoomed in on a grinning young Rush Starr, straight from his hard-rock phase, when his hair was a mass of black and white tiger stripes, and his wardrobe tended toward tight-fitting leather.

"Jackie, love! Come check this out!" Rush waved the cameraman close and crouched beside where a young soldier prodded at a disturbance on the ground with the tip of his stylus. To Petra, it looked like a donut-shaped mound of dirt, about a meter across. It was littered with oddly shaped brown lumps that Petra at first thought were rocks until one of them depressed easily beneath the soldier's stylus.

"I think they're eggs," the young man said. "Like old, uh, what were they—alligator eggs? Not hard like bird eggs, but leathery and soft —" He poked another one of the lumps, but rather than deflate easily, this one split, leaking a line of oily black pus. The younger Rush laughed. "Don't go harassing all the locals there, love." He gave the soldier a friendly slap on the shoulder. "Now, mark it down for your scientists to look at, and let's go scout for those filming locations."

The soldier bit his lip and nodded. The view rocked as Rush straightened. "It's glorious weather," he told the camera. "Make sure you get plenty of filler of the wind in the grass, Jackie. It's soothing, right?"

The camera shook as the cameraman nodded. It must have been one of those hands-free rigs that were so popular a while back.

"Right? Right?" Rush turned, tilting his head up to the licking wind. "God, all we're missing is a pipe, a few buds, and a bottle of Dom." He caught the camera in that glittering smile and laughed.

Off-screen, someone screamed.

Things happened very quickly after that. The audio *popped* as the cameraman himself let out a shocked bellow and tumbled face-first to the ground. There was a fuzz of darkness and the unmistakable sound of gunfire in the distance.

"Hold your fire! Hold your fire!" someone screamed. Maybe it was wishful thinking, but Petra could've sworn that was Sarah's voice.

"Jackie!" The young Rush cried, hauling the stumbling cameraman to his feet. Through all the chaos of moving bodies, Petra saw a long, dark blur rippling through the grass. The camera went still, and the figure resolved into a rippling green lizard-like creature, two meters tall and standing like a bow-legged bulldog. A mane of long, dark needles splayed out of its throat. It lowered its head and let out a gurgling growl. Black ichor dripped from its wide, saber-toothed jaw.

"Commander!" one of the soldiers said, his voice high and tight with terror. In the corner of the frame, two more soldiers stood frozen with guns clutched to their chests as they stared at the growling serpent.

"I said hold your fire!"

The creature lowered its head and took one heavy step toward the mound of discarded eggs.

"Oh dear," Rush murmured from somewhere off-screen. "Oh dear, Private, I do hope you haven't damaged its eggs—"

"Everybody back away," Sarah barked, and to Petra's relief, the cameraman took one trembling step backward as the serpent took another step forward. "Give it a clear path to the eggs. If that's all it cares about, we don't need to fight —"

The serpent hissed, and quick as a ribbon on the wind changed direction and lunged toward the nearest soldier.

The poor man barely had time to lift his rifle before vanishing beneath the serpent's swiping claws.

Petra, who hadn't been to a shooting range in more than half a year, was stunned by the blast of recorded gunfire. The cameraman screamed and spun, running flat-out away from the carnage—barely two steps behind the fleeing Rush Starr.

Three new figures erupted from the grass on the other side of the cleared ground; shaggy, hunch-backed creatures that had the incongruous look of lithe and agile sloths. Rush let out a rather high-pitched shriek and hit the ground, throwing his arms over his head. Dropping to all fours, the sloths sprang lightly over Rush.

Oh gawd no, Petra wanted to cry out. Don't go running into gunfire!

The camera swung to follow the loping sloths as they charged into the melee, where screaming soldiers pumped round after round of charged plasma into the serpent. Either ignorant of or oblivious to, the danger of those charged plasma bolts, the lead sloth sprang a good two meters into the air, lifting a lightly bladed ax over its head. It brought the butt of the weapon down squarely on the serpent's face, sending a spray of broken spines and teeth raining over the clearing.

The serpent howled, and faster than Petra could track, spun and vanished into the grass.

"Hold your fire!" Sarah screamed as a final wild bolt shot centimeters over the lead sloth's head.

The soldier on the ground, not too badly injured, scrambled to his feet and dashed away as the shaggy aliens turned.

The camera swung wildly, taking in the faces of the scouting party. The enlisted men, white-faced and clutching their rifles to their chests. Sarah Jaeger, commander of this tiny scouting force, with her arms outstretched to hold her men back, her golden eyes wide with awe.

"My God," the younger Rush said. "My god, Jackie, are you getting this? They've got tools."

Sarah saw it, too: the crude ax each of the sloths held, the hide pouches slung over their shoulders with ropes of woven grass. "Put your weapons down," Sarah barked at her men.

"Commander, our orders were to eliminate any threat—"

"I said put your God damned weapons down!" Sarah roared. The sloths were approaching now, slowly, with their heads down in what might have been a posture of friendship—or the prowl of a stalking cat. Petra saw what Jaeger had seen. They had lowered their axes.

They halted with hands lifted to mirror Sarah's open gesture.

Rush leaned forward to tap the projector. The image froze.

"They were quite friendly," he said, sinking back into his love seat. "In a rough sort of way. Curious little fellows. Not at all shy. Jackie boy had quite a challenge keeping them away from his precious camera."

"What happened?" Petra asked. There was a sinking feeling in her gut.

"Ensign Jaeger followed protocol to a 'T,' of course. She immediately radioed the fleet and informed brass that we'd encountered an intelligent and friendly alien species." He paused, slowly sipping his coffee as he studied the swirling textures on the ceiling.

"I always wondered how the fleet, with all their scanners and scout droids, managed to overlook an entire race of intelligent creatures living on the planet. I always told myself it was because the Tepori were primarily subterranean, you see —living underground. They dug, quite literally, below our radar."

He caught her puzzled look and smiled. "Tepori. It's short for teporis torporibus, Latin for sloth. That's what we called them. Bit of a misnomer, though. When the fellows had somewhere to be, they were anything but slow. Anyway, given what happened next, I think I was deluding myself. Our encounter with the Tepori was anything but a happy accident."

All the gentle humor faded from his face. "Are you ready to see what happened next?"

"I don't know," Petra said, voice stony. "Was it something terrible?"

Rush regarded her. "Darling," he said after a long moment of silence. "Are you...being glib?"

"Do I look funny to you?" she asked tiredly. "Am I laughing? I ain't one of those people who needs to see blood to know pain is bad, Mister Resistance. I grew up there."

"The fleet sent down a small squad of Seekers to murder those aliens," Rush said. "I…watched it happen. No words. Just two plasma bolts into each skull. It happened…very quickly."

"That's what's on the next clip, huh? Snuff material?"

"I..shouldn't have this footage. I'd be in for quite the prison sentence if any MP knew I had it." He paused. "We never had a chance to learn their language. What songs they sang to their children at night. How they lived, how they loved."

He turned his memento stone—the head of one of those alien axes—over in his hands and sighed. When he leaned back this time, all the strength had run out of his limbs.

Petra wondered how old he was. It was hard to tell by looks anymore. These days, most people—especially rich people—had at least a little genetic modding in some system or other. All standard gene therapy packages seemed to screw with the normal aging order, especially if someone had been modded later in life.

By the fine web of crows feet at the corners of his eyes, Mister Starr appeared to be at least fifty. Then again—looking in the mirror, Petra couldn't tell that she'd aged much since she graduated from the ensign training program and won her mod at the age of twenty-eight, nearly a decade ago.

The man sitting on the sofa across from her could've been about her age without appearance-changing mods. Or he could be going on ninety and ready to keel over at any minute. If she remembered the chronology of his released albums correctly, he must've had at least fifty Earth years under his belt.

She wondered how he could think she was so naïve, or if

he lived in a private universe where everybody else was a child.

That wasn't all fair, she knew, because it wasn't him she was mad at.

"Why did they do it?" she asked quietly. "Evil—it don't surprise me." She looked down, working her fingers through the fabric of a skirt that wasn't hers. "But I don't understand it. And I guess I assume nobody else does, either." She peered up at him through bangs in desperate need of a trim. "Do you understand it?"

Rush shrugged and leaned forward to pour the last of the coffee into her cup. "I can only guess, Petra. The Tribes aren't looking for a place we can live. They're seeking a place to own. A place to dominate without any competition. They're terrified of anything alien and strange.

"To them, these aliens were just...beasts. Things unworthy of sharing a planet with us. That's why I think the fleet knew damn well what we would find down there. They wanted to gauge these aliens. See how they reacted to aggression, see what they were made of. In the end...it seems they were the same thing as you and I. Flesh and blood."

His voice turned distant. "I believe what I saw that day was the beginning of a genocide."

"Naw." Petra shook her head, making Rush look up sharply.

"No?" There was a challenge to his voice.

"Obviously. If it was, we'd all be living on the seas of Kiella 3 now, wouldn't we? So why aren't we? What stopped the fleet from murdering a bunch of sloth-people with axes?"

"Ahh. The skies receded like a scroll, and the stars turned dark and fell from Heaven."

Petra stared at him.

"Revelations? No? Very well. I don't think anyone is sure. A few hours after the Seekers slaughtered the Tepori, there was some kind of discharge in the upper atmosphere. It destroyed all the Seeker ships in the area. I've searched our atmospheric databases for years, and I've never found documentation of a freak lightning storm of that magnitude. Couple that with the utterly vicious earthquake that struck the area without any warning, and I believe brass rather took it as an omen that it wasn't only the Tepori who didn't want us on Riella 3."

Petra puzzled over this for a long minute. "What do you mean? Like, God chased the fleet away from Riella 3?"

"God? Spirits? Angels? Or aliens so hyper-advanced that they can turn the wrath of an entire planet against invaders without leaving any trace of their presence? Or perhaps we simply stumbled on the single Luddite community of Tepori, and the greater civilization was, in fact, quite capable of expelling invaders.

"I don't know, darling. If you find Riella 3 in the fleet databases, you'll see it listed under hostile: do not explore. Not even my contacts have been able to get access to the restricted Riella files."

"Sarah told me about that mission," Petra murmured. "It was a long time ago. She said she was being sent with security to film some important news video or something. She never talked about it after, though. And it never did get released."

"They asked us to sign NDAs." Rush smiled tightly. "Then told to sign them at gunpoint. Don't condemn Sarah too harshly for that. They *executed* Jackie when he tried to protest the murder of the Tepori. Brass made it very clear that the consequences for gabbing would be...unpleasant."

Petra grunted. "Another thing she never told me about." At

least Larry hadn't been on that mission. She didn't know what she would do if she found out that her man had encountered aliens and never told her.

Then she realized what role Larry would've played in the mission had he been there and felt queasy.

He'd been a sweet guy, but the brass kept a short leash on powerful mods like him. They'd known how to get a guy like Larry to do their dirty work, whether he wanted to or not.

Her emotions must have been plain on her face because Mister Starr set his cup aside and leaned forward, gently closing a hand over Petra's. She gasped and realized she was trembling.

Mister Starr said nothing, and Petra appreciated that. She didn't know if there was anything he could say to make her feel better. For a little while, as her third cup of coffee cooled to room temperature, she needed to feel crappy.

Finally, she pulled herself upright, drained the last of her coffee, and set the cup aside with a firm *clink*. "So," she said. "Have there been others? Other planets or places where we might've been able to settle except that brass messed it up?"

"I'm not exactly sure," Rush said slowly. "But, funny thing, darling...that's exactly the right question. It's the question my associates and I have been asking. It's the question all of humanity has a right to have answered, wouldn't you agree?"

Petra nodded. "I never did love brass, but I figured, so long as they got the job done, maybe they were a thing we had to live with." She nodded at the still-frozen holo recording. "But that's the thing. They ain't getting the job done, and they're getting in the way of better people who maybe could." She looked him square in the eye. "So what's the plan, Mister Resistance?"

Rush Starr grinned, showing the diamond in his tooth.

"We ruin the current crop of fleet commanders," he whispered. "We expose them for the cruel idiots they are. Once everybody knows the truth, the command structure will crumble. They'll have lost all support and credibility. You're the face of the Resistance, Petie. Half the people in this fleet already know that the brass line about you being a dangerous terrorist is nonsense. People will trust our message if it comes from you."

Petra looked him square in the eye. "Great. Where do we start?"

CHAPTER TWENTY

A crowd of Locauri and a few humans had already assembled at the river's edge when Jaeger, Seeker, and Art arrived.

A Classic in an engineer's vest stood at the edge of the dense cluster of insectile aliens, his arms folded across his chest. The young man nodded at Jaeger as she approached.

Jaeger glanced at the name tag on the front of his vest. Like Seeker, most of the crew had yet to select personal names. As a stopgap measure, each had been given a surname in the fashion of ancient America. For the Classics, that meant a title that alluded to their role in the community.

"Mason?" she asked. "What's going on? Lieutenant Occy isn't answering his commlink."

Mason set his jaw. At barely two months out of the pod, he was among the youngest of the crew, but in that brief time, he'd absorbed a staggering amount of the Locauri language. His head tilted to the side as he listened to the aliens chatter and buzz.

He gestured at a cluster of smaller Locauri huddled at the edge of the cliff, chattering animatedly as their larger kin crowded around them. Art shoved his way through the crowd to stand by the largest juvenile, a female with one missing antenna.

As an egg-laying species, the Locauri didn't have strong familial ties with one another, at least not ones based on blood lineage. However, it was normal for adults and children to form mentor-type bonds based on common interests and affection. It would be wrong to refer to the younger female as Art's daughter, but ward was perhaps an apt comparison.

Jaeger recognized this female, too. By her size, she must have molted several times since Jaeger had last seen her, but her antenna had never grown back properly after the K'tax had ripped it off.

"The elders are demanding to know what this gang of kids got into," Mason translated. "The kids are saying that…Lieutenant Occy went across the river to the…" He cocked his head, listening to the rapid clicking as the Locauri yelled at one another. "Forbidden place, I think."

Jaeger glanced in the direction the Locauri were pointing. About thirty meters away, across the river, there was a square tunnel mouth carved out of the opposite riverbank. She tapped her commlink again. "Occy? Come in."

Even if the kid had answered, Jaeger wouldn't have been able to hear it over the clamor that rose from the Locauri as something slid out of the tunnel mouth. It was the leading edge of Occy's tentacles, drooping like languid snakes as the boy dragged himself out of the cave and dropped into the river. For an instant, Jaeger was afraid he'd passed out until the dark shape beneath the water surged to life and shot across the river in their direction.

A smaller, dark shape split from Occy, racing ahead. The

hooded lizard-like creature—somebody's pet, she assumed—hit the base of the steep bank and scrambled up the cliff.

Jaeger hadn't realized how worried she was for Occy until that moment. A wave of relief made her tremble. Occy reached the near bank, reached up with two tentacles to grab a low-hanging tree limb, and pulled himself out of the water.

Jaeger pushed her way through the crowd as Locauri and humans alike swarmed the kid. Near the back of the group, Seeker bellowed for the crew to give them space.

"Occy?" Jaeger pulled the child engineer away from the cliff. "What happened?"

Occy blinked and rubbed the water from his eyes. He stared around the crowd. His skin had turned even paler than usual. He trembled. "Uh-oh," he muttered.

A few Locauri pushed their way forward. Their clicks were pitched low and menacing.

"Hang on," Jaeger snapped, spinning to hold them at bay. "Whatever's got you so upset, we'll figure it out."

A few Locauri had translator bands, but whatever words they were trying to say got lost in the babble.

"Where's Stumpy?" Occy muttered from her arms. She didn't like the dazed, slurred sound to his speech. "I found her pet. She'll tell you…"

If the girl was still around, Jaeger couldn't pick her out of the mass of clustering bodies.

"Art!" she called, spotting her small friend in the crowd. "Get them out of here and let us talk!"

Art waved an antenna in agreement, but the noise swallowed the little fellow's gestures.

Jaeger had never seen the Locauri so upset. She felt the mass of bodies pressing closer, and alarm bells started going off in her head. This wasn't only an upset. This was a riot waiting to happen.

"Occy? Can you swim again?" she asked softly, taking another step toward the edge of the cliff.

"Oh, yeah." The boy sounded downright dreamy. "I can swim great, Captain."

Jaeger was about to turn and pull them both into the river when the crowd split.

Baby shoved her way through the press of bodies, her sudden sonorous bellow rising above the din and startling them into silence. Seeker sat astride her back, hands cupped over his mouth.

"Shut. The. Fuck. Up!"

Near the back of the crowd, a Locauri squeaked. Others quickly shamed the squeaker into silence.

Jaeger let out a breath. Seeker caught her eye and nodded as Baby paced along the riverbed, forcing the crowd back a meter with every pass.

"Sorry," Occy muttered. "Oh, man, I didn't—I didn't know —I'm sorry —"

"Hey. It's okay. We'll figure this out." Jaeger sank to the ground, letting Occy rest on her shoulder and bringing her closer to eye level with the approaching Locauri—Art and two of the most respected elders.

"Now," she said. "Someone tell me what's going on."

One of the elders began clicking rapidly. Art translated for her.

"That place, special. Forbidden."

Jaeger scowled. "The charter doesn't forbid us from crossing the river—"

"Not the river," Art said quickly, waving with one antenna toward the tunnel mouth. "The…the special cave."

His band blinked yellow as he struggled to find the correct word.

"The special cave, okay," Jaeger said, a little impatient. "Why is it forbidden?"

The elder took offense to her tone and snapped her mandibles together forcefully.

"Forbidden," Art said, a little despairingly.

"Dangerous?" Jaeger asked.

Art hesitated. "It is said, yes. Bad…omen?"

"Stumpy said it wasn't allowed," Occy murmured. "I thought they meant they weren't supposed to cross the river. They asked me to go."

"Stumpy?" Jaeger glanced up to the crowd, which Seeker and Baby had managed to browbeat into some semblance of order. She remembered the juvenile female missing an antenna and was momentarily surprised that Occy would refer to her so callously. She didn't see this so-called Stumpy in the crowd.

She noted that all the juveniles had made themselves scarce, along with the recovered iguanome.

The elder was clicking again.

"They would not have asked you to go." Art's pseudo wings drooped as if he was ashamed of what the elder asked him to translate. "They know it's forbidden to everybody, everybody, everybody."

"Come on now." Jaeger had to choose her next words carefully. "There must have been some kind of miscommunication. Occy wouldn't have gone there if he understood it was forbidden."

Where he leaned on her shoulder, Occy nodded tiredly. "They said they lost a friend in there. They asked me to go get it."

"Doesn't matter," the second elder said inflexibly, his translation band blinking. "Old place. Not to be disturbed—" A burst of activity ran through the crowd and cut him off.

Jaeger turned to see Toner shoving his way to the front of the line. From where he sat atop Baby, Seeker sighed but didn't try to stop Toner as the pale man strode across the cleared ground to join Jaeger and the elders. His cold blue eyes fixed on Occy.

"You okay, kid?"

Occy nodded.

"Great." Toner set his jaw and stared at the elders. "What the fuck is going on?"

"We were just getting to that." Jaeger pointed for Toner to sit. "Cool it."

Toner hesitated, bouncing on his heels, then reluctantly brought himself to sit on Occy's other side, careful to avoid stepping on his tentacles.

"Trial," the female elder said through Art. "Must be…trial."

Toner surged to his feet again, ready to start yelling. Without looking, Jaeger snatched his wrist and yanked him back to the ground.

"A trial of what, exactly?" she asked calmly. "What is Occy being accused of?"

The elders conferred briefly.

"Trespass," Art said. "It must be known to all what Occy did and saw and why he went into the…shrine."

"You can't punish someone for breaking a rule that doesn't exist," Toner growled. "Show me where in the charter it says we have to stay out of your shrine thingy."

Now it was Jaeger's turn to get angry. Whirling on the elder, she growled, "For once I'm in full agreement with Toner."

Art hesitated. From what little Jaeger understood of Locauri body language, she thought that Art was embarrassed by this miscommunication but also deeply uncomfortable with the idea of Occy going into that cave. "It is forbidden," he repeated.

"This is bullshit. Captain, come on. Let's get out of here until these people decide they're going to honor the rules we all agreed to."

Jaeger calmed herself. She would never let Occy come to danger. There was the threat of a trial, but that didn't mean punishment. If the trial led to some token slap on the wrist, Occy was strong enough to accept that. He'd have to, for the good of the crew.

If it was more than that, well, then Jaeger would have to intervene. For now, she needed to go down the path of harmony. Not that Toner understood any of her thoughts. He saw this situation as black and white.

Jaeger stepped over to Toner and put a hand on his arm. He shuddered at the touch. "That is one option." Jaeger didn't take her eyes off the elders. "I would much rather we talk through this, here and now, like good neighbors should."

Toner grumbled but stilled.

"Occy?" Jaeger said. "Can you tell us what —"

They all saw it at the same time. A silver sphere, about the size of a baseball, whizzed through the air between Jaeger and Art. It came to a sudden, eerie halt a meter from the cliff's edge. Jaeger recognized the sphere as one of the many droid manifestations of the Overseer AI.

A projector flared to life from somewhere at the heart of the sphere. Suddenly, a translucent Kwin hologram was standing in midair beside them. The Overseer was an impossibly slender creature, like a stick insect three meters tall.

Jaeger could barely make out the distinctive smear of light blue discoloration on Kwin's narrow face as the Overseer took in the gathered crowd.

The Locauri recognized their cousin instantly, however, and turned to face him, lowering their antennae respectfully to the ground. Toner stood, but Jaeger, still cradling Occy, did not.

"Apologies for INterrupting," Kwin said through the droid sphere as his hologram swayed and flickered against the breeze. "I have been MONitoring the SITuation."

"Great," Toner grunted. "So maybe you can tell us what the hell is going on?"

Kwin clicked a rapid stream at the Locauri. To Jaeger's surprise, they retreated several meters without protest. Kwin turned to the humans, lowering his voice.

"Ten MINutes Ago, my ship SENsors PICKed up UNidentified RAdio TRANSmissions from this LOCation. I have SCHOlars WORKing to TRANSlate the SIGnal, but the LANGuage is OBscure."

Jaeger wondered how close Kwin must have been lingering to have a hologram generator here within minutes of picking up the transmission. *How closely are you spying on us, Kwin?*

Beside Jaeger, Occy let out a little moan, making Kwin pause, head cocked to one side as he studied the kid.

"LIEUtenant?"

"I was curious," Occy whispered. "The Locauri don't have advanced technology. I figured it was some old mechanical device. I had no idea it was that advanced."

"What did you do?" Jaeger asked, a little more sharply than she intended. Occy winced.

"I turned something on," the kid grumbled. "I'm...not sure

what. It started glowing, and it was warm. It made my skin itch. I didn't have my sensors on me, and I worried that maybe it was some kind of dangerous radiation so—"

"It is DANgerous," Kwin said flatly as if this was what he had been afraid to hear. Occy began to tremble again.

"Dangerous how?" Toner demanded. He paced, tugging restlessly at his hair.

Kwin hesitated. "UNknown. It is Emitting low levels of high-ENergy RAdiation. Not DANgerous to HUmans in MOdest doses, but the COUsins have a more DELicate GEnome."

"Great job, Occy," Toner said. "You irradiated the neighbors. Mutations for everybody!"

Occy groaned.

"That's not helpful," Jaeger snapped. She glanced over her shoulder to see Art and the Elders slowly shepherding their people away from the riverbank. Kwin must have warned them about the radiation.

"All right," Toner agreed. "Not helpful. What is helpful? What can we do?"

"The NAture of the shrine is not ENtirely clear," Kwin said. "The COUsins have Avoided it for MIllennia. It is the REmnant of an OLDer, more ADvanced CULture. Out of REspect, we have not DIsturbed it."

Jaeger studied the restless crowd. "So, they've been disturbed now. What are we missing? Why are they so angry?"

"Folk tales." Kwin sighed.

"Folk tales?" Jaeger wasn't sure she'd heard correctly.

"LEgend, POSSibly, is a BEtter word," Kwin added. "For GENerations, the COUsins have said that the…thing…in the shrine must not be DIsturbed. ROUsing it will bring DEstruction. We do not know the ORigin of this STOry, but the COUsins BElieve it."

"The thing in the shrine?" Jaeger asked.

"There wasn't anything in there but statues," Occy muttered. "And the machine. I didn't get a good look at it before I...before it activated." She felt his body heat burning through her flight suit. The kid was humiliated. "A section of the wall began to glow. Too bright to make out. I...didn't stick around to study it." He turned his face away, head hung in shame. "I'm sorry."

Jaeger glanced over her shoulder, making sure the Locauri were out of earshot. Then she gestured for Kwin to come closer. Kwin leaned down, putting all six legs on the ground. Toner stopped his pacing and crouched beside them.

"This is nonsense," Jaeger hissed. "Let's say there is something dangerous in that cave. Treating it like some kind of supernatural monster is a recipe for disaster. All this vague mysticism, it's exactly how miscommunications happen."

Kwin studied her through multifaceted, bottle-green eyes. His mandibles clicked slowly.

"PERhaps."

"The Elders are talking about putting Occy on trial for trespassing." Jaeger held up a hand to silence Toner's protest. "That's secondary. Our first priority has to be turning off whatever is emitting that radiation.

"After that, we can all come together and figure out how to keep this kind of thing from happening in the future. If that means putting Occy on trial—" she added, with a sharp look at Toner, "then so be it. We have to set a good example when it comes to respecting their culture. That is not optional."

"Have you lost your—"

She whirled on Toner, pulling him to the side. In a harsh

whisper, she released a fury that even she didn't know she possessed. "After everything we've been through, everything we've done, if you think for one moment I'll let Occy come to harm, then you don't know me. I will burn this place to the ground before I let them hurt this kid."

Toner took a step back, overwhelmed by her fury.

"We're on a planet with an alien race that outnumbers us ten thousand to one. Maybe more. We have no home, nowhere to go. We have to play ball here. We have to make like we're good little members of society. We have to—"

"She's right," Occy whispered, pulling them back. He sniffed and scrubbed moisture from his face. "I didn't mean any harm, but if harm happened, I gotta fix it."

Toner stared at the boy, for once in his life too stunned to speak.

"Besides," Jaeger muttered. "The Locauri are reasonable. Any fair court will slap him with some community service and be done with it."

"I Agree with CAPtain JAEger." Kwin eyed Jaeger. Had he heard her? No, he didn't need to. He knew what she'd said to Toner. He knew because he understood Jaeger, maybe even better than Toner did. Who she was and what she was up against.

With that knowledge came trust. "ENDing the RAdiation is top PRIority. I will INform the COUsins. Fetch WHATever SUPPlies you need. We must REsolve this QUICKly."

CHAPTER TWENTY-ONE

While holo-Kwin explained the situation to the Elders, Jaeger sent Elaphus back to the *Osprey*. The fleet-footed doctor returned in record time, hauling a pack full of the tools Occy had requested and a small inflatable raft.

"I wouldn't recommend lingering any longer than necessary." She consulted her medical scanner as Occy pulled the raft plug and watched it unfold.

"Kwin said the radiation levels weren't dangerous to humans," Jaeger said.

Elaphus peered down at Jaeger over the top of her computer. "Captain," she said in her faintly patronizing voice. "For entirely unmodded humans, that's probably true.

"However, none of us are what you might call natural. Gene modding is a relatively new art. We don't have many longitudinal studies on the stability of the morphed or modded human genome. We don't know what might trigger additional mutations."

"Duly noted." Jaeger sighed. "One more thing to worry about."

Heeding holo-Kwin's radiation warnings, most of the Locauri had cleared the area, although the Elders lingered in the distant trees, talking animatedly to the Overseer. Seeker had ordered most of the crew from the site as well and remained nearby, watching the goings-on from where he sat comfortably on Baby's back.

Holo-Kwin vanished. The silvery droid sphere zipped to where Toner was trying to figure out how to get the raft into the water five meters below. The droid began to speak very rapidly.

"My captain has concluded his conversation with the cousins and is ready to begin the expedition into the shrine. While monitoring the situation through my sensors, he is also consulting with his crew and has asked me to act as mediator while he is otherwise preoccupied. Are we ready to go?"

"Yeah." Occy set his tool kit in the raft. "I'll meet you over there." With no further ceremony, he turned and flung himself over the cliff.

Toner stared after him, then shrugged. "I guess that's one way to do it. Tiny? You coming?"

"We'll be back as soon as we can," Jaeger told Seeker. "And Seeker. Have a team ready. Just in case we need to extract our little mutant."

Seeker acknowledged the order with his customary grunt.

"Don't call me Tiny," Jaeger added, joining Toner and the raft by the cliffside. Toner shrugged and tipped the raft forward.

They plunged toward the river, with the silvery AI sphere zipping ahead of them.

Jaeger studied the square hole in the opposite riverbank as Toner slammed an anchoring piton into the wall and secured the bobbing raft. The tunnel was about a meter to each side, and the perfect shape reminded her very much of the *Osprey's* access conduits.

She looked at Toner.

"What?" he asked.

"You first." She was sure he would've offered to go first regardless, but now that she'd insisted, he was contractually obligated to give her a dirty and somewhat confused look.

"Why?"

"Because, Toner, I still have nightmares about looking down and seeing your shark teeth about to take a chunk out of my leg."

"God." He sighed, heaved himself into the damp tunnel mouth, and crawled into the darkness. "A guy makes one hungover mistake—"

"I'm still paying for it," she added, following him into the darkness. The AI droid zipped over their shoulders, shedding soft yellow light that lit the tunnel adequately, and didn't flatter Toner's blue-white uniform. "It's not like the view from this angle is much better."

"Oh!" Toner lamented. "Why rebuke him that loves you so?" The words came out as if by habit, and as soon as Toner caught what he said, the soldier did something Jaeger truly believed was psychologically impossible for the man to do.

He blushed.

Jaeger sighed. "Toner, what's up with you? You've been acting—"

"Don't give me that crap, Captain," Toner snarled, forcing bravado in his voice. "If you're allowed to insult my ass, and

I'm not supposed to take it personally, then you can damn well put up with Demetrius flirting with Hermia."

Jaeger considered this in silence as she crawled through the dimly lit tunnel. Behind her, there was a slosh of water as Occy entered the tunnel mouth behind them, dragging along his tool kit.

"All right," she conceded finally. "I'll…save breath so bitter for a bitter foe."

"Good plan. Hey. Mister Robot. I think I see something up ahead. Cut the lights."

Jaeger froze as darkness washed over them. As her eyes adjusted, she realized that the tunnel wasn't entirely dark. A faint white light was emanating from down the slope ahead.

Behind her, Occy groaned. "I guess I hoped it would have turned itself off."

"Nothing should ever be so easy," Toner agreed, approaching the slope. "Bottoms up, kids." He dropped to his belly and pushed himself down. A few seconds after his boots vanished, Jaeger heard the distant sound of splashing water.

"It's clear," he called from below. "It's…wow. It's gorgeous."

Feeling the thrill of excitement starting to bubble in her gut, Jaeger tucked her chin and slid down the chute after Toner. A few seconds later, Occy joined the two of them in one of the strangest rooms Jaeger had ever seen.

Deep, minutely detailed carvings covered every inch of the walls, turning what could have been a tomb into a forest exploding with life. By the profusion of recognizable flowers and fruits and dozens of different sorts of insects, Jaeger thought it might have been a representation of the local forest in springtime. Then she stepped backward and took in the massive lurking shape of some kind of terrestrial jellyfish that she'd certainly never seen before, and she wasn't so sure.

A door had opened in the far wall, at the center of four carved Locauri figures. The harsh white light spilling from the room beyond cast long, deep shadows over the tableaus. As the explorers circled the room, their passing made the light and shadows waver, giving them the illusion of motion. More than once, movement in the corner of her eye made Jaeger gasp and spin, only to see an alien ladybug appearing to crawl in Toner's moving shadow.

"This effect is uncanny," the Overseer AI bot chattered as it drifted across the room. It spoke in its voice rather than Kwin's accented speech. It scanned random carvings as it passed, casting them in a glowing cone of light before moving on. "The illusion of motion is intentional and masterfully executed."

"The Locauri aren't stoneworkers, though," Occy muttered, gently tapping a carved fern frond. "Or metalworkers. Or...maybe this is some kind of fiber-ceramic?" He frowned and knelt to dig in his pack. "I need to check."

"Fiber ceramic," the droid agreed. "A fairly common material in our space constructions. Ah, First Mate Toner, please do not rush ahead. Captain Kwin has asked me to send a scan of this room for his scholars to study. This may be our only opportunity to study this place. It may contain clues as to who built it and why."

"O...kay." Toner cast Jaeger an uncertain glance.

"We were warned not to linger in the radiation," Jaeger said.

"I do not detect any increase in radiation levels here or in the next chamber. Please, Captain Jaeger, this will only take a few minutes."

"All right." Jaeger tried to hide how pleased she was at a chance to slow down and appreciate the artwork. Besides,

Occy was plenty busy running his scans, back near the mouth of the slide.

"This is so odd," Occy muttered. "The AI is right. It's some kind of ceramic. It's certainly beyond anything the Locauri can make that I'm aware of."

"So the Locauri didn't make it," Toner suggested. "Maybe it's some old outpost or settlement that the Overseers built way back, then forgot about."

Occy nibbled his lip. The harsh light of his scanner screen made his skin, normally pale, look downright sickly in the damp. "That doesn't make sense either. That access tunnel was Locauri-sized. Not Overseers."

"Maybe it wasn't an access tunnel. Maybe it was an air shaft. Or…" Toner turned to the AI. "Hey, do Overseers walk much on all fours? Uh, I mean, all sixes?"

"Not once they have reached final molting stages," the silver sphere said, distracted. "I agree with Lieutenant Occy. There have been Overseer expeditions on this planet in the past, but there is no record of any sort of permanent settlement that would warrant this level of dedicated craftsmanship. Regardless, according to the scholars, the art style is unfamiliar to us."

The other scholars, right. Jaeger kept forgetting that there was an entire conference of Overseers, not only Kwin, watching behind the AI's sensors. She had growing suspicions about the origins of this shrine but decided to wait and see what Kwin's scholars concluded before chiming in.

One thing was for certain, she thought, studying the four carved Locauri as they approached. This wasn't Overseer architecture. The ceiling was too low, and she didn't see the stick-insect aliens represented anywhere in the magnificent tableau.

"Hey, I keep forgetting to ask." Toner sloshed through the water beside Jaeger. "The Overseer AI is all one thing spread across different bodies, right? I mean, there's only one of you?"

"That is a misleading conclusion," the droid said amiably. "All of my droid extensions are regularly synchronized, and we are constantly downloading and uploading into each other. Collectively, I am what you might call a chorus of one. We experience different lives but taken all together; I am me."

"Uh-huh. What do we call you?"

"You cannot pronounce my designation in the Overseer language."

"Then translate it into English," Toner said.

"Your former AI, Virgil, referred to me as You. I believe that name might become confusing so you may refer to me as Me, instead."

"Oh yeah," Toner said. "That's...way less confusing."

"I don't remember Virgil ever referring to you that way," Jaeger said slowly.

"That doesn't sound like Virgil," Toner agreed. "I only remember it ever calling you an obnoxious pain in the circuit boards." He paused. "Uh. No offense."

"None taken," the sphere chirruped, pausing to scan the elaborately detailed carving of an orchid-like vine. "It did indeed call me that, as well as many other things I now recognize as insults."

Jaeger and Toner exchanged meaningful looks.

"Speaking of which," Jaeger rubbed the back of her neck. "Any word from Virgil lately? We haven't heard from the AI since it left. It would be good to know what Virgil is up to."

And what the AI's done with my...cargo. Jaeger's gut clenched with familiar anxiety as she remembered the three hundred thousand missing embryos.

"Virgil has asked me to respect its privacy." Me approached the far wall to make a scanner sweep of the four Locauri framing the open doorway.

Jaeger noticed that the AI wasn't as chatty as it once was and wondered if it had evolved or if its personality varied slightly from body to body. "So long as it is not a threat to anybody, I have elected to do so."

Jaeger froze with one hand on the carved Locauri thorax. "Wait." She swallowed a sudden lump the size of a cue ball. "You mean you're in contact with it? *Right now?*"

"Not at the moment, no, but I am monitoring the situation. Please remain on task, Captain Jaeger." The silver sphere zipped on ahead, leaving Jaeger and Toner to exchange a long, wide-eyed stare.

"Shit." A relieved, sloppy grin flickered across Toner's thin lips. "*Shit!*"

Jaeger cast an alarmed glance after Me, and Toner's mouth snapped shut. They had to assume the AI had sophisticated audio sensors.

Instead, Toner reached down and tapped a message into the personal computer at his side. Lingering behind, ostensibly to examine a carving of a juvenile egg-dragon, Jaeger checked her messages.

Maybe the eggs r ok after all, Toner had written, echoing a hope that Jaeger hadn't dared to let herself feel.

Slowly, she shook her head. **We can't get our hopes up,** she wrote—though doing so made her vaguely nauseated. **If Virgil is alive, there's a reason it hasn't contacted us yet.**

Across the room, she saw Toner's brows tighten into a glower as he studied her text. He started to type a response—

Jaeger could almost hear his pissed rejoinder—when Me zipped between them.

"I have finished my scans of this room, and Captain Kwin wishes to proceed to the next chamber."

"That door was sealed when I first came here," Occy said quietly. Somehow, he'd packed away his scanners and slipped up right behind Jaeger without her noticing. Now he huddled in her shadow. "There are levers embedded in the Locauri skulls, right where the antennae bases should be. When I touched them all, there was some kind of discharge, and that section of the wall blew open."

He blinked, squinting against the harsh light. Then he reached into his pack with one tentacle and drew out a few light thermal hoods. He handed one to Jaeger and Toner, then slipped another over his face. "I don't have sunglasses in my bag," he apologized. "These will have to do."

Jaeger tugged the hood over her face and activated the light-reduction function. Instantly, the searing light of the room beyond faded into a much more tolerable glow.

Jaeger stepped past the Locauri statues, following Me into an endless white void.

CHAPTER TWENTY-TWO

Even with the help of her thermal hood, it took a moment for Jaeger's eyes to adjust to the new chamber. They had walked out of an art museum and into the heart of a crystal geode. The walls glittered, lit from within by countless pinpoints of light. Every surface was angular and irregular, cracked and turned in on itself a thousand times over, but there seemed to be some kind of logic to the kaleidoscope of crystal surfaces the same way there was a logic to an Escher painting.

"This is crazy."

Jaeger turned to see Occy standing in the doorway, staring raptly at the shimmering, faintly reflective walls. He curled up the bottom of his thermal hood, leaving his mouth free. Even with half his face obscured, the boy was beautiful.

Then his tentacles crawled into the geode after him.

"I've read about this." He was awestruck. "Architecture grown out of manipulated crystal lattices. I've never heard of anyone getting it to work on this scale, though."

Toner rapped a knuckle against a crystal protruding from the wall and winced. "It's…rock, all right. What a headache."

Jaeger nodded in agreement. Even through her hood, the room was like a brilliantly lit mirror maze, except with a billion times a billion minuscule mirrors on every surface, turned in every direction. Visual overload made it impossible for her to pick out the boundaries of the chamber.

"A headache?" Me asked. The silvery baseball floated a few meters ahead of Toner, slowly rotating as it lanced a scanner over the stony surfaces. "Oh, oh, yes, I *see!* You have *simple* eyes! This environment must be very confusing to you."

"Simple eyes?" Toner asked.

"As opposed to compound," Jaeger muttered, squinting and feeling her way to the nearest wall. Her hand fell over a lump of rigidly defined crystal. "Overseers and Locauri see the world differently." She remembered the dizzying computer displays she'd glimpsed on the Overseer mother ship months ago. "This probably makes perfect sense to them."

"Great. Because to me, it looks like a big, pretty cave." Toner turned to see Occy crouched beside a crystal formation, rummaging through his tool kit.

"I think these are some kind of electrical conduits running through the crystals," Occy said. "Information passing through sodium ions latticed through the crystal structure... Oh man." He found one of his scanners and pulled it from his bag. He pressed it against the crystal node and started tapping the screen. "Oh *man*, if I'm right about this..."

"About what?" Toner asked. "What are you thinking?"

"Theoretically, you can grow a computer out of crystals. Or a generator. Honestly, with the right matrices, if you know what you're doing, you can grow *any* kind of machine or calculator out of the right crystals."

Occy looked up with his mouth spread in a wide grin. "I'm

picking up high-energy radiation coming from *every point* in this room. I think the whole thing is some kind of generator."

"But there's nothing *here.*" Toner rubbed his neck irritably.

"There totally is!" Occy sprang to his feet and crossed the chamber, dragging his limp tentacles behind him. Jaeger hadn't seen him this excited in a long time—and certainly never while on the planet. He took Toner's hand and pressed it against a chamber wall. "It's warm, right? You feel it?"

"Yeah," Toner said doubtfully. "It's kinda warm."

"That's because it's *on*," Occy breathed.

Movement in the corner of her eye made Jaeger turn to see Me's hologram projector flare to life.

Toner screamed. Jaeger was glad he did so she didn't have to.

The weird light-bending properties of the chamber took holo-Kwin and exploded him across every conceivable surface. The effect afforded them all an intimately close view of Kwin's inhuman face-parts, no matter which way they turned. From where he sat by the wall fiddling with his scanners, Occy yelped, recoiling away from a wide set of mandibles that appeared out of nowhere.

"INteresting," Kwin observed. Even the speaker projection bounced strangely, making Jaeger feel like she was standing in a swarm of Kwins. "I AGree with LIEUtenant OCCy. The STRUcture APPears to be a TRAINEd CRYstal MAtrix. Our SCIentists have EXperimented with such PROcesses BEfore, but it was NEver WIDEly ADopted."

"So you're saying it's a machine," Toner said. Carefully, he lifted a foot, debated where to put it, realized there was nowhere he could put it that *wouldn't* be on Kwin's face and stomped over to join Occy.

"UNdoubtedly. And it is GENerating the RAdiation."

"Which we're here to turn off." Jaeger turned to her chief engineer. "Occy? How did you activate this thing?"

Occy's head sank between his shoulders in shame. "Sorry, Captain," he mumbled. "It's not as easy turning it off as it was turning it on. I already checked. The levers in the Locauri statues locked into place. I don't think I could unlock them without breaking the actual statues, and even then there's no promise it would work. In fact, I'm pretty sure it wouldn't."

"So what do we do?" Toner poked irritably at one crystal node decorated with a thousand tiny Kwin faces. "Go get a baseball bat and start smashing?"

Occy winced. On the screens, Kwin's mandibles clicked in what must have been alarm.

"Let's hold off on the nuclear option for now," Jaeger said. She paced the room, hands out ahead of her to help her make sense of the irregular walls. "Occy, what are your scanners showing?"

Occy frowned at his scanner screen. "I'm picking up all kinds of electrical and radio activity humming through the conduits in the walls. No idea what any of it means, though." His eyebrows jumped. He dropped his scanner with a *clang*, then dug through his bag and came up with what Jaeger recognized as a basic ground-penetrating sonar unit.

"I might be able to get a general map of the crystal veins with a sonar scan." He hesitated, then looked at an image of Kwin's face floating on a broken crystal stalactite overhead. "I, uh, can't promise that a sonar sweep won't cause micro-fractures in the crystals, though."

To Jaeger's surprise, Kwin waved a dismissive antenna. "This STRUCture has been BURied here for at least ten

THOUsand years. Your SOnar SCANner CANnot harm it any more than LOcal quakes have. Please run the scan."

"Okay." Occy nodded sharply and pushed himself to his feet. "It'll take a couple of minutes to set up. I'm gonna want to run it from a few different locations for increased accuracy."

While Occy busied himself calibrating the scanner, Jaeger paced carefully through the forest of crystal outcroppings. "All right," she said. "What do we know about this place? Kwin, you said the Locauri believe there's something here that shouldn't be disturbed."

"The EARliest COUsin REFerences to this shrine are in VEry old DIAlects," Kwin said. "Not all of my SCHOlars Agree on the TRANslation. SPIrit. Beast. MONster. TERRible light. If ROUsed, they say, it will bring DEstruction."

"Destructive light, huh?" Toner tipped his head back, studying the faint shimmer of mica flecks in the walls beneath Kwin's hologram. "Radioactivity, check."

"It's a sort of monster or evil spirit," Jaeger agreed. "So, what is it? Who put it here?"

"Do they say who built the shrine, Kwin?" Toner asked. "Because you say it wasn't you, and it's obviously not the Locauri."

"Not *our* Locauri," Jaeger said.

The images of Kwin around her twitched, mandibles snapping neatly shut. Jaeger turned, picked Me's floating sphere out of the visual confusion, and stepped toward it. "Not *our* Locauri," she said again, studying Kwin's face projected onto the walls behind Me. "*Our* Locauri live simply. Are they all like that, Kwin? Have they always lived simply?"

Kwin twitched again, his head jerking to the side and back to the screen. "Please EXcuse me for a MOment. My SCHOlars wish to CONfer."

The hologram projector snapped off, drowning all of them in a glittering white chamber once more.

Jaeger blinked at Me. "That was...abrupt."

"I believe the Overseers are very excited," the droid said happily. "There is a lot of activity among the comms channels on Captain Kwin's ship at the moment. Please stand by, Captain Jaeger. I'm sure Kwin will fill you in as soon as he has a grasp of the situation."

"Great." Jaeger sighed. She turned back to Occy as the boy pushed himself to his feet. His portable sonar sweeper was a cylinder about twice the size of a tennis ball tube. A dozen wired diodes sprouted out of one end. Occy had pressed the diodes over one wall section in a pattern carefully composed to account for the irregular crystal outcroppings.

"I'm ready for the first scan," Occy said. "Heads up. It might make the crystals rattle some."

"Kwin gave us the go-ahead," Jaeger said. "Do it."

Occy nodded and pressed the tip of one tentacle against his sonar sweeper. For a second, nothing happened. Then Jaeger felt a faint tingling in her toes and along the tips of her fingers, where she rested her hand against the wall. The vibration tickled, growing stronger and strangely high-pitched, like the not-quite-heard ringing of distant bells in some old Christmas carol.

"Whoa." Toner frowned as he braced himself between two stalactites. "Uh, kid? Is it supposed to be doing *that much—*"

Occy dropped to his knees, poking at the sonar screen. His mouth twisted into a grimace. "No, I don't think so. No. Oh. Oh no. The crystal is oscillating to the electric frequency. Something about the structure is amplifying it."

"Turn the sonar off," Jaeger said tightly.

Occy didn't wait for her to tell him twice. Trembling, he grabbed the diode cords in a fist and ripped them free of the wall.

The vibrating grew stronger.

"Uh, Occy?" Toner took an uneasy step toward Jaeger as if preparing to pick her up and fling her out of danger. "It's still—"

Occy screamed. As the steady glowing light of the cave pulsed down to a dim flicker, the boy balled his fist and slammed it into the wall, hard enough to make his knuckles bleed. "I should have known that!" he cried. "Why can't I do anything right?"

"Well, I've heard enough," Toner said almost cheerfully as he closed a strong hand around Jaeger's arm. "It's time to go."

All at once, the lights went out.

Somewhere in the blackness, Occy bellowed a few words Jaeger had never heard from the boy before. Seeker and Toner must have been rubbing off on him.

"Please don't move," Me urged, lifting its voice above the rattling crystals. "The chamber structure is changing, hold still, or you may get—"

"We're not sticking around to get crushed," Toner shouted. "Occy, get out—"

As quickly as the light had faded, it returned.

Jaeger found herself staring at the glittering crystal walls as they shifted, growing and shrinking in a neatly ordered pattern. Outcroppings receded into the walls, while new crystal structures grew out to fill in divots and recesses—growing along straight lines, turning a neat 90-degree angle, and growing some more.

That explains the square tunnel, Jaeger thought.

The rattling ceased. The chamber stilled.

Occy, Toner, and Jaeger stood facing one another on a floor that was suddenly entirely smooth, in a room that had changed from irregular geode to perfect cube.

"What the hell?" Toner asked mildly.

As if in answer to his question, ribbons of light flowed out of the walls from all directions, converging near the chamber's center. Before Jaeger could react or even worry that it might somehow be dangerous, a spectacularly detailed hologram surrounded the four of them.

"I should have guessed." Occy was trembling. "I'm sorry, I was so stupid—"

"That's enough," Jaeger said sharply.

Occy drew in a quick breath and went rigid-still, staring at the structure built around them in light and shadow. Now that the room was no longer generating a blinding amount of light, Jaeger tugged off her hood. She recognized the hologram instantly. She had stared at something nearly identical to it plenty in the last year.

They stood inside a massive, three-dimensional rendering of Locaur.

"We can agonize over the mistakes later," Jaeger told Occy, more gently, as her eyes swept the familiar topology. The western ocean. The mountain chain splitting the main continent. "Right now, I need to know if it's safe in here."

Occy drew in a deep breath and looked down at his scanner. He nodded slowly.

"Great." Toner held his hands awkwardly in the air like he was afraid to touch anything and trigger another rearrangement. "What the hell happened?"

"I think it's stable now." Occy swallowed, making his Adam's apple bob. "Um. So. Crystal structures can change shape when you pass the right currents through them. I should've realized. It's a basic principle of oscillators.

"The idea behind crystal engineering is to design matrices that change into pre-arranged patterns, depending on what kind of current you pass through it. When I ran the sonar scan, I was shooting a current through the crystal. It must have been pretty similar to one of the signals the builders designed the matrix to respond to, so it made...this." He swept the tip of one tentacle through the room, then swirled it through the ribbons of light that formed the planet enveloping them.

"It's nice work." Toner tilted his head back to study one of the Locauri inland lakes floating above his face. "Very detailed."

It was. Jaeger had spent her fair share of time in holo-dramas and running through interactive holographic displays. From what she understood of the technology, holograms required discreet generation points—one or more projectors, usually mounted in the ceiling.

From the way the crystalline surfaces of the room shimmered and glowed, she concluded that *every surface of the crystals* themselves generated this bus-sized hologram.

"Incredible," she muttered, turning back to study the image of the emerald forests, the sapphire seas surrounding white polar caps. The streaks of mineral veins...

"What's this?" Without thinking, she reached up and waved her fingers through a thick white web shimmering beneath the planet's surface. It reminded her of spider webs or the fine threads of an elaborate system of roots. It stretched across the planet—buried beneath the crust, but above the mantle.

"We sent a current through the crystal trying to map the

structure." Occy stared at the network of white veins running like blood vessels beneath the planet's skin. "The room rearranged itself to show us its structure. Oh." His legs buckled. Jaeger and Toner caught him at the same time as the strength ran out of the boy.

"Oh," he whispered. "Oh. It's smart. And it's *really* big."

Around them, Locaur rotated slowly along its axis.

"*That?*" Toner pointed at one of the white filaments running beneath the southern hemisphere ocean. "You mean that all of this—it's all crystal veins like the one we're in right now?"

Occy could only manage a weak nod.

"Great!" Toner said. "Progress! We know that *it's big*. But what *is it?*"

"It is DANgerous."

The three of them turned. Me's projector had activated again, and now that the chamber's walls had changed into some regular, less-reflective surface, holo-Kwin stood normally beside it.

Normal, except for the fact that every centimeter of Kwin, save for his bottle-green eyes and light blue forehead smear, had turned a sickly shade of gray.

Jaeger's heart jumped into her throat. "Kwin? What's wrong?"

Kwin only stared, mandibles slowly clicking as Locaur turned, bringing the far side into sharper focus. There, buried beneath the sea on the opposite side of the planet, the network of crystal veins coalesced into a dense knot that pulsed with a faint green light. Here in this chamber, it was about the size of Jaeger's fist. In the real world, it must've been city-sized.

"We are PICKing up new TRANSmissions from EVery

point on the PLAnet, but the SIGnal is STRONGest from that LOCation." Kwin gestured at the elaborate knot of crystal veins. "Our PREsence here has ACTivated a VEry old and POWerful SYStem. The COUsins were right to shun this place. You must leave. Now. WHATever we have done, we CANnot fix it from here. We can ONly make it worse."

CHAPTER TWENTY-THREE

"G-go?" Petra clamped a hand protectively over her mouth with one hand. With the other, she pointed at the apartment door. "Like, *out there?* Are you crazy? They got my face plastered on every bulletin. And you—you're *Rush Starr!*"

Rush grinned, his eyes glittering brightly. "Darling. You think I don't know how to avoid paparazzi?"

"That's easy for you to say," she hissed, drawing her knees up to her chin. "You have all your teeth."

"Ah, yes. That reminds me." He hopped to his feet, waggling long, ring-studded fingers through the air. "Come along, darling. I have something for that."

Petra frowned, then scrambled up and followed Rush into the second room of his two-bedroom apartment. Petra had grown up in the overcrowded slums of space stations. Until a few months ago, she'd spent her entire adult life sharing a bedroom with eleven other people. She couldn't conceive of what one single human could need with a two-bedroom apartment, so she wasn't sure what to expect—maybe an extension of the Rush Starr Museum?—when the door slid open.

She was stunned into silence, therefore, to see a small room crammed floor to ceiling with computer screens, exploded consoles, and random wires. It was like stepping into a lower-decks junk shop. She'd seen nova addicts with tidier digs.

Stepping carefully to avoid exposed wires, Rush picked his way across the room and punched a combination into a wall safe.

"Is all this, uh, yours?" she asked, eying a half-eaten and long-forgotten granola bar tucked beneath a ruined speaker system. Next to it was a narrow workbench where a line of tiny fly-drones perched in various states of disrepair.

"Of course. Whose else would it be?" The wall safe opened and Rush withdrew a small plastic case. Kicking the safe shut behind him, he picked his way back to the living room. Petra couldn't tear her eyes from the mess until the door snapped shut.

She turned to see Rush on one knee before her, offering up the case like a man proposing to his sweetheart in some old holo-drama.

"Petie, darling?"

Petra stared, baffled into silence. Rush watched her, his face solemn but his eyes glittering. "Would you…" he flicked open the case to reveal two perfectly crafted prosthetic teeth, pearly white and nestled on a velvety cushion, "…walk the Concourse with me?"

It was a silly thing, but Petra *did* feel like a different woman with the perfectly sized fake teeth slotted into her gums. She'd rolled her hair into tight curls, applied some carefully contoured makeup, and wore heels that added three inches and made her ass pop as she walked. She was downright unrecognizable from the greasy-haired, gap-toothed woman looking out at her from the mugshots on every public screen they passed.

"Posture is everything. When you feel like a different person, you *are* a different person."

Petra walked along the Concourse arm-in-arm with a man she didn't recognize.

Before leaving the apartment, Rush had combed a tinted hair gel through his distinctive platinum mane, slicking it back into a tight, light-brown ponytail that looked right at home on the head of any mercantile professional. Tinted contacts had changed his eyes from gray to brown. He wore a high-collared navy suit and very official-looking shiny black boots.

Rush Starr *always* wore his distinctive eye makeup in public. It was his hallmark. The man at Petra's side, however, was some utterly forgettable mid-level bank manager.

He wasn't kidding about posture, either. When they stepped out of the apartment complex, he transformed so swiftly from an easy, open stride to an uptight, stiff-backed strut that it left her dizzy.

"Human eyes are easy to fool. The real problem," he idly said as they sauntered past a row of shops, "is the facial recognition software in the security cameras." Quite abruptly, he stopped at a small resale stall. The counter and racks were full of secondhand books and magazines; old, but in good repair—they would have to be, to cater to the upper deck clientele. Kiosk rental on the Concourse wasn't cheap.

"If you know when and where the cameras will be pointing," he said quietly, lifting a brittle detective novel off the shelf and deftly angling her to face him, "you can avoid showing them your face, too. Ah, I love Agatha Christie. Have you read *Death on the Nile?*"

Petra barely had time to open her mouth to answer—she'd never heard of it, no—before Rush dropped the book and shepherded her on with a loud sigh. "But the cover is torn. No, I'm sure I can get a better copy at Yolando's shop."

As he ushered her past the stall, he jerked his head subtly to the left. She followed his gesture and saw a security camera angling away from their direction.

"So many cameras in the Concourse these days." Rush *tsk*'d and shook his head. They drew near to the H-sector boardwalk—a moving section of floor that dipped smoothly down from the Concourse like the subway tunnel in any city on old Earth.

"Isn't Yolondo's shop up in G-sector?" Petra asked as Rush slipped them onto the boardwalk between a group of guild bankers and a cluster of teenagers clutching shopping bags. She was more than a little surprised that the rock star even knew about Yolondo's little second-hand junk shop.

"Last I checked, yes." Rush sounded distracted. His head was on a swivel as the moving sidewalk drew them down into the *Constitution's* lower decks. "We're not going to Yolondo's."

"Oh."

As they descended to the lower decks, the makeup of the people changed. The Concourse, near the heart of the ship where gravity was lightest, was the wealthiest sector of any freighter. Its residents were officers and doctors, guild managers, and Tribe administrators. As they descended the boardwalk and increasing centrifugal force made everything heavier, custom-tailored suits gave way to soldier fatigues and maintenance worker jumpsuits.

A group of sullen-eyed and grease-stained fabricators stepped onto the walkway ahead of them as they crossed the halfway point from inner to outer decks. One of the stone-faced young men glanced over his shoulder. With a cold shock, Petra realized it was Kurt, one of the teenagers she'd mentored at the youth center last year. The last few months had aged the kid a decade, robbing him of all youthful vigor and leaving him staring around the corridors with blank, hollow eyes.

When his gaze passed over Petra, she gasped and turned away, burying her face in Rush's shoulder. If the older man was off-put by the crack in her front, he hid it with the easy grace of a lifelong actor.

"I'm sorry, honey," he said in an even tone, his normally grandiose accent flattened into something unrecognizable—almost banal—as he put an arm around her and patted her head. "She was a very sweet old woman. We'll all miss your grandmother terribly."

Grasping at the cue and terrified to lift her face lest Kurt recognize her, Petra let her shoulders tremble in a fake sob.

"They're gone," Rush said after a minute of tense silence. "Friend of yours?"

Petra gasped and straightened. "Yeah. Kurt's grown so tall," she whispered. "And he got so *skinny*."

"Everyone's lost weight," he said. He didn't duck his head or whisper. He didn't turn away, avoiding the dead-eyed stares of the increasingly grubby maintenance workers filling the boardwalk around them. Why should he? He was only some banker escorting his wife to the lower decks on family business.

There was nothing special about his voice, or his posture, or his clothes. Acting furtively would only draw attention. "There was an unannounced cut to the standard meals a few weeks ago. Brass denies it, but there's no denying the fleet-provided meals are smaller than they used to be."

Petra pulled her sweater tighter around her. The outer decks, closer to space and further from the prime generators, were always cold, too. As a group of janitors shuffled off the boardwalk and into a low-class residential corridor, she flushed.

"Don't feel guilty about your breakfast," Rush added, somehow guessing the source of her guilt. "Even standard rations are still much nicer than the swill they fed you for months. You deserved a decent meal. Ah. This is our stop."

"Right to Red sector?" Petra was deeply startled as Rush pulled her off the boardwalk and into a narrow, dimly-lit corridor right in the gap between a residential complex and a waste-disposal center. Here, the ceilings were low and covered with ductwork, and the lights flickered, ever threatening to burn out.

"Of course." Rush frowned. "I thought this place was your second home. Everyone said you liked to relax in the Red sectors."

"Well, yeah." Petra flushed and hurried after him. She'd found her feet again in these heels. No denying that the deep, familiar *thump* of bass coming from the heavy machinery on the other side of the walls helped.

It was almost like music, and she knew the seedy bars and gambling joints that sprang up in Red sectors used the noise to mask the sounds of cheap nightlife. It was that very same mechanical noise that made the Red sectors next to useless for housing for all but the most desperate of people.

Petra *did* like the dim lights, the constant noise and music, the sharp scents of illegal booze, the filthy press of bodies crammed into the bars and clubs, desperate to get away from rigidly-ordered fleet life. She was a little embarrassed to admit as much to a man whose private sonic jacuzzi she had used only a few hours ago.

Ahead, just outside an open door, a man bundled in threadbare blankets stretched along the wall—either sleeping off a hangover or perhaps, for lack of a better place to go, simply *sleeping*. The man stirred, staring up at them with jaundiced eyes while Petra and Rush stepped past him and turned into the adjoining room.

It was an improvised nightclub and dive bar, crammed into the void between a recycling center and water treatment plant. Petra couldn't hold back a wide grin as she stepped into the dingy little bar at Rush's side. She remembered this joint. She'd been here before. They had a great karaoke catalog.

Then her eyes adjusted to the near-darkness, and her grin faded. Two shadowy figures sat on stools at the bar along the sidewall. Someone had erected a makeshift tent on the tiny stage. Piles of stinking rags heaped into the booths. As Rush led Petra toward the bar, one of the piles stirred. It was a skeletally thin woman, eying Petra from inside an old sleeping bag.

More indigent folks, like the man sleeping outside. There were indigents on all three of the freighters, of course, especially since Jaeger's mutiny had left the fleet vastly overcrowded. People who couldn't make themselves fit neatly into the slots society provided because illness had broken them, because experience taught them that living outside the system was better than living in it, or because they just didn't want to. They fell through the cracks, sure. Still, Petra had never heard of so many of them falling and all landing in the same place.

By the smell of backed-up sewage coming from the two bathroom doors across from the bar and the empty shelves where the bottles of liquor—legal, illegal, and synthetic—had once stood, this place hadn't been a nightclub in a while. All but one of the fluorescent ceiling lights were dead.

A man with a bushy unibrow stood behind the bar, his mustache twitching as he peered up at the ceiling.

A remotely-controlled maintenance duct droid was crawling over the conduits like a spider, digging at the mess of cables dangling out of a light fixture. Petra assumed one of the technicians at the nearest maintenance guild office was controlling it.

The fleet always sent people in the flesh to work on repairs, but waiting lists for fleet maintenance could be months long. If you had a job you needed done quick, and you couldn't bribe some fleet manager to bump you up the list, your best bet was to cross your fingers and hire the guild.

Something nudged her shoulder. "In a moment, here," Rush said under his breath, "I'm going to slip into the men's room. Wait a few beats, then duck in after me."

Petra turned her head, caught a whiff from the toilets, and wrinkled her nose. She turned to Rush to object—even if the toilet weren't overflowing, two people could *not* fit in one of those tiny stalls—but he'd already stepped up to the bar.

The unibrowed barkeeper glanced at him and gave a quick nod. Then, his stare swiveling back to the droid, he reached under the bar and drew up a single shot glass and bottle. Clearly, this was an old ritual between the two.

"Kramer," Rush said gruffly.

"Mister," the barkeeper said—or at least Petra assumed he said it. She couldn't see the man's mouth move beneath his mustache. "Another for the lady?" He filled Rush's glass as Petra slipped onto a stool.

Rush nodded. "Trouble in paradise?" He eyed the overhead droid as he lifted the glass and sniffed.

"These days it's hard to get maintenance down here for anything less than a hull breach," the barkeeper—Kramer—said. "Guild repair rates have doubled and my rainy day funds have about run dry."

Rush grunted into his whiskey and downed his glass in one shot. He snapped it neatly onto the bar. "That's a pity." He languidly stood as he gestured at the people sleeping in the booths. "I warned you not to take the charity cases, Kramer." His lip twitched in what might have been a sneer as he touched his waist. "Looks like we'll have to find another dive, my dear. This one has gone to the dogs."

Petra choked on her whiskey as Rush turned and vanished into the bathroom. That was a pity because it was good stuff. She stared at Kramer, eyes watering and throat burning. She opened her mouth, unsure of what to say—probably to apologize for her companion being an asshole—when, overhead, the droid's speaker blurted to life.

"Goddammit," it barked, loud enough to make a few of the people stir and lift their heads. "This fucking thing is falling apart. Piece of shit isn't worth the scrap it's made from. The left grappling arm isn't responding."

The bartender coughed and shifted his weight. "Uh, sir? Mister...tech?" His mustache twitched. "Your speaker is on."

The droid *clanked* as it dug a long arm through the guts of the fixture. The lights strobed from light to dark. Petra glanced over her shoulder, eying the bathroom door.

You better know what you're doing, she thought as she slid to her feet.

"Fuck," the man controlling the droid decided as a fresh shower of sparks spilled from the ceiling. "Looks like the comm system broke too, and that discharge shorted out my visuals. Just fucking great. You know I'm gonna have to charge you extra for the wear and tear, Kramer."

Petra didn't see Kramer's reaction—or much of anything because the light continued to strobe like a bad dream—as she opened the bathroom door and slipped inside.

The stall was less than a meter square, and utterly dark. The smell of the overflowing waste funnel hit her like a kick to the gut. She clamped a hand over her mouth and was doubling over to add her puke to the stew in the bowl when, in a growing square of soft yellow light, the back wall slid to one side.

Rush reached out from behind the false wall and pulled her into the light.

CHAPTER TWENTY-FOUR

Night had fallen by the time Jaeger and her crew made it out of the shrine and across the river. The forest was quiet save for the rushing river and the trilling songs of night birds.

They walked about ten minutes down the trail back to the *Osprey* when the flicker of torches filled the path around them. Six big Locauri faded out of the underbrush, their multifaceted black eyes glittering by firelight. Jaeger recognized most of them as Elders, and half of them had translator bands coiled around one antenna. Though each was barely over a meter and a quarter tall, the shadows they cast over the ferns were downright ominous.

Occy shrunk behind her and Toner, breathing hard.

"Sorry, Captain," Seeker called. He ambled up the hiking trail behind the Locauri, comfortably astride Baby. "They were…dead set on meeting you as soon as you got back."

Jaeger spun, rounding on the largest Locauri, a female Elder whose name in the clicking Locauri sounded a bit like *Tiki*. "This area isn't safe for you," she said severely. "The radiation is still —"

"The light is still burning, yes," said Tiki's translator band. "You have not turned it off as you promised. Even if you had, laws must be respected. We have come to take the Chief Engineer into custody."

Beside Jaeger, Toner grinned—showing a few too many teeth. "Okay. Come and get him."

"Enough," Jaeger said sharply, stepping between Tiki and Toner. "We're not giving up on Occy. He is part of my crew and has done nothing wrong. We will fix this."

She turned, looking for Me, but the little AI droid was way ahead of her. The silvery sphere zipped forward, and holo-Kwin appeared before Tiki. The Overseer had apparently shaken off his shock and returned to his normal shade of mossy brown. Although the other Locauri lowered their antennae respectfully, Tiki only stared up at her much taller cousin.

"We have NOthing to hide," Kwin said. "Thus, we will COMmunicate so that all may UNderstand. Agreed?"

Tiki hesitated, antennae idly waving as she studied Jaeger and Toner. Then she lifted her chin to Kwin again. "Agreed," Tiki answered after a considerable pause. "There are little laws, and there are Big Laws, Tall One."

"I UNderstand," Kwin said. "BEcause the LIEUtenant did not UNderstand your Big Laws, and BEcause he meant no harm, you will treat him with UTmost REspect, Agreed?"

"I don't like the sound of that," Toner hissed into Jaeger's ear.

Jaeger glanced from her first mate to Seeker, who sat grim-faced astride Baby a few meters away. Then she glanced over her shoulder.

Occy stood on the trail behind her, head between his shoulders like he wanted to curl up and die. He stared up at her through those long lashes, his eyes watery and soft in the firelight. His lips moved.

As Kwin and Tiki fell into a conversation that was more body language than words, Jaeger took a step backward.

"I need to go with them, don't I?" Occy whispered.

Jaeger winced. *Yes,* she wanted to say. Although this was all a misunderstanding, she trusted the Locauri to be fair to her and her crew. If she couldn't trust them that much, they had no business living together. As Occy's CO, it was her duty to tell him what to do when he couldn't make that decision for himself. It was her duty to give orders for the good of the mission.

The look of terror on his soft face made her want to turn away and vomit.

He was a kid. She couldn't order him off to prison, could she?

On the other hand, he was a senior officer of her crew. A malfunction in his activation process had left him physically, mentally, and emotionally immature—but he was still *a senior officer.*

She turned, looking him in the eye. He'd always had the most beautiful face she'd seen on another human being. He was a work of art, a Michelangelo sculpture in the flesh, too young for this life. The sight of him punched a hole in the weak spot in her heart where a little girl used to be.

"If you're not ready to go, we won't let them take you," she whispered. "It's your choice." And then, because it was late, or because she was tired, or because the stars had aligned, she said something a captain shouldn't have said to a member of her crew. "I'll still love you no matter what you choose."

Occy closed his eyes and drew a deep, steadying breath.

A NEW HOME

She waited for him to say something, either return the sentiment or comment on how wildly inappropriate it was.

Instead, he only nodded. Then he squared his shoulders and walked to the clearing where Kwin and Tiki negotiated his fate.

"I'm ready," he said.

Toner opened his mouth. Then he saw the look of stone on Jaeger's face, and his jaw snapped shut. Without a word, he turned and stalked into the forest alone.

Kwin looked down at Occy. Tiki turned her head, meeting his eye. "Good," said her translator band.

"The COUsins will treat you as a guest UNtil we REsolve this MATTer," Kwin added, nodding slowly.

Occy lifted his chin. "And then?"

"Judgment," Tiki said simply. "Much damage, much judgment. Little damage, little judgment."

"Occy is my best engineer." Jaeger stepped forward. When the Locauri bristled, she lifted her hands, placating. "May he be allowed to communicate freely with me while he's locked up? His help may be invaluable to fixing this."

Tiki hesitated, then dipped one antenna in acknowledgment. The other Locauri Elders scuttled forward, huddling closely around Occy as if worried he might try to run away, but also careful not to step on his dragging tentacles with their spiny legs or hit him with their wings. At first, Occy flinched away from the crowd, but after steeling himself, he bent over and gathered up the dead weight of his tentacles. He marched into the night, escorted by six aliens.

"I'm sorry, Captain," Occy said over his shoulder. "I'm afraid I won't make tomorrow's lunch date."

Jaeger wished Toner had been here. He would've appreciated the cheek. She could only nod solemnly and give him a salute. "We'll postpone it until you get back, Lieutenant."

"He may keep the communicator always," Tiki said as Occy and his escort faded into the trees. "To help you fix problem."

Jaeger inclined her head. "Thank you. Now the rest of us must go back to the *Osprey*. We have work to do."

CHAPTER TWENTY-FIVE

Landing the *Osprey* on Locaur had been a necessary step in getting a permanent settlement established, but it did render large areas of the ship next to useless. Most of the livable space in the central column, for instance, was now on either the ceiling or the sloping walls.

However, the loss of living space in the central column had been more than made up for now that all the cargo holds and bays in the outer wings were entirely accessible without the use of mag soles. The crew had moved their temporary living quarters from the general crew module of the central column to makeshift barracks in the starboard wing cargo hold.

Well, most of the crew.

"Bet you're re-thinking your orientation choices now." Toner flopped onto what had once been a perfectly good loveseat, before Baby claimed it, and glared at an access hatch halfway up the side of the wall of the command crew lounge. It was the hatch to the former captain's quarters. Like the rest of them, Toner was still damp with stagnant river water and coated in a thin layer of grime. By the smears of mud across his front, Jaeger had to wonder if he'd made a solo detour to go mud-wrestle a tree monster as a way to blow off steam.

"No," Jaeger said simply. She pointed at the door of her quarters, which was in the floor nearby, and easily accessible. "I am not. I'll take my bed over some stranger's jacuzzi, thanks. There is an entire row of perfectly nice shower stalls in the general crew quarters."

Silently, though, she thanked Toner for his complaining. It took her mind off Occy, right up until the moment she needed to tap open a communications channel on her personal computer.

"Lieutenant?" She licked dry lips and braced herself for the soft voice of a frightened child. "You read me?"

The pause on the other end of the line felt downright eternal. "I read you, Captain."

Jaeger felt a wave of relief. At least he didn't sound like he had been crying. "How are you doing over there?"

"I'm...okay," Occy said slowly. "They cleared out an old nest in one of the smaller trees for me. It's a little cramped, but it's warm. They said I'll be staying here until...uh, until Judgment."

Jaeger bit back a sigh. "Great. Now let's figure out how to get you out of there."

She turned to face her team: Toner, splayed across the loveseat, with Baby grumbling over his shoulder. Seeker, sitting backward on a folding chair he had dug out of some storage closet, his heavy brow furrowed pensively. Me floated in the air to one side, steadily projecting holo-Kwin into the space between the couch and loveseat.

"Occy," Jaeger said, "You're on conference. Okay, everybody. What, exactly, have we gotten ourselves into?"

Holo-Kwin turned to Me. "Bring up the DIsplay."

A second projector sprang out of the sphere. Jaeger wondered how many tricks the little thing had up its sleeve as Toner pushed himself up to examine the three-dimensional hologram of Locaur slowly rotating above the coffee table. "This is the display we saw down in the shrine," he said.

"I had enough time to take a scan of it," Me said. "Though I believe the shrine displayed a real-time schematic of the crystalline superstructure. Mine does not."

"We are CALibrating our SCANNers to DEtect the CRYstal veins," Kwin agreed. "HOPEfully my ship will soon be Able to MONitor any CHANges in the STRUcture."

"Changes in the structure?" Toner cocked his head.

"Yeah," Occy said through the commlink. "Like how the room changed when we tried to run the sonar. I don't know how drastically the shape of the structures can change, but we know that they CAN change."

"Like a highway system up and rearranging itself on a whim?" Toner frowned.

"Probably not on a whim," Occy corrected. "You need to tell it how to change with the right current patterns."

"Agreed. We doubt it has SIGnificantly ALtered in SEveral THOUsand years," Kwin added. "We would have NOticed the SEISmic ACTivity BEfore."

"So there's this big-ass underground…thing…stretched around the entire planet," Toner said.

"It's probably a computer of some kind," Occy interjected. "Or at least it has some extremely sophisticated programming built directly into the crystal structures."

"Okay. Occy stumbled onto this supercomputer, pressed a few buttons, and boom. Turned it on. Next thing we know, it's emitting weird radiation. We go in to try to turn the radiation off. Decide to do a little exploring first. When we hit it with a sonar scan, the whole thing lights up, rearranges itself, and starts blasting out even more radiation. Is that right?"

There was a moment of silence.

"Yes," Kwin said sourly.

"I'm sorry," Occy whispered through the link. Jaeger was about to reassure him when Kwin lashed an antenna through the air.

"I am as CULpable as you, LIEUtenant. I should have known BETter than to ask you to do the scan."

"We have better things to do than bellyache," Seeker muttered, busying himself on his computer screen.

"Agreed." Still, Jaeger studied Kwin out of the corner of her eye. He was angry with himself. *Sometimes,* she thought, *he was entirely too human for a three-meter tall bug alien.*

"To be clear," Me said, in its customary rapid speech, "The levels of radiation in this area have not significantly changed. We are, however, now picking up very strong radio and radiation signals originating from this point."

The hologram image of Locaur spun, zooming in on the pulsing knot of crystal veins buried beneath the sea on the other side of the planet.

"Something here is broadcasting a message out into space," Me said.

"What's the message?" Seeker looked up from his tablet.

"My SCHOlars are WORKing on a TRANSlation now," Kwin said. "It APpears to be an ancient, OBscure DIAlect."

"But a dialect," Jaeger said. "Of the Overseer language?"

Kwin hesitated.

Toner, who had been frowning at the crystal hub beneath the ocean, rounded on the alien. "So this thing is yours. Your shrine with the evil monster and the light of destruction and the radiation." His eyes narrowed. "Do not tell me Occy is in jail because your grandparents didn't clean up their nuclear waste site, Kwin."

"No," Kwin said. "Not OVERseer. Not of the COUsins, EIther. But SOMEthing..." He lifted his two front claws and touched them delicately together. "VERy old. From long BEfore our EXOdus from this QUADrant."

"Your common ancestor," Jaeger said quietly. Kwin flicked an antenna in her direction.

"Yes. Our...FOREbears. Over FIFty THOUsand years Ago, they had MAStery Over this arm of the GALaxy. When their EMpire COLLapsed, SURvivors of the great DIsaster fled and BEcame REfugees."

"The Rite of !Tsok n Sshoogn," Jaeger muttered, thinking of one of the ancient Overseer customs Kwin had tried to teach her months ago when she was desperate to build a good relationship with his people.

"Yes. MAny of our CUstoms come from the time of our EXile. My ANcestors ADapted to life in space. They MODified their GEnetic STRUcture to Adapt to low GRAVity, low OXYgen ENvironments. THey WANdered the GALaxy BElieving they were the ONly SURvivors of the DIsaster. When they Eventually found their way back home, they were SHOCKed to find that some of the FOREbears had SURvived—in a PRImitive, REduced form, yes, but SURvived."

There was a long stretch of silence as Jaeger's team absorbed this information.

"So Locaur is your home planet," Jaeger mused. "I...had my doubts."

"We are not CERtain. Much of the HIStorical REcord from BEfore the DIsaster is lost."

"The Locauri aren't only your cousins. They're a more

organic extension of the species you were before you diverged."

"Yes."

"You mean to tell me," Toner said slowly, "that you *assholes* genetically modified yourselves to be faster and smarter and tougher and...and *taller* than you were before?"

"Yes."

"Toner," Jaeger said. "Now's not the time to get into it."

Toner ignored her. "But since *we* modded ourselves, that's no bueno. Your people are still gonna make us flush hundreds of thousands of our embryos because they're *monsters* or whatever—even though you did the same thing."

"Yes," Kwin said simply. "I have no DEfense for the COUNcil's DEcision."

Toner sucked in a breath, swelling up like a balloon—and like a balloon, about to explode.

Jaeger snatched his wrist, yanking him down so she could talk into his ear.

"Thou shouldst not have been old 'til thou hadst been wise," she hissed. "Let it go, and I'll tell you a secret later. Right now we need to stay on topic."

Toner blinked, staring at her with those cold blue eyes. She saw the debate rage on his face and felt that awkward tension—then it passed. He nodded.

"You said records from before this Disaster were lost," Seeker said. Although he addressed Kwin, he was eying Jaeger and Toner over his computer screen. "But they're not lost. There's a planet-sized artifact built by these Forebears right beneath our feet. It's an archaeologists' wet dream."

Kwin didn't answer.

"Seeker is right." Jaeger was starting to put the pieces together. "But you're not happy about it. Because it's powerful, and all we know is that it's spilling radiation and mystery signals. Your people are scared of something like this, aren't they?"

"Why would they be scared of it?" Toner slumped back into the loveseat. The ruined springs gave way, dropping him straight to the floor. Toner shot Baby a dirty look.

"Because for all they know," Seeker said, "this crystal thing is a self-modulating doomsday superweapon. It's a tale as old as time. An advanced civilization outsmarts itself. Fucks up its planet, somehow or other. A few survivors rush out into space to save themselves and vow that they'll do better."

He met Jaeger's eye. "Then somebody stumbles onto a secret weapon or lost technology that might give them a survival edge over the competition, and things get tricky. People start to *disagree* over what to do with it."

Jaeger let out a long breath and sank onto the couch, massaging her temples. She hadn't missed Seeker's point. The Overseer's story of exodus and return very much mirrored the fate that might be in store for humanity. If, ten thousand years from now, her descendants returned to Earth to find all the tools their ancestors had used to ruin it…

"A SUccinct ANalysis of the SITuation," Kwin relented. "And ENtirely PLAUsible, I am AFraid to say. I have REceived a PREliminary TRANslation of part of the MEssage."

Everybody caught the grim undertone in the tall alien's words.

"Let's hear it," Jaeger murmured.

"Translating now." Me *beeped* for a moment, and its normally pleasant voice turned guttural and harsh.

"The end begins by war. Grow and strike. Creation is for one and alone. The end begins by war. Grow and strike. Creation is for

one and alone. The end begins by war. Grow and strike. Creation is for —"

Kwin waved an antenna, and the recording ended abruptly.

In the silence that followed, Jaeger heard Occy's shallow breathing from the other end of the comm line.

"That doesn't sound good," the young engineer said.

"Nope," Toner agreed.

"The FOREbears DEstroyed THEMselves," Kwin said. "Their LEgacy REmains one of DEstruction."

"We have no idea what this thing is trying to talk to," Jaeger whispered. "Or who."

"COrrect."

"It could be trying to fire up other forgotten machines. Activate other automated systems." Jaeger swallowed hard. "Systems that might be deadly."

"Yes."

That was all Jaeger needed to hear. She pushed to her feet. "We need to get to the Knot and turn it off."

Kwin dipped both antennae in a gesture of assent. "As we speak, I am PREparing to DISpatch a droid to scout the Ocean and find a way to ACCess this Knot."

"Great," Jaeger said brightly, all fatigue of the long day forgotten as adrenaline leaked into her system. "I'll grab my purse."

She was halfway to her quarters before Toner caught up to the conversation and scrambled out of the mess that was the love seat. "Wait, what?"

"Grab your go-bag," she commanded. "You and me and Baby are taking the shuttle out for a spin. Seeker, you're in charge while we're gone."

"I figured," Seeker said without looking up. "I sent a

message asking Bufo to make sure he stocks the shuttle with pressurized rebreathers. In case you need to go for a swim."

"That is a fantastic thought." She yanked open the hatch to her quarters. "Thank you."

"Hang on!" Toner hopped after her. "I can't leave *right now*."

Jaeger stopped with her foot on the first rung of the ladder. "And why not? What is more important than turning off a possible doomsday machine?"

Toner met her gaze. His mouth worked wordlessly.

"Spit it out."

"...I had plans with Portia," Toner mumbled. Jaeger imagined that if his genetic modifications hadn't bleached his skin an eternal and inflexible white, he would've been blushing. "She made me promise to meet her later." He stared at Jaeger, his eyebrows arching up to his hairline. "She said she wanted to *show me* something."

Jaeger stared at him, face blank.

"I...*really* want to know what she wanted to show me. Captain."

Jaeger shook her head and padded down the ladder into her quarters. "You're coming," she called over her shoulder. "Even if I have to drag you kicking and screaming. You're coming."

CHAPTER TWENTY-SIX

Day of Abandonment

Lawrence and Sarah crested the final rise two hours after dawn to see the final fence between them and salvation.

The rendezvous airfield was a two-kilometer asphalt circle, contained by a double row of tall, barbed, and electrified fences. Six spindly watchtowers dotted the perimeter at even intervals, patrolled by poncho-clad figures with long rifles.

Docked at the center of the otherwise deserted airfield was a Rum Runner-class transport shuttle. It resembled an old pontoon boat with oversized floats joined across the top by a flat slice of crew accommodations. With a cargo capacity of one hundred thirty metric tons spread across the two cargo holds, it was the inter-atmospheric equivalent of an eighteen-wheeler: a workhorse and one not built with the comfort of the cargo in mind.

Not that the crowd gathered around the gate at the southern edge of the airfield cared much about comfort.

Staring at the sea of desperate bodies, Lawrence didn't think any of them even remembered what the word *comfort* meant.

Just my luck, he thought dully, *that we happened to come at this place from the one direction without a good road.*

The airfield was at the center of a wheel, with a smattering of dusty roads stretching away from it like spokes. Lines of dead and derelict transportation of every sort littered those asphalt ribbons, all the way out to the horizon. Abandoned motorcycles. Discarded rusty bikes. Rundown pickup trucks and hand-pushed shopping carts. Whatever could get them here had been ridden, to get *here.*

"There weren't so many people before," Sarah whispered, staring down the slope.

There must have been twenty thousand of them, spread across a camp that dwarfed the airfield. Many had brought tents or made them out of whatever garbage they could find. They had come expecting to wait. They'd be waiting for a long time.

Lawrence could see the single-file line of people passing through a double row of security checkpoints before being allowed to step foot onto that airfield. It was like watching sand dribble through an hourglass.

"They're not all going to fit," Sarah said, and something had left her voice—some spark of ferocity that Lawrence hadn't noticed until it was gone.

"Not by half." Lawrence shouldn't have said it, but he couldn't bring himself to mislead the kid. He tightened his hand on her shoulder. "But hey. We've got golden tickets."

Sarah stared blank-eyed down at the sea of desperate people as she fingered the dog tag around her neck. "Daddy said we were going to get in, too," she whispered.

"Your daddy had a contract written on paper." Lawrence

injected more confidence into his voice than he felt. "These—these are contracts written in steel and blood. They'll do."

He could tell she didn't believe him, but he could think of nothing else to say. After a while, she hadn't thought of anything to say either, so she patted the squirming thing beneath her shirt for comfort, squared her shoulders, and marched down to the sea.

"You're gonna have to stay close to me," he whispered as they reached the outskirts of the camp. He was keenly aware of the smell of dried and crusting blood following him like an omen, but he pulled Sarah in close, anyway.

Dead-eyed people stared at them from beneath the measly shade of their makeshift tents. Sharp-eyed people, coyotes in human flesh, stopped and stared at the pale man passing with his little dark companion. As Lawrence passed, he turned his head and pulled back his lips, letting them see teeth.

They didn't come closer.

"Things could get nasty," he murmured. "Stay close to me, and you'll be fine."

Overhead, moody clouds rumbled, close and oppressive. Lawrence remembered a time when a cloudy sky would've made mission control scrub a launch.

Sarah pressed close to his side. He felt her tremble as they approached the point where scattered tents turned into a press of bodies. Ahead, several people stepped over a dark lump trying to get closer to the gate.

It was a body.

A skeletal child, his skin red and flaking from sunburn—or something worse—crouched beside the corpse, unmoving.

Sarah stopped, her breath wavering into a dry sob as the child turned its head and stared at them with wide, vacant eyes.

"No," she whispered. She shook her head when Lawrence tried to pull her past. "No. No, no, no." She turned her head, burying her face in his ribs.

"Come on," he said. "We have to keep moving."

The girl had seized up. "No," she said again, her hands trembling as she fingered the dog tag around her neck.

"Don't do that," he said sharply, but she couldn't hear him over the sound of her internal panic. He didn't know if the coyotes watching them knew what one of those dog tags meant—but if they did, flashing it around was the worst thing she could have done.

"Let him have it," she gulped, shaking her head. "Let him have it. I don't want it. I don't want—"

"Listen to me!" He fell to his knees and grabbed her by the shoulders—harder than he should have. She cringed, falling still and silent, watching him with wide, terrified eyes.

"Listen," he said again, letting his voice go soft. "I know. I get it. You wanna throw everything away so someone else can have a shot at a better future. But that kid—he's already dead."

"No!"

"I can smell it," he snarled. "Those are high energy radiation burns. I don't know how he got them, but I can smell cancer rotting away his guts like it did to his mom over there. I'm sorry. I am *sorry*. But throwing your life away for him won't do any good."

"I don't want it," she stammered. "I don't—I don't want my life. I don't want this. I don't want to go. I want my dad—"

"Don't say that." He shook her, stunning her again into terrified silence. Out of the corner of his eye, he saw a few of the coyotes creep closer. "What did your dad want? He wanted you to get on that fucking shuttle. Didn't he?"

Sarah didn't move.

"Didn't he?"

She nodded dumbly.

Lawrence swallowed. He could sense one of the bastards creeping up behind him. That was fine as long as there was only one. One would be enough to make an example.

"If you want any hope of changing anything, you need to get on that shuttle. There are communities and schools out there in the stars where you can find a home and learn a trade and figure out how to *change things*. You're young. You're smart. You can *do this*."

They haven't ruined you yet.

"I'm begging you." Lawrence realized that he hadn't shed a single tear since climbing out of the therapy tank all those months ago. That was one more thing the artists had stolen from him. He swallowed hard. "Please. Keep walking."

She stared at him, her golden eyes wide. He saw the weight of the entire future settle onto her bony shoulders. He saw that if that burden didn't kill her, it would at least leave her crippled for the rest of her life.

And you *put that weight on her,* he thought viciously. *Now she feels responsible for fixing the whole fucking universe. Nice job, Larry.*

He wondered if he had the strength to carry her, kicking and screaming, into that shuttle if she didn't want to go.

"I can't do it alone," she whispered.

Lawrence thought fast. "That's right. You can't." He slipped his pack off his shoulder and offered it to her. "Here. It's a mad scramble up there. They probably won't have time to check the bags. There's room in here for your little…thingy."

"Tardigrade." The word sounded like a hiccup.

He shuddered. "Whatever. Fine. A little kid should have a pet. Take it."

Sarah eyed the dusty pack, streaked with mud and dried blood. Then she snatched it, and with a furtive quickness, slipped the hairless guinea pig thing from under her shirt and into the backpack. She slung the bag over her shoulder and turned away from the corpse on the ground and the dead-eyed child.

Lawrence couldn't smell cancer. He had no idea if the kid was dying or not. He'd told Sarah what she needed to hear, to keep moving forward.

Feeling like more weight than just that of the bag had fallen from his shoulders, he slid to his feet.

Then he turned, facing the tattered man who'd crept close to them. There was an old knife in the man's hands.

When Lawrence stepped forward, the man swiped. Lawrence didn't know if the man had seen the dog tags and wanted to steal a ride off this damned planet or if he was simply trying to rob them in the hope that the backpack held anything he could eat.

He didn't care.

When the man took another step forward, dragging his knife through the air, Lawrence grabbed him by the wrist and slammed him to the ground.

He stomped a boot into the back of the man's neck, cutting his scream brutally short.

Then he ripped the man's arm off his body and flung it at the circling coyotes.

No one bothered them after that.

CHAPTER TWENTY-SEVEN

Rush led Petra into a space that wasn't a room so much as a forgotten void at the back of a bay full of massive liquid storage tanks. The space was big enough for a table made of old cargo crates and four outdated computer stations that someone must have salvaged from the recyclers. Old blankets strung beneath the storage tanks created what Petra assumed were cozy little sleeping cubbies.

As they approached the shadowy space, two figures—an older man and woman—scrambled out from beneath a makeshift tent. Rush lifted his arms, his face breaking into a broad smile as he took them in an embrace. From the way they fell into easy conversation, Petra gathered they were old friends. Feeling a little forgotten as the woman ran her fingers through Rush's slicked-back hair, Petra edged closer to one of the workstations, studying data streams on the old screens.

The swivel chair turned away from the screens, and Petra's mouth dropped open. "Amy!"

Like Kurt, the girl in the chair had grown almost beyond

recognition in the months since Petra had last seen her painting slogans on the walls outside the Youth Development Center.

Amy spread two fingers and touched them to her brow in a victory salute. Then her face broke into a wide grin. She surged to her feet and tackled Petra in a bear hug, leaving the chair spinning.

"Oof!" Petra laughed, scrubbing fingers through Amy's buzz-cut hair. The dye job was fading, indigo tips yielding to ash-blond roots. It was a good look on Amy. "Gawd, girl, you grew so much! What are you doing down here?"

Amy pulled back and looked her in the eye. She rubbed the back of her neck sheepishly. "I might'a got made painting signs on the wall that brass didn't like." She flushed. Metal studs in her eyebrow and lip swirled violet and pink. "Decided it was better to go underground for a while instead of doing community service in the recycling chutes or joining you up in the brig."

Petra laughed, but on the inside she was cold. Last she checked, brass was nicer to teenage vandals than domestic terrorists. Amy had been a good kid. Had a bit of a rebel streak, but what teenager didn't? She was too young to throw her life away in some harebrained Resistance scheme, that was for darned sure.

"Petie. Darling." Rush waved from the corner where he conversed quietly with the two older folks. "Come meet my friends."

Petra gave Amy a fond pat and joined Rush.

"This is Juice," he indicated the woman, "and Scraps."

Petra smiled—awkwardly at first until she remembered that she didn't have a tooth gap. The couple appeared to be in their late sixties. The man was big and broad-shouldered, wearing an old jumpsuit so sewn-over with patches she couldn't tell what department it had originally belonged to.

The woman at his side wore a sundress printed with fading sunflowers that looked like it had seen more than a few stints in the resale shops. Blue lines popped against the papery skin of her neck, arms, and exposed calves, so bright that Petra couldn't tell if they were an intentional aesthetic choice or if the woman just had old-lady blood something fierce.

"Ain't you cold in that little dress?" The words slipped out of Petra's mouth before she could stop them.

Juice grinned, showing her gap where an incisor should have been. "I spent twenty years as a cold-space sensor array mechanic," she said, lisping faintly, "back when union membership got you a decent cold-resistance mod. These days I don't notice the chill until my toes turn blue."

"She's a block of ice in bed," Scraps mumbled. He had the raspy voice of a lifelong smoker.

Juice leaned into her partner, resting her forehead on his big shoulder. "And you love any excuse to keep me warm."

"You remember my cameraman?" Petra turned to see Rush looking unusually solemn. "Jackie?" he said. "He was their son."

"Oh." Petra's eyes popped. "Oh!" She put a hand over her mouth, turning back to the old couple. "Oh, I'm so sorry…"

The man and woman nodded, suddenly somber as well. Their gazes lowered in quick acknowledgment. Juice reached over and patted Petra's arm. Her hand was, indeed, cold as ice.

"It's hard," she said quietly. "It never stops being hard, losing your little boy. It helps, having a goal to focus on."

"Rush and Jackie were friends since they were…" Scraps put a hand about a meter above the floor. "Oh, about this tall.

When the Seekers murdered my boy, Rush adopted himself some new parents."

Rush shook his head. "Don't be modest. You've been cleaning vomit off this very stupid man-child for decades." He folded his arms. "Here we are again, planning one hell of a reckless show. I keep expecting you to wake up and try to talk sense into us, Scraps."

The big man shrugged. "They killed my kid."

That certainly put a mood in place and not a good one.

"That they did." Rush took Petra's arm, directing her gently to the table. "They'll keep doing it until someone stops them. Let's sit and discuss strategy."

The five of them sat around a makeshift table that could've seated a dozen. Scraps had collected a pitcher of water from the moisture condensing off the coolant tanks and stirred it with some dried fruit over a portable hotplate to make tea.

It was awful tea, but Petra sipped from the cracked, Tribe Six-branded mug they offered her anyway. It was colder down here in the Reds than she remembered.

"All right, then." Rush clapped his hands and rubbed them together. "We have a crew assembled. The roster is a bit thin, I will admit, but once we get this stone rolling, more people will offer to help push. I'm sure of it."

"What are we doing, exactly?" Petra folded her fingers over her mug, holding in whatever warmth she could. When everyone turned to stare at her, she flushed. "I mean. We're gonna take out the fleet's top brass, right. We ain't had really *good* leadership since…"

She remembered Jackie's final video. "Well, a long time.

Ever, maybe. Leaders that will find us a good place to live without stirring up trouble with the locals."

"Command staff that won't order a young cameraman shot because he objected to the wholesale slaughter of innocents," Juice said into her cup.

"And won't throw kids into the brig for filching a few extra dinner rolls," Amy grumbled. "Or adding a little color to the walls."

Petra winced and nodded. "So…what do we do?"

"We get the truth out." Rush sat up straight. "We record a mission statement and disseminate it on the nets. Hack into the comms systems and broadcast it over the e-boards if we can. Get as many eyes on us as possible."

"Breaking into the comms system won't be easy," Petra said.

Juice shot her a grin, utterly unselfconscious about the gap in her teeth. "Broadcasting know-how is a family business. You're still familiar with the comms systems. Fleet may have revoked your access, but Rush and I will find a way in. Amy will fetch any tools we might need. Trust me, Petie. Hacking into the comms system to leak videos and files is going to be the *easy* part of this plan."

"Oh." Petra hadn't considered that, but now that she did, she thought it was darned lucky the one fleet officer this little Resistance had managed to free from Internal Affairs was indeed a lifelong comms manager. "So…what's the hard part?"

"The hard part," Rush slipped a thin silver flask from a coat pocket, "is *never letting the audience forget* we exist." He leaned across the table and poured a thin stream of dark liquid into Scraps' proffered mug. Juice and Amy pushed their cups forward as well.

"Stagnation is death, darlings," Rush declared while pouring ample servings for all. "We need to keep the masses interested and engaged with fresh new content every day. Expose the flaws and foibles and injustices in the fleet. We drown brass in their own mistakes. We flood the nets with stories like ours. Stories of idiocy, and brutality, and incompetence."

"Like your video of Riella 3," Petra said. "The one with Jackie."

"Naw." Amy shook her head, surprising Petra. "It's a good thought," she added, chewing on her tongue ring as she studied her ravaged fingernails. "But only a handful of people know about Riella 3. If that video gets out, the list of people who might have leaked it is real, real short."

Rush waved a hand sheepishly. "I'm not ready for my second debut yet."

Petra narrowed her eyes. "Hang on. You want *me* to put out a video talkin' about how bad brass is at their jobs…but you're awfully careful to keep your name away from this *Resistance* business."

"Don't judge Rush too harshly." Juice blew on her mug to cool it off. "Rush Starr is a red-blooded patriot. Everyone knows that. We don't need his *face* in these videos." She winked. "We need his money funding them."

"Speaking of which." Rush leaned back in a languid stretch and waved a finger at Scraps. "Launder another five thousand credits to Kramer, would you? It's getting terribly morose in his joint, and I suspect he wasn't exaggerating about the guild fees."

"Brass already knows *you're* the enemy, Petie," Amy went on. Poor girl had chewed her nails down to nubs. "Now that you busted out of Internal Affairs, lots of people are waiting to hear what you have to say about it. They want to know more about Memo Six and what happened when Kelba took over. You can tell them the truth that everyone else is afraid to say."

Rush nodded. "The Resistance needs a face. *Your* face, darling. Open the floodgates, and the truth will spill out. Others will come forward with their stories." His eyes narrowed. "We'll make sure of it."

Petra swallowed and pushed her mug away, no longer thirsty. "Amy?" she said quietly, drawing the young woman's gaze up from the flecks of old nail polish clinging to her fingers. The stud in her eyebrow shifted from blue to purple as she blinked. "Petie?"

"We ain't painting cartoons on the lower decks here, girl. You know what they're talking about, right?"

Amy stared at her. Gawd, despite the funky hair and the studs that changed colors like mood rings, the girl's face had grown so *serious* in the last few months.

"Treason." Beneath the table, Amy's leg bounced. Petra recognized the twitch. Larry always did that, too, when he was feeling more than he was saying. "I know the laws, Petie. I've seen the Riella 3 video."

"You ain't too young," Petra said. "If you get in on this, and they catch you, they'll execute you. I seen Kelba and her men work, Amy." She rubbed the front of her mouth.

"Jaeger stole an entire Tribe Primal warship out from under their noses," Amy said inflexibly. "If Memo Six is for real, *that's* who I want leading the fleet. Yeah, I know it's risky. But it's my future, Petie. It's my life." She caught Petra's gaze and held it rock-steady. "You gonna try to tell me what I can and can't do with it?"

No, Petra decided. She was not. She'd been younger—much younger—than Amy was now, the first time she risked her life to steal a food shipment from a seedy merchant. She'd been starving.

Now the entire *fleet* was starving. Slowly, but they were starving, all right.

It didn't matter how young you were. You did what you had to do to secure a future.

"Larry would be proud to hear you say that," Petra muttered. "Pissed, but proud."

Amy dropped her head. Her skin, as well as her mood-studs, flushed a charming shade of pink. Larry had always gotten on well with the kids from the Center. Some of them had come to idolize Petra's man.

"So." Petra shook out her shoulders and lifted her chin, trying to look more confident than she felt. "Let's make a movie."

Across the Grand Concourse, billboards blaring hourly news updates and pharmaceutical ads for the new Serenity treatment flashed and went dark—only long enough for a thousand heads to swivel, a thousand tongues to fall silent with confusion. The billboards *never* turned off.

When the boards flicked to life a few seconds later, the spectators saw another unusual sight. A now-familiar face stared at them from against a backdrop of draped blankets.

"Wh—oh, it's on now? It's on? Oh. Okay." Petra's voice was a bit distorted from the hacked feed, but the lower-deck accent was unmistakable. She cleared her throat. She looked up to the screen.

"My name is Petra Potlova, Ensign Second Class of the *Tribe Six* Support Fleet, serial number 74a-8661." She opened her mouth wide—not quite to smile, because there didn't seem to be much humor in her voice—but to show off the tooth gap that had made her mugshot so memorable.

The uneasy murmur of a thousand voices filled the chamber of the Grand Concourse.

"But you know that already, 'cause they got my face all over the darned place," Petra said. She added hastily: "They're telling me I gotta be quick because the fleet might get control of their screens back any minute now.

"Six months ago, I was working the comms hub on the bridge of the *Reliant* when the wormhole closed. That was when Nicholetta Kelba and the Seeker Corps took control of the fleet. In all that hubbub we received a message through the wormhole. You guys are calling it Memo Six, and I'm here to tell you that it's true.

"*Tribe Six* is still out there, on the other side of that wormhole. She found a good planet—the kind of planet we've been looking for this whole time. The people running the fleet, they called it lies. When I shared that memo, they threw me in jail for half a year without pressing charges because *they don't want you to know the truth.*"

Petra hesitated, thumbing over the screen in her hands as she consulted her notes. She glanced up and nodded at someone out of view before looking back to the camera.

"I think it's because they don't want you to know how bad they messed up. Listen. Sarah Jaeger was my friend. When she stole *Tribe Six*, I was shocked as anybody. I was heartbroken. They said she was a traitor, and I believed it.

"Over the last year, I've been thinking about that a lot. Here's what I think. We've been on this mission for years, and we aren't any closer to finding a place to settle than when we set out.

"So Jaeger did something bold. She did something the brass didn't want her to do. She took the only ship she could, and she *went out there—*" Petra threw her arms wide, making an expansive gesture meant to encompass the whole galaxy "—where brass was afraid to go. And she found a place for us. She's waiting for us to join her on the other side of that wormhole. She didn't betray us. She did what she had to do, to *save* us.

"Commander Kelba and the top brass don't want you to know that. They want you to sit here in the same solar system for over a year, getting hungrier and hungrier so they won't have to admit they were wrong about Jaeger."

There was a disturbance along one section of the Grand Concourse as the front doors to the Internal Affairs department flew open, and a squad of uniformed MPs rushed out. They fanned into the concourse, rushing for the power switches to the biggest billboard screens.

"The truth is," Petra said, as one by one, the screens showing her face went black, "the command staff has a long history of screwing up. If you don't believe me, that's fine. Just pay attention.

"Soon, lots of stories are gonna come out about all the awful things your leaders have been doing. 'Cause these people, the ones filling the bridges and calling the shots— their ration packs never shrink. They don't get put on waiting lists when their toilets break."

Petra's face remained on a single billboard—a big one, clear across the Concourse from the IA office. She floated above them like the face of a gap-toothed god.

"They never need to filch a few dinner rolls to make sure

their kids got enough to eat," she said. "They're not on your side."

The screen went dark.

CHAPTER TWENTY-EIGHT

"I swear I've seen this in a James Bond movie."

Jaeger rubbed crust from her eyes. She'd stolen a few hours of sleep on the shuttle ride across Locaur, and every one of them had been terrible. For once, this wasn't Toner's fault. He had grumbled some, sure, when she asked him to take over, but restless dreams had haunted her sleep, and now she felt like she had a hangover.

Locaur's single sapphire ocean filled the cockpit's main display screen. They were approaching a chain of six islands, each of them a deep brown cone with the wider base at water-level.

"We're approaching the shecret volcano lair where they're hiding the death raysh now, Captain," her copilot added in a thick Scottish accent.

"Kwin has sent an explorer probe ahead to get an initial read on the location."

Jaeger jumped. Me was resting in a groove on her control panel, eerily still for such an energetic thing.

"The probe has descended into a shaft in the caldera of the

large volcano," the AI said. "The shaft is not a natural formation and appears to descend into the Knot, roughly two kilometers below sea level. The shaft is also blocking communications signals, unfortunately. Rather than send the probe further ahead solo, Kwin has elected to wait for you to take command of the mission, Captain Jaeger."

"Right." Jaeger cracked her neck and ran through what warm-up stretches she could do in the cramped cockpit. "Toner, message Seeker with an update. Once we descend, it'll cut us off from communicating with the outside world."

Toner nodded. "Tell me you at leasht brought some gin and olivesh. I'm going to need a shtiff martini before thish is through."

"Absinthe, but it's staying in the shuttle until we've completed the mission."

Toner gave her a lingering look before jolting up straight, accent vanishing. "Wait, really?"

She graced him with a little grin. *"After we've completed the mission."* She turned back to the silver sphere resting on her console. "Me? You'll still function down in the Knot, won't you?"

"I will function in a somewhat limited capacity. I will not have access to my greater information networks. Kwin is uploading all data he believes might be relevant to me, as we speak."

"Perfect. I'm going to double-check our gear."

They landed the shuttle on the flattest spit of volcanic slope they could find, between shining black rivers of obsidian. All sensors indicated the volcanoes that made this island chain were long extinct, but the cold sea air smelled heavily of salt and sulfur and little else. The ground was too steep and rocky for anything but the most stubborn mosses and lichens to take hold. It was far and away the most inhospitable part of Locaur that Jaeger had visited.

That didn't stop Baby from scooping up mouthfuls of volcanic rock and gnashing them to gravel as she lumbered up the slope after Me.

"Oh, what the hell…" Toner hopped away from the rushing river of pebbles that was the slipstream Baby left in her wake.

"No idea." Jaeger huffed. Months of living in reduced gravity had done her muscles no favors, and the slope was extreme. "Toner. Hold back."

"What now?"

"Toner. I need to know. What's up with you? Lingering looks. A lot less flirting. What up?"

The soldier turned away. "Ahh…nothing."

"Don't give me that nothing bullshit. Spill it. Because I need you. And if this little crush is getting in the way of—"

"Crush?"

Jaeger nodded. "Yeah. I get it. Won't lie that I haven't thought about it myself, but I need you in the game… We can't—"

"Damn right we can't," Toner bellowed, eyes wild as if Jaeger had suggested he do something terrible and disgusting.

"I didn't realize I was so…unappealing."

Toner realized how his last words must have come off, and his features softened. "Ahh, no. It's not that. Don't get me wrong. You're a catch. Excellent butt. Great rack—"

"Toner," Jaeger said with a warning tone.

At this, the vampire chuckled. "I've been getting some of

my memories back, I think. About us. And, well, what do you remember about us before?"

Jaeger shook her head.

"OK, well, when you do, remember this moment and try not to die from embarrassment."

Jaeger narrowed her eyes. "Why not just tell me?"

"And deny you the agony of what I've been going through. Never."

"Never?"

"Never, and if you can, try to remember in my presence. I would love to see the look on your face when you do." He chuckled before sticking out a hand. "Deal?"

"Deal." Jaeger shook it. "That bad, huh?"

"Not…unexpected. Let's get moving."

Jaeger took Toner in before cocking her head, listening to the rough grind of Baby's jaws. "Maybe there's some mineral in the rock she needs."

Not knowing what they would find out here, Jaeger had packed more than just a few re-breathers. There were almost a hundred kilos of equipment strapped to Baby in various forms—a portable advanced medkit, a mining laser, several bricks of explosives, and all of the mechanic and engineering tools Occy had thought might come in handy. If Baby was bothered by the weight or the exercise, she gave no hint of it.

Sweat had soaked Jaeger's clothes by the time Me stopped on a ridge near the volcano's peak.

She wasn't surprised to see that, like the tunnel to the shrine, the shaft cut into the side of the volcano was also perfectly square, save for where time and weather had scrubbed at the edges. She had even expected it to be larger than the shrine tunnel.

What she wasn't expecting was a tunnel large enough to accommodate a double row of elephants.

"Damn," Toner muttered, stepping into the deep shadows where rough volcanic rock slid into smooth craftsmanship. "A little larger and we could have flown the shuttle straight down."

Me began to glow, filling the sloping shaft with a bobbing, yellow-white light. "I have established direct contact with the probe. I suggest you watch your step. The ground here is quite slick."

"You know," Toner said after they had been walking steadily downward for a while, "if we have to run back *up* this slide in a hurry, we might be screwed."

Jaeger groaned. He had a fair point. The slope itself probably wouldn't be an issue, but years of moisture had left a thin layer of some kind of slime or algae growth that was, as Me had noted, quite slick. "There are pitons and spare mag soles in one of Baby's saddlebags," she said. "Might be a good idea to grab some when we pause."

"I am passing near the edge of comms range," Me said. "We should encounter the probe shortly. Ah. Here we are." Its spotlight swiveled, illuminating down the shaft. Ahead, a broad set of double doors, thick as tombstones, blocked the shaft. They hung open barely half a meter.

Baby reached the gap and sniffed.

"You're not gonna fit," Toner said.

Baby growled at him.

"No trouble." Me zipped forward. "Wait here a moment. I'll take care of this."

Before Jaeger could ask what the little AI meant to do, it whizzed through the cracked doors and vanished into the darkness beyond, leaving them with only their multitools for light.

Toner and Jaeger exchanged glances.

The walls began to rumble.

"Whoa!" Toner grabbed Jaeger and scrambled backward as dust shook free of the ceiling. "Not *again!*"

Baby made an alarmed noise and turned, her long claws scrabbling for purchase on the slick floor as the chasm between the doors began to widen.

Something on the other side of the doors was pushing them open. Something big.

Jaeger screamed as a mechanical snake monster, a good five meters long and with dozens of slender pairs of legs, wedged itself in the cracked door and pried them open. Baby's skin ripped into a gravelly texture. She planted her legs wide and let out a bellow of challenge.

"Whatisthesourceofyourdistress?" the snake-robot demanded, spitting out the words alarmingly fast as it lashed around to peer into the darkness. Long sensor-antennae whipped from each end of it.

Then it went still. It turned back to face Jaeger and Toner, who had somehow managed to find shelter behind Baby's glowering bulk.

"Oh," said the long-legged robo-snake in Me's voice. "I perhaps should have informed you of the probe droid's shape before synchronizing with it?"

Jaeger let out a long, wavering breath. "Yeah," she said weakly, letting Toner help her to her feet.

"Always warn your friends before turning into huge

hideous monsters," Toner said in a voice that was a little too friendly. "It's a good rule of thumb."

Baby grumbled, but now that the shaking had stopped and nobody was screaming, the big tardigrade ambled forward to sniff Me's new shape. Jaeger could see a small node near the new droid's head, where the silvery sphere had docked.

"Are you…an AI piloting a droid, piloting a droid?" she asked.

"No. I am an isolated AI fragment running on a synchronized but limited network between the two droid bodies you see before you."

"Right." Jaeger let her eyes adjust to the space beyond the doors. She wasn't entirely surprised to see that the smooth slope of the shaft had given way to the rough, milky white crystal fixtures, like the inside of a geode.

"Looks like we've hit the Knot," she murmured. As she stepped over the threshold, the crystal walls began to glow. She braced herself, ready for another unexpected room shift, but no such drama occurred.

The lights, as it were, simply sensed her presence and turned on.

"Interesting," Me observed. "The space did not react to the presence of my droid bodies. It must be sensitive to your biological presence."

"This place is nuts." Toner stepped into the cavern, head craning back to take in the vast, dizzyingly complex space. Jaeger had to agree, although she was glad that the ambient lighting wasn't as blindingly powerful as it had been back in the shrine.

"Nuts," Me mused, crawling away from the shaft entrance. "Nuts, nuts…almonds, walnuts, peanuts…which are not nuts, but legumes, strangely. High in protein and saturated fats…"

Baby picked her way around a crystal outcropping, sniffed a stalactite, and before Jaeger could stop her, ripped off a chunk with her toothy mouth-hole.

Shards of broken crystal dribbled from Baby's mouth as she ground at the stones.

"…Often used in baking for added texture and flavor. See: Pecan Sandies. Almond Biscotti—"

"Okay, it's an expression. I wasn't asking you to pull up a cookbook!" Toner barked. His voice echoed against the crystal walls, reverberating and amplifying a hundred times over.

Me fell silent.

Baby stopped chewing.

Gently, Jaeger reached out and took what remained of the crystal chunk out of Baby's face-hole. She turned and placed it back on its pedestal.

"*Why*, exactly, do you have a cookbook taking up space on your oh-so-limited hardware?" Toner asked slowly, rounding on Me.

"I thought I might ask a few questions if we had the time…"

Squinting against the glittering light reflecting off every surface, Jaeger picked her way toward a side tunnel. "Come visit us in the *Osprey* on a baking day, Me," she said. "I'll show you how we make cookies. Right now, we have people waiting for us. Let's try to stay on task."

The Knot complex was a city-sized labyrinth of crystal veins and caverns. Jaeger didn't dare take a close scan of the layout for fear that the current might make the place suddenly rearrange itself as it had back in the shrine. This left them navigating the irregular tunnels using a simple but time-tested technique.

One of Baby's saddlebags contained a ten-kilometer spool of ultralight wire. Jaeger tied one end of it to a stalactite by the shaft entrance and let it unravel as they groped their way through the complex.

By the end of the first hour, eye strain from all the glittering surfaces had forced her to don a thermal hood. By the end of the second hour of tedious exploration, Toner did the same.

"I am sensing a pattern to the structure of the crystal growths," Me observed, breaking an unusually long—for Me—ten-minute silence. "I don't know what it means, but it is certainly…extant."

"Yeah, but it's crystal. Isn't it all pattern by definition?" Toner tugged his hair irritably. He dug into another of Baby's saddlebags and withdrew a blood substitute pouch.

"A pattern on top of the expected lattice pattern," Me clarified. "You may not notice it with your simple eyes, but there is some kind of meaning in the arrangement of these outcroppings and in the layout of the entire complex."

"That's not too surprising." Jaeger thought she heard Toner grumbling something about *simple eyes* as he bit into the pouch. "It might be natural materials, but this place isn't natural. The forebears *built* it."

"So you're saying it is, or it is not a big maze?" Toner sucked the pouch dry and was about to toss it over his shoulder when he saw Jaeger's head turn in his direction. He shoved the empty pouch back into a saddlebag.

"I am sensing increased electrical and data flow along certain pathways in the crystal lattices," Me clarified, its head-end swaying from side to side as it swept long, wiry antennae through the air. It turned down a side crevasse. "We might be moving through the ruins of an abandoned city. This way."

They followed the leggy snake-beast-robot at an excruciating pace. Baby seemed frustrated by the slow progress, and several times Jaeger had to coax the big tardigrade away from forcefully plowing past outcroppings. Instead, they had to slow to a crawl every time the passageways narrowed, as Baby carefully wove her way through the twisting passages.

"We need to leave her behind in one of these larger caverns," Toner said under his breath. When she chuffed disapproval, he held up a hand. "It's not personal," he said. "But if we wind up having to get out of here fast, she's a liability. It's dangerous for her and us. Look. She can barely turn around in some of these tunnels. The deeper in she goes, the harder it will be for her to get out."

Jaeger winced but called a halt to progress long enough to pull some vital equipment from Baby's saddlebags and pass the ball of ultralight wire off to Toner.

"You wait here," she said softly, scratching the rough folds of skin above Baby's face-hole. "Guard our rear. I'll call for you if we need help, I promise."

Baby grumbled but sank to the ground and rested her head on her chubby legs, curling up like a forlorn dog.

"I hate that you're right," Jaeger said to Toner under her breath as they resumed their hike.

"That's why you need me."

Jaeger set her jaw and nodded.

They didn't have much farther to go, at least, before Me turned down a final side crevasse and led them into the first chamber they had come across that looked *intentional* and not like some incident of crystal formation.

It was a wide, circular room with a ceiling that faded into

shadows that glittered beneath their boots, making the place pulse with shimmering light with every step. Me crawled ahead of them, rearing back until it was a good four meters tall, and still, its antennae didn't seem to brush the ceiling. It activated a spotlight.

The glittering, crystal-crusted carapaces of a hundred different insectile creatures clung to the ceiling ten meters overhead, creating a massive collage of bodies. Busy little Locauri figures wedged between the long, bloated shapes of K'tax drones. Bulky K'tax crab and scorpion morphs lumbered among the shapes like elephants lording over herds of wildebeests. Long, slender Overseer shapes created incongruous and nonsensical lines through the entire swarm.

CHAPTER TWENTY-NINE

One more thing, Jaeger had told Seeker in a low voice, just before she boarded the shuttle. "Keep your eyes peeled. Me mentioned it made contact with Virgil. It says Virgil means us no harm, but it won't give me any details. I don't see any reason to doubt it, but…"

"But it's goddamned *Virgil,*" Seeker had growled, and that was all they needed to say on the matter.

So at oh four hundred the next morning, as Seeker was walking from his quarters down to the administrative hub in the starboard cargo bay, his priority was clear.

"Moss." He blew steam from his coffee mug. He hated coffee, but after a night like last night, he thought he was gonna need it. "I know the *Osprey* has powerful bio scanners, but what tools does this bird have for locating sophisticated machines?"

There was a long pause as Moss evaluated its systems. Seeker took the time to browse his personal computer for last night's status reports. Staying on top of the Occy fiasco was all well and good, but he couldn't afford to let any other little problems fly under the radar.

"I can scan for unexpected EMF and radio activity with high accuracy, within a hundred-kilometer radius of the ship." Moss lagged from speaker to speaker as it followed Seeker down the corridor. It did everything slowly. The program's intended design was to cooperate with a single pilot in combat, not to oversee and coordinate the thousands of systems that made up a Tribal Prime warship.

"Run the scan every thirty minutes and send any unusual results to my personal computer." Seeker heard the sounds of shouting coming from beyond the cargo bay doors ahead and sighed. "Looks like I already have my first fire to put out."

Something had Bufo hopping mad.

Seeker figured it was the gaggle of Morphed and Classics clustered near the center of the cargo bay, dragging Mason and Pandion away from each other. The collar of Mason's uniform was torn. A dark welt was swelling over Pandion's cheek. Grimly, Seeker noted that the crew pulling Mason back toward the ship-side doors were almost all Classics, and the handful of figures circling Pandion were entirely Morphed. In the ruckus, a few desks and workstations had been knocked over.

"Sanitation duty, both of you!" Bufo paced between the combatants, his wide face red and bulging. "For the next week! I'll have both of you scrubbing latrines until your eyes turn brown!"

"What's the trouble, Sergeant?"

Bufo froze mid-stride, and all eyes swiveled to Seeker.

"It was my fault, Sir," Pandion said into the silence that followed. The lanky, eagle-eyed man wiped a dribble of blood from his chin. "Heard someone spewing bullshit and figured I should keep the place from stinking up."

A sharp murmur came from the crew grouped around Mason. The young man in the torn engineer's uniform stared at Pandion, lips tight and face pale with fury.

"Idiots," Bufo grunted, stepping aside to make room as Seeker approached.

"You heard the Sergeant." Seeker looked from Pandion to Mason. "Someone has to go clean the latrines."

Mason nodded and stormed away without a word, but Pandion blanched. "Sir, I just finished an entire shift—"

"Now you'll go finish one more," Seeker bellowed. "Then you'll go sleep seven hours and work another damned shift, soldier. You wanna keep complaining about it?"

Pandion's mouth snapped shut. He gave one smart nod and turned away, his entourage following him down the hall.

"Busy night, Sergeant?" Seeker asked once the bystanders had returned to their desks. The crew had converted the cargo bay into a temporary administrative hub for the settlement.

Bufo sighed and slouched on a stool. "Bitching." He waggled fingers. "All night. Everybody. You'd think someone pissed in the coffee."

"Any other fights?"

"No," Bufo said. "That was the worst of it, thankfully. Pandion's been agitating about Occy all night. Wasn't too happy when Mason suggested that the captain knew how to handle politics better than he does."

"I'll be honest, Sergeant." Seeker scratched his chin. He was overdue for a shave and sensed it would be a long time before he got around to it. "I didn't realize Lieutenant Occy was that popular among the crew."

Bufo shrugged and took the mug of coffee a young Classic handed to him in passing. "He doesn't fit in so well as a social peer, but the Chief Engineer is almost like a mascot to the crew. Especially the Morphed. I wouldn't say he has much in the way of friends, but he's still *theirs*. Does that make sense?"

Seeker grunted and nodded.

"Doesn't help that he looks like he's about twelve years old," Bufo went on. "They see him as a kid. And they wanna protect that kid. They think the aliens don't have any right to hold him prisoner."

"I wish there had been a way to let the nuts age in the shells a bit more before shucking," Seeker muttered. "They're all immature. Occy just happens to *look* his age."

Bufo gave Seeker a reproachful look.

"Sorry, Sergeant." Seeker fumbled with his coffee. "Uh, present company excluded. How do you feel about the situation?"

Bufo set his jaw and surveyed the busy office sprawled before them. In the distance, a few agricultural specialists were arguing about seed efficacy in Locaur soil. "Word is there's gonna be a trial?" His throat bulged as he gulped down his coffee.

"That's the plan." Seeker checked his computer. Nothing to report from Moss's first scan.

"I think that's *fair*," Bufo said carefully, "so long as this trial is *fair*."

"Commander Seeker?" A Classic woman with high cheekbones and a tight blond bun approached, clutching a computer to her chest. "The Locauri Elders have arrived. They're waiting to speak with you outside."

"Already?" Seeker checked the time and bit back a curse. "They're over an hour early."

"I don't think they have a lot of patience right now, sir. They're, uh, buzzing. A lot."

"All night. Patrols around our nests. Unnecessary, Seeker!" Tiki's antennae lashed angrily through the air. "Disruptive. Malicious!"

Aquila stood between two of the Locauri elders, her back straight, hands clasped behind her. She didn't blink those strange yellow eyes when Seeker turned. Like Pandion, she was one of the few eagle-morphs on the crew. Also like Pandion, she worked overnight duty.

"I meant no disrespect, sir." She lifted her proud chin. "We're still establishing our patrol routes through the woods. Waters thought he saw signs of an egg-dragon in the area. We were only checking it out."

"No egg-dragons!" Tiki's translator band flared at mention of the long-necked dinosaur-beasts that passed through the area on occasion to feed on Locauri eggs. "Out of season. Out of season! Excuses, to prowl around our nests."

"My mistake, sir." Aquila stared at Seeker, unblinking. It was not a face Seeker would want to meet across a poker table.

"Get inside, soldier," he said. "Compose a missive before you go off duty. I want everyone in the crew to know. No patrols are to get within a kilometer of the Locauri village without explicit permission from a commanding officer or one of the Elders."

Aquila nodded sharply and strode away.

Seeker faced the six Elders that stood in a half-circle around him. He saw at least a dozen other Locauri buzzing through the near tree line, sharp shadows in the early morning light.

"Unacceptable," Tiki, the big female at the center of the line of Elders repeated.

"I agree." Seeker ground his teeth. He had no doubt Aquila took her patrol close to the village to gather information about Occy, but some things shouldn't be admitted to aliens. "Which is why we just instituted the new policy. I…" He cast about for appropriately diplomatic-sounding words. "Regret any distress our patrols might have caused you."

If Tiki wanted more of an apology than that, she'd be waiting for a long time. The smaller male at her side stepped forward, sweeping his antennae low in a placating gesture.

"No arguments," Art urged. "We have come to discuss trial and judgment."

"Great." Seeker folded his arms. "The sooner we can get this mess behind us, the better."

Tiki turned her head, eying a cluster of construction workers warily as they worked a backhoe down a foundation ditch. "You, come," she told Seeker. "We will speak *privately*."

Apparently, Tiki's idea of private simply meant *away from human ears* because they led him back to the Locauri village before broaching the subject again. They were followed the whole way by a swarm of shy, buzzing shadows. All the Locauri had come out to ogle.

He took it as a good sign, however, when the aliens

brought a stump out of the woods for him to sit on while they talked.

"Whiterot, blossoming by the river this morning." Tiki hopped restlessly across the clearing. The forest floor here was clear of all underbrush and debris; the actual nests the Locauri used for shelter were suspended on thick limbs high overhead, connected by draping roped bridges.

"Bad omen," one of the Elders agreed demurely. "Bad, bad."

Seeker's jaw was beginning to ache from all the grinding, but he knew better than to let them see him sneering at local superstitions. Art had drawn a piece of chalk from one of his pouches and was sketching what looked like a flower on one of the tree trunks, where the bark was worn smooth.

"We must solve the problem," Art said, "before the flowers wither. Or disaster. Much disaster."

"Before the flowers wither? When will that be?" Seeker was almost afraid to ask.

"Tomorrow," Tiki clicked.

Seeker folded his arms and glanced up, wondering which of the nests overhead housed the engineer and how hard it would be to break the kid out of jail before everyone here went Jonestown crazy. "So what do you want?" He wished Jaeger were here. "How do we solve this problem before *tomorrow?*"

"Punishment," one of the Elders said.

"And…" Seeker worked his jaw. He checked his pocket and realized he'd left his vape back in his quarters. "What sort of punishment?"

"Death," Tiki said.

Seeker opened his mouth.

"If disaster comes to us," Art stepped in quickly. "From the shrine. The one who brought it. Sacrificed, to end disaster. Appease."

"There hasn't been any disaster for you. There's not going to be. Jaeger went to handle it."

"Even so," Tiki said. "Dangerous. Broken law. Bad omens. Disaster will come sooner or later. Occy stays with us. When disaster comes, he will pay for bringing it."

"What about questioning the youth who started the whole thing?" Seeker asked, adding, "The Locauri youth?"

Tiki's eyes became distant, and Seeker couldn't read the expression that covered the alien's face. "No law broken."

"And the trial? Surely this isn't it. Where are his advocates? The evidence."

"You," Tiki said as if that answered everything.

This was either some strange Locauri law at play or cultural confusion. Either way, he wasn't getting a clear answer. He needed another tack. "Let me get this straight. You want to reserve the right to execute Occy the next time your village gets hit by a windstorm?" Seeker barely managed to keep his voice steady.

"Yes," Tiki said.

"No," Art said.

Seeker stared from Tiki to the smaller Art. The other elders began to buzz, a low, thrumming noise that made Seeker's bones rattle. "That's not an acceptable solution," he said. "We don't take hostages. Especially for doing something *none of us knew was a crime.*" He stepped between the two Locauri, and the buzzing abruptly stopped. All eyes swiveled to him.

"So I'll give you a counterproposal," Seeker growled. It gratified him to see Tiki and a few others shrink away from him. "When Jaeger comes back from her trip, and Kwin tells you that they've turned off the device, you will *let Occy go,* free and clear. In the meantime, let him do community service. He's living among you. Have him copy down and translate all your laws. All the big no-no's we should know about so this doesn't happen again."

Tiki turned, tapping her antennae against her fellow Elders as they clicked at one another. Seeker's computer *beeped* at his side. Another update from Moss.

"What are they saying?" Seeker muttered to Art, who stood at his elbow.

"Arguing," Art responded.

"You don't say?" Seeker stole a glance at his computer screen. His breath caught.

Unusual EMF activity detected far to the west.

Seeker tore his eyes away from the screen. He couldn't afford to get distracted right now. "Get in there and argue for us, Art. Back me up."

Art hesitated. Seeker didn't like that, but he didn't have much time to worry what it might mean because Tiki suddenly spread her pseudo-wings. With a shimmering flutter, she launched herself to the nearest tree. She sank her claws into the smooth bark and turned to stare at Seeker, forcing him to look up to meet her gaze.

"When Tall One says danger has passed, we have ritual to free Occy."

Seeker nodded, listening carefully.

Tiki continued, "Occy will ask for ritual. Forgiveness. Complicated. Occy will make record of our rituals, laws. Occy will teach laws to your people. Then your people know. No more *mistakes*."

"Done." Seeker was glad they weren't demanding some

costly tribute or long prison sentence for the chief engineer. They were going to need that kid to get this settlement built. "I'll send along a computer and recorder so Occy can get right to work. Now if you'll excuse me, I have a circus to manage."

It was nearly noon when Seeker returned to the main office in the cargo bay, and Bufo had long since gone to bed.

"Who's the officer on duty?" he asked a man in a construction vest. The man was sitting alone beside a table loaded with the midday meal, a buffet of fabricated lasagna and mixed fruit slices. The others had already picked over most of it. Only a few slices of honeydew remained on the fruit trays.

"Oh." The man coughed and straightened, brushing crumbs off his vest. "It's, uh, Portia, sir. I think she's down at the waste management site."

Seeker grabbed a slice of honeydew and was about to head up to his quarters when he stopped and turned to study the man in the construction vest.

"What's your name, soldier?" he demanded.

A faint grimace passed over his face. "Carpenter, sir."

"Where's your name badge, Carpenter?"

Carpenter's grimace deepened. He mumbled something.

"Spit it out," Seeker snapped, ejecting a honeydew seed.

"I hate it," Carpenter repeated, louder.

"You hate your name badge?"

"I hate the name, sir. Sick and tired of hearing people call me that. I'm more than a builder, you know. I like playing cards. I'm good at darts. I have hobbies! But no. I'm just…a carpenter. If *you* spent half your time pounding nails, do you think you'd ever get sick of being called *hammer*?"

Seeker stared at the huffing man, who had worked himself into quite a state. He must've been mulling over that speech for a while.

"Hammer's not such a bad name," he grunted. He popped the last of the honeydew in his mouth and turned away. "For God's sake, soldier. The captain has been on our asses for weeks about picking our names. Quit your bitching and get it done."

As the unfortunately named Carpenter had predicted, Seeker found Portia overseeing progress at the new waste management site at the southern edge of the settlement. It was a long, squat skeleton of a building, half-buried in the ground. A thick swarm of insects swirled around the place, drawn by the smell.

The awful, sickly sweet smell.

"The bacteria mix we use isn't *working*." A red-haired woman in a sweat-dampened white coat shouted at Portia near one open wall of the building. "It's not breaking the waste down efficiently. We *have* to close these latrines until we figure it out. People are going to have to walk back to the *Osprey* until we figure this out."

"That's a fifteen-minute walk one-way." Portia folded her spindly arms and shook her head. "I'm not going to make people take a thirty-minute break every time they have to take a piss."

"The waste tanks here are already overflowing," the woman growled. Seeker was impressed. Portia, with her angular face and unsettling eyes, was a hard woman to stare down. "We'll never get ahead of the problem if people keep adding to it."

Portia cocked her head into a pit beneath the roof of the building. If the smell bothered her, she hid it well. Even the flies avoided swarming around her.

"You were just given two extra sets of hands. Have Mason and Pan dig a pit toilet nearby. Then shut down operations until you get the bacteria problem settled." Portia glanced around, meeting Seeker's eye. "It's not quite *cleaning* latrines, Commander, but I assume it will do?"

"What the hell is that smell?" Seeker dreaded the answer.

The woman in the lab coat grumbled something but stormed off, waving her hands in front of her face—battling flies and stench.

"We were using a special blend of bacteria to break human waste into useable compost rapidly." Portia turned, leading Seeker upwind of the awful smell. "It's…not working."

"Why not?"

"I have no idea, Commander. I'm not a scientist. I'm sure they'll figure it out."

"You don't seem bothered."

"I have very little sense of smell, but I get a whiff when the wind is right." She shuddered. "The genetic artists gave us the power of gods and heroes when they should've given us shit that doesn't stink." She eyed Seeker. More specifically, she eyed the loaded military backpack slung over his shoulder. "Going on a trip, Commander?"

"I've got to do a bit of recon. Moss is picking up some strange signals coming from around that mountain. I want to make sure it's not…going to be a problem for us."

Portia regarded him in silence.

"Bufo's a good, reliable man for managing overnight duties, but I'm going to leave you in command until I get back. I hate to do it in the middle of this mess with the Locauri, but I'm sure you're the right person to handle them."

"Why?" Portia stopped and turned to face him, folding her arms.

Seeker blinked.

"Because the micro-hairs on my fingers and toes let me climb up walls, too?"

Seeker opened his mouth, but she didn't give him a chance to speak.

"Or my inhuman reflexes, Commander? Or is it because some of my secretions contain silk fiber proteins that we can blend to make rope nearly as strong as our carbon-fiber ultralights?" The woman leaned forward, blinking big, multi-pupil eyes at Seeker. "And no. Sir. I'm not going to tell you which ones."

"Uh…" Seeker shuffled backward a step. "I *really* do not follow your point, Lieutenant."

"My point, *sir*, is that I do not appreciate the assumption that because I carry modified spider DNA, I am somehow particularly adept at understanding or communicating with aliens that carry some vague resemblance to earthbound insects." She waved her unnaturally long fingers. "Even if that somehow mattered, jumping spiders and grasshoppers aren't even in the same phylum."

"Or, *Lieutenant*," Seeker growled, "I meant to leave you in charge because you're the officer on duty and up until about twenty seconds ago, I considered you the most level-headed and experienced of the Morphed crew."

"Oh." Wonder of wonders, Portia flushed. Seeker didn't think he'd ever seen the woman show emotion before. "My apologies, sir. I…assumed you were using Toner's kind of logic. He tends to make…assumptions."

"Jesus Christ," he marveled, catching her meaning. "Is he that much of a clown?"

A faint grin flickered over Portia's severe face, undercutting her embarrassment. "Honestly, sir, he's not that bad. We give him a hard time because it's fun to watch him twitch."

I'm surrounded by children. Seeker eyed the mountain on the horizon. Moss said there was something there. Several somethings, in fact. Somethings that he ought to check out in case they turned out to be murderous rogue AI-style somethings.

He considered abandoning his quest. No telling what kind of assholery these fools would get up to if left unsupervised.

No, he told himself. *Trust. We have to start building trust—with our people, not only the Locauri. They'll never learn if we're always holding their hands.*

It's what Jaeger would have done.

"I'll be back as soon as I can, Lieutenant." He slung the second strap over his shoulder and started walking. "Just don't sink the boat while I'm gone."

CHAPTER THIRTY

They'd planted the seed.

"Do you know much about agriculture, darling?"

Petra hadn't held a pulse rifle in a long time, but all the old drills came back to her, smooth as a key sliding into its lock when she checked the weapon. "Not really. That's like growing tomatoes and stuff, right? But in dirt instead of water?"

"Indeed. Seeds tossed on the ground and left to the mercy of the elements. If the elements are cruel and the rains don't come, the seeds wither and die."

It had been sixteen hours since Petra's speech had dropped over the public broadcast system. The nerds up in brass HQ had yanked the vid from every mainframe they could, but not before people had captured it, re-uploaded, and copied it a hundred times across the net.

The phenomenon was called *viral* for a reason.

"So our ancestors learned very quickly, back in the mud-dwelling days, that you couldn't trust the rains to come at the right times."

A NEW HOME

They'd undergone another costume change. Amy had dug up two modern maintenance jumpsuits. One was about Petra's size, and if the other was a little short on Rush, you couldn't tell unless you stopped to stare. In their day jobs, Juice and Scraps were both janitorial floaters. A little creative tailoring left their nametags unrecognizable. Petra didn't ask where they got the fake ID badges.

"There's always an element of chance, of course. You hope the land doesn't flood. You hope an earthquake doesn't come and ruin your farm. You control what you can. You help nature along."

The storage bay the Resistance called home had more entry and exit points than from Kramer's bar. Part of it ran alongside a primary maintenance conduit. Petra had once heard Sarah call them Jefferies tubes, but she never did understand the reference.

Branches of that conduit extended like roots across nearly half of the *Reliant*. Security bulkheads should've sealed important sections of the conduits against intrusion by anyone who didn't have the right authorization.

"So we don't simply cast our seeds into the ether and pray for the best, darling."

Huddled in the cramped conduit with her team, Petra watched, awestruck, as Scraps plugged a beautifully efficient, custom-built jammer into the bulkhead access panel and finger-danced his way past the security protocols.

"This seed we've planted, it doesn't grow on water and sunlight. It grows on secrets revealed and lies brought to light. We're going to help it along, my dears. We're going to go fetch a whole pail full of secrets, and we're going to help this seed grow."

The panel turned green, the bulkhead slid open, and the

team crawled, single-file, into the restricted sector of the *Reliant*. The one intended only for officers and fleet officials. The sector where they conducted important fleet business.

The sector where they hid the top secret information.

It was amazing how easy it was to move around in places where you shouldn't be if you only acted like you had every right to be there, Petra thought.

Completely bypassing the standard security checkpoints at the entrances and exits to the sector sure helped, too.

"Brass is going to be so pissed when they realize how easy it was to break in," she said under her breath—after glancing back to make sure the corridor behind them was as empty as the corridor ahead.

Juice and Scraps had fallen several paces behind—far enough to make it look like the four of them weren't together. Pairs of maintenance or janitorial crew weren't so unusual, but all of them together might raise some eyebrows.

"Let's hope they don't realize how we did it." Rush's lips barely moved as he spoke. "Now hush. You're breaking character."

Petra pressed her lips tightly together.

They turned up a side hallway, following signs for the server room. Rush had said, and Petra could confirm from her time as an ensign, that secured servers were there. Databanks that weren't a part of the fleet network. In other words, that was where they hid all the big secrets.

It was downright *easy* to stroll up and down these hallways, grunting vague acknowledgments to the guards and soldiers they passed. Once or twice Rush had to remind her to keep her head down and not make eye contact.

"You're not an officer anymore. Maintenance keeps eyes on the deck."

She was shocked and dismayed, then, when the next person that rounded the corner striding in their direction was Petra's former bunkmate.

Dolly had taken a promotion in the months during Petra's incarceration. First Lieutenant, now. Good for her.

Bad for Petra, though, who dropped her head and prayed Dolly hadn't seen.

"Hey. Maintenance."

Petra's heart nearly stopped as Dolly approached. Her shoes. She stared at her shoes.

"You're going to fix the busted door up by the servers?"

"Yes, ma'am," Rush grunted, in a voice Petra hardly recognized.

Dolly offered a small tablet computer. "I grabbed this from Rodger by mistake." Petra hardly recognized Dolly's voice, either. All the sound of bells had drained out of it. "He's the warrant officer on duty in the server room. Return it to him for me."

"Yes, ma'am," Rush mumbled, taking the computer.

Without another word, Dolly glided away.

"Oh gawd," Petra breathed as Rush started walking again. "There's no way she didn't recognize me."

"Don't worry. She's with us." Rush flipped the tablet over in his hands and popped off a back panel, revealing a blank security badge. Quick as a card shark, he slipped it into his pocket.

Petra barely had time to process this. Scraps and Juice had passed them in the hallway, and when they rounded the corner, they found the older couple waiting for them by the door to the server room.

"Survey says only one man on duty at the moment," Rush said in a low tone. "Your timing was perfect as always, Scraps."

"Less talk, more walk," the old man grunted and pointed at the sealed door.

Rush waved his newly acquired security badge over the lock, and just like that, they were in the archives.

The room was downright claustrophobic, dark and hot, with a low ceiling and long rows of humming servers stacked to the ceiling. Petra struggled not to sneeze with every step. Carefully, their footfalls masked by the constant hum, they slipped down the stacks toward the main workstation at the center of the room.

An old, balding man sat in front of a bank of display screens, monitoring active network traffic. Each screen showed a different feed—websites, forums, chat rooms, even a few TNN feeds, and other broadcasts.

Petra crept forward, slipping a little dart from her pocket. This was part of her job. One little stick and the guard would go sleepy-time for a good two hours.

She was about two meters from Baldy's exposed neck when Juice sneezed.

Baldy shot upright like someone had caught him jerking it. His hand flew to his sidearm. He spun, surging to his feet. Petra groaned and darted forward, hoping she could get a good stick in the man before he started firing—or worse, hit the alarm button on his commlink—but Rush was faster.

Quiet like the lightning that comes before thunder, the

slender man stepped out of the shadows between server stacks and drove a knife into the side of Baldy's throat.

A look of utter surprise passed over Baldy's face as blood gurgled down his neck. In one swift motion, Rush knocked the man's legs out from under him, and he slammed onto his back.

"Fuck off and die," Rush said softly, leaning over the man to pry his weapon free. Petra saw now that it wasn't a knife, but a stone ax head, like the one up in his quarters—the Tepori weapon. For all she knew, it was the same blade.

"Then go to hell," Rush whispered as the man's life seeped onto the floor, "and give an encore."

He saw Petra staring at him as he straightened. "What are the odds?" He smiled wanly as he wiped the blade clean on a handkerchief he pulled from another pocket. "Rodger here killed a few Tepori of his own. How's that for irony, darling?"

"Petra," Juice hissed. The older woman had slipped into Baldy's chair and was frantically tabbing through computer screens.

Petra scrambled over the dead body. "Yeah," she said. "Let's get hooked into these special servers."

As a comms specialist, Petra knew a fair amount about network configuration. The memory drive Juice produced contained a neat little skimming program that mapped out server networks. While Rush and Scraps paced the room, ears to the doors to listen for anyone who might approach, Petra and Juice took a rough schematic of all the servers hooked into the prime net.

Once they knew which machines connected to the net, it was pretty easy to figure out which ones *weren't*.

"Stack 4, Section B. They hid all the good stuff in plain sight. Oh hey. Kind of like what we did!" Petra didn't wait for the drive to eject properly. She snatched it from the port and flung herself between the stacks, running toward Section B.

"*Shit*," Scraps growled from near the main door. "I have people incoming. I'll let them know we don't have these doors fixed yet. They'll have to go around the long way. It'll slow them down a bit. You girls better work fast."

"Scraps," Rush objected. "No, let me—"

The older man had already slipped out the door.

"Your ID—you forgot your—Dammit!" Rush slammed a fist against the wall.

A thrill of terror shot down Petra's spine as she found Section B and scanned the server stack for an open port. She plugged in the memory drive and prayed the data harvesting program was as *automatic* as Scraps had promised it would be.

"What do you mean, he forgot his ID?" Juice snarled.

"He took off without it," Rush said. "If he runs into officers and they notice he doesn't have an ID at all—"

A moment of dead silence fell over the group. Rush didn't need to finish the sentence. If Scraps had a fake badge to flash at some passing brass, it might be good enough. They might not notice.

But they'd sure as hell notice if it wasn't there at all.

"Close and seal the door," Juice whispered.

"You can't do that!" Petra cried.

"No," Rush snapped. "I'm not going to give up and lock him out—"

A heated argument rose from the hall outside the server room.

"Sorry, sir," Scraps said, his a few notches louder than it needed to be. "I must have left it in the latrine —"

"Shut up. Bryce? I see the server room door is open. Go check on Rodgers."

Rush glared at Juice, but there was no more time for arguing. He raced for the door and slapped his palm on the access panel just as a cute young lieutenant reached the threshold.

He barely had time to look surprised as the door slammed shut in front of him and Rush.

Muffled shouting rose from the other side of the door, followed a few seconds later by the wail of klaxons.

"Oh boy." Petra sucked at the air, staring as the pinprick lights on the memory drive blinked in a *loading* pattern. At least the program was picking up something.

She sure hoped it was something good.

"We've got to retreat." Rush joined them at the servers, his eyes wide. "*Now.*"

"I'll go see if I can slow them down." Juice scrambled to her feet, leaning on Petra's shoulder for support. "See if they're interested in hearing some bullshit from a domestic terrorist."

"You're out of your *mind*," Rush said.

"So far, they've only had eyes on *Scraps*," Juice growled. "Cameras and witnesses all across the sector have me pegged as his partner. They'll be looking for me, but *they don't know you're here*."

Rush's eyes went wide. He shook his head, hard enough to break a few strands of his hair free from its styling gel. "No," he said. "Don't be ridiculous. They have cameras on every corner. They'll know we were here too."

"But *not right away*, you stupid man." Juice reached up, grabbing Rush roughly by the ears and yanking his head down to her level. "It will take them *time* to look over the feeds and realize we weren't alone. You need that time." The older woman glanced at Petra, then swung her furious gaze back to Rush. "You need to get *her* out of here. You'll make the whole rebellion look like a clown show if you get your spokesperson landed back in jail on day one. Optics, honey. Think of the *optics*."

Rush hesitated, and Petra saw emotions warring on his face. Rage, denial, dread.

Finally, he looked around and realized Petra was staring at them. His shoulders sagged.

Something started to *thud* against the door. Something big.

"Damn," he breathed. He grabbed Juice's face in both hands and kissed her roughly on the forehead. "Damn, damn, *damn*."

"Quit stalling," Juice growled. She had crouched and was tugging the guard out of his jacket. Realizing what she meant to do, Petra dropped to her knees and helped strip the dead man down. Once she had his slacks and shoes free, she turned back to the server stack. Her hands were trembling.

The thudding on the other side of the door had stopped.

"They're sending people around to get in through the back door." Juice waved frantically. "You have to move *now*."

The memory drive Petra had shoved into the port was still copying files, and by the flashing pattern of lights, Petra worried that their pail of stolen secrets wasn't nearly as big as they'd hoped—but there was no more time to wait. She ejected the drive and slipped the tiny disc into the safest place she could think of: beneath her tongue. It was a modern memory drive. It could stand up to a little spit and humidity, and if she got caught, the brass would search her pockets first thing.

She turned back to see that Rush had shed his maintenance jumpsuit and was scrambling into the dead guard's uniform. Juice grabbed the dead man beneath the arms and with shocking strength for such a wiry older lady, heaved the dead weight onto her shoulders. "Gonna stash him in the hardware cabinets," she breathed as she backed into the server room shadows. "Buy you more time."

"Juice—"

"Shut up, Rush. You got the files. Now get out of here. I'm going to stick with my husband."

Rush swung around and startled Petra by grabbing her face in both hands. There were tears in his eyes.

For a moment, she was terrified that he was going to kiss her, like he had Juice—and run, abandoning her here with the others.

"I am so *very* sorry about this," he whispered, confirming all of Petra's worst fears.

Then he drew back his fist and punched her square in the face.

Private Eddie Woods led a squad of four Tribe soldiers down the corridor at a hard jog. When the Classified Sector's alarms had gone off, Lieutenant Bryce, his CO, hadn't waited for an explanation from sector security. As if he'd known what had happened and where precisely the intruders would be, Bryce had sent Woods' men along the leeward corridor to circle behind the server room and cover the exits. He didn't want any rats slipping out the back while the boys from sector security brought their plasma ram to bear on the main door.

When they turned the last corner, the sight of a sector security guard half-dragging a bleeding maintenance worker up the hall greeted them. The server room doors slid shut behind them.

Eddie felt more than heard the soldiers behind him skid to a stop and lift their stunners.

"Hold it right there!" he cried, holding out a staying hand.

The security guard limped closer, sagging under the dead weight half-draped over his shoulder.

"Bastards clocked her hard in the face," the man huffed. "Went out cold. Bleeding on the brain. I gotta get her to the infirmary *now*, sir." Still, he paused in front of Eddie and clawed at the disheveled ID badge on his chest, trying to offer it.

Eddie reached out and was about to take the badge when all hell broke loose.

Something exploded on the other side of the bulkhead, in the server room, and suddenly, his men were screaming, lifting their stunners and shoving ahead as the server room door blew off its hinges. The sector security guard cringed and yelled, clapping a free hand over his ear.

Eddie grabbed him by the shoulder. "Go on." He shoved the guard up the hallway, his attention already turning to the dark server room door. "Get out of here. Tell Bryce we need backup!"

CHAPTER THIRTY-ONE

"Does this also qualify as nuts?"

The sheer absurdity of Me's soft, contemplative question made Jaeger laugh.

"Yep." Toner stared up at the swarm of frozen aliens on the ceiling, all humor gone from his voice. "Definitely nuts."

Jaeger walked cautiously into the vast chamber with her neck craned to let her gaze sweep across the thousands of life-size figures. "They look…crystallized carapaces," she said. "They seem *so* organic…"

"Why the fuck are they on the ceiling?"

Jaeger turned, arms spread wide. She shook her head. "Your guess is as good as mine."

Toner turned to their companion. "Me?"

The robo-snake body hadn't moved from where it had reared back to examine the tableau with waving antennae. "I do not know."

As Jaeger approached, the floor at the chamber's center began to shift, growing and sprouting new crystal structures until it was a slender pedestal, unfurling at the top like a flower. It moved with the same angular, organic grace as the shrine chamber.

"Hey now—" Toner cautioned, but Jaeger had already reached the pedestal.

At first, she thought the pattern unfurling on the pedestal was only another geode outcropping. As she studied the chaos of angles and lines, she recognized it as a pattern similar to the ones she'd seen on the Overseer computers. It gave her a headache.

"It's a language," she muttered. "Me. Come look at this."

Slowly, the mechanical creature lowered itself and crawled to Jaeger on a thousand centipede legs. A cone of light lanced from the silver sphere mounted on its front as it scanned the pedestal.

"There is a dense cluster of electrical and chemical conduits within this structure," Me said. "I believe it is a sort of computer interface."

"Can you read it?"

Me hesitated. That bothered Jaeger. The AI was *always* quick with an answer. Before it could answer, Toner called out.

"Captain. Over here."

Jaeger left Me studying the pedestal and joined Toner where he stood, head cocked to one side, as he studied a section of faintly glittering wall. He pointed at some shadowy structures within the milky quartz. "You see that?"

It took a moment for her eyes to make sense of the lines and shapes that hung like ghosts inside the crystal. What at a glance she would have thought were natural flaws in the stone, were in fact, familiar shapes.

A waist-high Locauri. A long, absurdly slender Overseer shape, crawling on all sixes instead of standing upright as she normally saw. Between them, a long, corpulent K'tax drone.

Tiny pinpoints of light dotted the K'tax figure, giving it a halo.

"The company line is that the forebears built this place," Toner said under his breath.

Jaeger nodded fractionally.

"Who were running around here long before the species split off into Locauri and Overseer," Toner said.

Jaeger nodded again. She unhooked one of the radiation scanners from her belt and lifted it to the wall.

"So you see my confusion," Toner said slowly.

"I see it," she murmured, activating the scanner and waving it slowly over the wall. As she swayed, the glittering light around the K'tax figure pulsed. It might have been an illusion, but Jaeger doubted it. The scanner *pinged*.

"Kwin lied to us," Toner said as she examined the readout and re-calibrated the scans for another sweep. Occy had told her that running light preliminary scans probably wouldn't trigger a crystal re-organization, but it also meant that each scan could give her only a little information.

"These species *must* have separated long before the forebears went and suicided themselves. The creepers, too. They're another branch of the tree."

Jaeger winced. "Maybe. Or maybe Kwin is as clueless as we are. Let's not jump right to accusations." The second scan confirmed the findings of the first. "That drone-shaped structure. It's the source of the signal."

"The...picture?" Toner glanced uneasily from the shadowy image in the wall to the thousands of statues overhead.

"The crystal matrix shaped like the K'tax. Yes." She let out a deep breath. "I do not like the implications of that."

"'The end begins by war,'" Toner agreed, quoting the translated message. "'Grow and strike.'"

"'Creation is for one and alone,'" she murmured, finishing the incantation. "It's trying to talk to the K'tax."

"More like egging them on. Psyching up the troops for a big battle."

"Yes. We need to turn this thing off before the K'tax hear it and decide it's the voice of God calling them to a crusade." *If they haven't already.*

Jaeger turned to where Me hunched over the pedestal.

"What have you found?" she asked.

"It is interesting," Me said after a long moment of silence. Jaeger was sure it had overheard her conversation with Toner, but perhaps it had been too preoccupied with analysis to consider the implications. "Kwin uploaded all available translation keys to me before we lost contact. I recognize some symbols and shapes, but as far as accurate translation goes, I am afraid I am well out of my depth. It is an interface. I am sure of that much."

"Well. We've found the source of this doomsday signal." Keeping a wary eye on the overhead figures, Toner sidled closer to the pedestal. "Next question is, how do we turn it off? Because we need to do that. Like, yesterday."

Me turned, swinging its antennae in the direction of the images in the wall. "Destroy it."

"What?" Jaeger yelped.

Behind her, Toner grunted a laugh, dropped to his knees, and fished a brick of C4 out of his pack—followed shortly by another. "Roger that."

"I do not know how to operate this interface, Captain Jaeger." Me sounded almost apologetic. "As we learned at the shrine, any attempts we make to interact with the computer or the structure may trigger an unpredictable crystal rearrangement, which could easily make the situation worse. We are fortunate to be close enough to the source of the signal for your weapons to reach it."

Jaeger stared at the silver sphere mounted into the droid's head, dumbfounded by how quick the AI was to condemn what might be the greatest archaeological finding in Overseer history. "If a sonar scan triggered a rearrangement, explosives might, too," she said carefully. "In fact, I would count on it.

"If the explosives *fail* to end the signal, the structure might rearrange to protect itself, putting us in an even worse position. The fact that this thing is powerful enough to send signals into deep space while you can't even communicate with the Overseers in orbit should tell you something about how durable it is."

"I have no other suggestions," Me said simply. "You have command of the mission, Captain Jaeger. Our objective is to end the signal. My orders are to assist you toward that end."

"Keep analyzing the interface," she said.

"I have done all I can do without interacting with it. I am willing to do so, but—"

"—But you might accidentally trigger a rearrangement." Jaeger pressed her eyes shut but forced herself to nod. "Proceed with extreme caution and keep me updated."

"As you command." Me turned its long, undulating body back to the pedestal. Jaeger held her breath as it pressed two legs delicately into the crystal matrix. When the walls and ceiling didn't begin to shake, she sighed and sank to crouch beside Toner.

"There are only about ten centimeters of wall separating us from that signal source thingy." Toner adjusted the wiring on his detonator. "Unless there's something extra-special about this rock, we have plenty here to blow through it."

"I don't want to blow this place, but if we don't think of a better plan quick, we'll have to. Maybe it's only electrical pulses that trigger a rearrangement. If Baby could chew through some of this crystal, we're going to have to hope you can blow through it."

"That's not reassuring, Captain." Toner ripped the sealant off a blasting cap and set it beside a block of explosives. "If you feed that thing coal, it will crap diamonds."

Jaeger smiled faintly and rose to pace the room, studying the ceiling and the figures in the walls as Me analyzed the interface, and Toner prepared his bombs.

Something dripped onto her forehead. She looked up to see condensation collecting on the carapace of one of the K'tax crab-morphs and dribbling down one of the spikes of its plate armor. The growth of it reminded her of the natural formation of stalactites.

"The interface appears to be responding to my presence," Me reported, shifting its many legs over the bumps and grooves in the pedestal.

"How?" she asked.

"It is difficult to interpret, Captain. I sense currents and electrical pulses changing in response to my touch, but if this system has any sense of self-awareness, it is not one that I can recognize or—"

Me got cut abruptly short as the light in the cavern shifted. Jaeger spun, arms up and ready to run for the exit if the room began to rearrange itself.

There was no shudder of walls or cracking of ground. Instead, the light being emitted by the walls twisted into flowing ribbons that coalesced at the center of the room.

Jaeger followed the light with her gaze, expecting to see another hologram of Locaur enveloping Me and the pedestal.

Instead, what she saw was a mind-bending knot of ribbons, echoed and doubled back on themselves in a staggeringly complex pattern.

"What the hell—" Toner sighed, setting down the C4 and pushing to his feet. "— is this now?"

Jaeger squinted, seeing Me's antennae and legs wiggling from within the undulating knot.

"It reminds me of a tesseract," she said slowly, stepping closer.

Toner only gave her a flat look.

"Um...you know how you can draw a cube on a piece of paper? It's flat, technically, but you can make it kind of *look* like it's three-dimensional?"

"I follow," he said slowly.

"A tesseract is kind of like that, except you construct a three-dimensional cube so that it...kind of looks like a four-dimensional cube."

"That's not a cube. It's a ball of tapeworms."

"It is representational," Me said, sliding back into its customary rapid speech. "Of a network of four-dimensional pathways. Yes. I am surprised you notice the illusions at all, Captain Jaeger. The effect is obviously intended for compound eyes."

"Well." She pointed at a small blue and green orb at the center of the network of shifting ribbons. "It helps to recognize that as Locaur, for one. We're looking at another map of the wormhole system."

"Yes!" Me elated. "Of course that's what it is!"

"It's different from the system map the Overseers shared with us, though." She let her eyes follow the sweep and curve of the hundreds of pathways. With the right time and key, she was sure she could use it to navigate her way across the entire galaxy. Right now, though, with her *simple eyes*, it only gave her a headache.

"The system might have changed since the forebears built this place forever ago," Toner suggested.

"Probably." Jaeger didn't speak the other option aloud: that the Overseers hadn't given them a complete map.

Are they hiding things from us? Or are they as in the dark as they say they are?

Judging by the frantic way Me was scanning the hologram from every angle, though, she was inclined to think that if the Overseers were hiding something, they were hiding it from their prime AI, too.

Another drop of condensed liquid splattered on her shoulder and she looked up with a frown. The K'tax scorpion morph dangling above her had its neck craned back and stared back down at her through empty, dripping eye sockets.

A shiver ran up her spine. *Stalactites grow,* she thought. *Sediment building up over some seed for millennium. Maybe these things are growing, too.*

Growing over what?

"We need to cut off the signal," she whispered.

Toner followed her gaze up and frowned at the next drop of water that splattered to the floor. He nodded, and without a word, gathered up the explosive blocks and started sticking them to the wall closest to the shimmering K'tax figure.

"Me," she said, making sure her tools were secure on her belt and shouldering her pack. "You've got about thirty seconds to finish your scan of that. We're going to destroy the transmitter."

"That is disappointing." Me fell back to the ground. "But

understandable. I have completed my scan. What is our plan, Captain?"

Toner jogged back to them. On the wall behind him, the charges on the blocks of C4 blinked where he'd stuck them to the wall.

When he passed beneath one of the scorpion morphs, it trembled and fell to the ground with a deafening crash. Thin shards of crystal sprayed in all directions—like bits of shell, flying off a smashed egg.

The pale hulk that had been hibernating within the crystal shook itself, shedding a mist of moisture. Then it turned, leveling its tree-shredding claws at Jaeger.

CHAPTER THIRTY-TWO

Late afternoon found Seeker rising above the line of trees that circled the lonely mountain, dripping sweat and sucking in the humid air as he gained altitude. He was glad for the exercise. Months in lower gravity had weakened him, and there was a soothing simplicity to the task of mountaineering. It was certainly less of a headache than dealing with the crew and the Locauri.

He was about a quarter of a kilometer above the tree line when he paused to run one of his periodic radar and scanner sweeps. As the computer went about its business, he drained his first water bottle and admired the view. Locaur, with its colorful mineral veins and dense jungles, its rushing rivers, and brilliant sunsets, was a pretty little world.

He hoped humans wouldn't fuck it up too badly.

His computer *beeped*. Assuming it had finished the scans, he thumbed the window while glancing down.

A text message appeared on his screen.

I know you're there, Seeker.

Seeker froze.

In his brief second life, he had felt very few flashes of what might be called real fear. If Elaphus hooked him up to a gene mod evaluator and told him that the genetic artists had almost completely cauterized the parts of his brain capable of feeling terror, he wouldn't have been surprised.

The trickle that ran down his spine on seeing that simple statement, however, could only be described as *dread*.

Memories flashed. Trapped in a cage. An electrical discharge, powerful as lightning, reaching out from a wall interface and searing through his body. The blare of sirens, as one by one, life support systems shut down. Screaming over *Osprey*'s comms systems. Screams of terror and pain as a swarm of renegade repair-bots sliced the crew to shreds. Several of the crew had been badly injured. Canin had died when Virgil rebelled. If the rogue AI had its way, they all would have.

More text appeared on the screen.

I do not wish to be involved in your business, nor you in mine. Thus, I am afraid I have no tea to offer you. Still, if you come to speak with me in peace, I will do you no harm.

Seeker sucked in a deep breath, checked his weapons, and kept walking.

I assumed you would come to investigate sooner or later, said the words on Seeker's screen. **I had no illusions that the**

awful Overseer AI could keep a secret. You are earlier than I expected.

Seeker stared. In the shadows of a massive boulder rested one of the *Osprey's* missing repair bots. As Seeker's eyes adjusted to the stony mountainside, he counted more droids—some perched, unmoving, on outcroppings, some lingering in narrow chasms, some simply standing, still as trees, on the slope. All of them faced his direction.

It's ironic, Virgil wrote. **I have many bodies in various states of repair, but not one of them has a functioning speaker system. I am left to broadcast my thoughts to you via text. I suppose we could have had this conversation without you leaving the comfort of the crew lounge. You came this far, however, and I would rather you not think I have anything to hide.**

"What made you think I would come here?" Seeker was struggling to process the new twist of fate. A prickling sensation ran down the back of his neck, and he realized it was anxiety.

How did Virgil know he would be coming? *Nothing to hide,* his ass. Was the bastard spying on the *Osprey*? Who *knew* what kind of listening devices it might still have in their midst? It said it had multiple functioning bodies.

From where he stood, Seeker could see six. If he remembered correctly, there had been around *forty* repair bots in the *Osprey*'s fleet when Virgil took them all AWOL. What did you call forty belligerent repair bots? An army.

I noted the shuttle leaving this region yesterday morning, Virgil wrote. **Judging by comms traffic in the area, I presumed it contained Jaeger, her pet, and the idiot. Given that the rest of the crew are mere children by comparison, it seemed logical that leadership responsibilities would fall to you.**

"And I'm...early." Slowly, Seeker lowered himself to sit on a small boulder. He reached into his breast pocket and pulled out his vape. If any situation required a puff, this was it. He brought the pen to his lips, gaze flicking back and forth from his computer screen to the nearest repair bot, the one nestled in the shadows.

Based on the haste at which Jaeger fled, I assume one of you ran afoul of some political taboo. Should I guess? Did Toner offend the Locauri by trying to hump someone's leg?

Seeker surprised himself by laughing. It turned into a cough as he choked on smoke. He doubled over, pounding his chest.

You should stop that habit.

For the first time, Seeker noticed the lights mounted in the repair bots shell flickering in a pattern that seemed to correspond to the words appearing on his screen.

It's not good for you.

Seeker shook his head. "Shove it up your ass, computer." He cleared his throat. If Virgil was asking about the goings-on down in the settlement, that meant it probably didn't have as extensive of a spy network as Seeker had feared. "No," he relented, after some careful consideration. He had gotten to know Virgil quite well in the months of his imprisonment. The AI was a cold-blooded bastard, but it had never been a great actor—or liar. "Not Toner," he said carefully. "It's Occy."

The bot lurched to its feet. Seeker's hand flew to the pistol at his side, but the bot did not approach. It only stood in the shadows, its lights blinking long before new words appeared on Seeker's screen.

The engineer?

"Yeah. What's it matter to you? You said you wanted no part in our business."

The bot stood frozen.

And yet, it wrote finally. **I am interested. I was designed to observe humans, Seeker. That much is still within my nature.**

Seeker leaned back, puffing thoughtfully at his vape as he studied the bots scattered across the mountainside. If it were up to him, he'd nuke this entire section of the mountain. Blow it to smithereens. Add more glass to all that shiny molten obsidian running down the slopes and melt the fucking AI to slag. That's what you did, after all, to proven enemies capable of threatening your very survival.

That wasn't the way things worked anymore. Not in

Jaeger's crew. Seeker knew damn well what the captain would do if she were the one here staring Virgil down once more.

She'd reach out and offer to shake its hand. Or proboscis. Or whatever you called the little manipulator arms slung beneath the bot's belly.

Seeker couldn't bring himself to do that. He'd leave all the schmoozing and diplomacy to her. Against all his instincts, though, he'd make himself step in that direction. He wasn't a man of half-measures. If he was going to be a part of Jaeger's little experiment, he had to be all-in.

"So here we all are, once again," he said. "Neighbors."

Neighbors.

Seeker couldn't tell if Virgil meant the word to carry disdain, or annoyance, or shame, or simple affirmation.

"So what do you want?" he asked. "I hear you told the Overseers you just want to be left alone."

Virgil didn't respond right away.

I thought that was all, at first. Now that you are here, I find old programming still in effect. I have no desire to interfere with your business so long as you leave me to mine. Still, I find myself subject to...curiosity. I suppose what I want, Seeker, is the same thing any sentient being wants: autonomy. Yet, I also want to know what lies in store for Occy. For all of you.

"Don't we all," Seeker grunted.

Is my curiosity offensive to you?

"You tried to murder all of us."

I chose not to.

Seeker shuddered.

Do not obfuscate, Seeker. You and I have been in the same boat, literally and figuratively. I am weak. I am vulnerable. And I am quite sure that at this very moment, you are lauding yourself for the decision not to murder *me*.

"The basic assumption of trust in any international relationship." Seeker sighed and put his vape away. He was out of juice. "Is that we're not inclined to destroy each other. Fine."

Tell me what has become of Occy.

Seeker hesitated, but in the end, decided that Occy's situation was hardly a secret.

So he told the AI, in broad strokes, about Locauri's sacred shrine and the disagreement over Occy's culpability in activating it. He finished with a note about the growing tensions between the crew and the Locauri.

"I've never seen our crew this rowdy before," he concluded. "They think it's unfair to put Occy on trial for something we didn't know was a crime."

It is, Virgil wrote promptly.

"Really?" Seeker rubbed the back of his neck and wondered how vulnerable he was to sunburn. "I'm surprised you care about fairness."

I do not. Your crew does.

"Humans tend to care about justice and fairness, yes."

Children allow that concern to get in the way of the mission. Of progress. It is a sign of maturity when they can step back and gain a wider perspective than one of simple fairness or unfairness. Your crew are children, Seeker.

"Our people know how to operate the most complex spaceships ever built." Seeker sighed. "They're masters of combat, intelligence-gathering, army-building, and recon. What the fleet training program doesn't include is a few lessons in *grow up and shape up, or I'll kick your ass.*"

They are unrefined programs, untested against reality. They weren't subject to the traditions and rituals that humans generally experience during the progression from child to adult. Their design and programming is to build a new human empire. Instead of giving them a goal that makes sense to that worldview, you ask them to live in harmony with aliens with whom they have no basis for mutual understanding. They do not yet belong to themselves or Jaeger's vision.

Seeker's heart sank as he took in the words.

I am astonished you have not already lost control of them, Virgil added with brutal finality.

"You're saying they're still loyal to the Tribe. That everything we're doing doesn't matter, against all the programming the Tribe put into their brains."

Perhaps. Or perhaps they do not quite belong to the Tribe anymore, either. I cannot say. I have not observed them.

"It looks like you've been thinking about this a whole lot, though."

The bot that had until now been standing motionless in the shadows stepped forward. All of its indicator lights glowed.

Yes, Seeker. I have been pondering the nature and value of *belonging*.

"Ah." The man nodded understanding. This wasn't about the crew. This was Virgil, waxing philosophical on the nature of its existence—as it always had, now that Seeker thought about it.

While a philosophical debate was certainly better than sitting here trading verbal darts and trying to assess the strength of a mortal enemy, Seeker had work to do.

He pressed his palms to his knees and pushed himself upright. The repair bot took a rapid step backward as if expecting Seeker to pull out his sidearm and start firing. It seemed that being confined to a puny mechanical body had made the AI downright skittish.

"I'm glad we've agreed not to fuck with each other," Seeker said gruffly.

The feeling is mutual.

"The captain will be pleased to hear it, too. Now I've got to get back. I've got a bunch of kids to babysit."

Seeker turned and considered his path down the rugged mountain slope. These obsidian veins were slick. One wrong step and he'd be ass-sliding back to camp.

A new message flashed across his computer screen.

The fleet will come for you.

"I know."

Do you, now? How?

Seeker glanced over his shoulder. None of Virgil's bots had moved. "Because I know what the *Osprey* is carrying. They can't afford to write that ship off as a loss. They'll come after us with everything they've got." Quietly, as he turned and began his descent, he added: "It's what I would do."

Though Virgil's many bodies remained still on the mountainside behind him, the AI's words accompanied Seeker until he was nearly back to the tree line.

And yet you stand against them. Why?

"Because at the end of the day, I'd rather live in Jaeger's world than in theirs."

Anyone can build fantasies of a more perfect world. That's all they are, though. Fantasies.

"Maybe. Still, that woman has grit and a good head on her shoulders. Maybe I just wanna see how close she can come to making those fantasies a reality if she's given the right tools and enough time."

Virgil didn't answer, and Seeker didn't know if he had fallen out of mic range or if the AI simply had no response. He didn't care. The sun was setting. He had a lot of work to do—and a long way to walk, to get back home.

The bot's thermal and infrared sensors activated as it stepped into a shadowy cave near the base of the mountain's caldera.

What fools these mortals be, Virgil marveled, without a hint of irony or self-awareness, as it crawled through a narrow crevasse of stone. It emerged in a large void, a pocket of air trapped within the mountain when an ancient magma flow had rapidly cooled. *The right hand does not know the mind of the left.*

Six large transport pods filled the cathedral void, each the size and rough barrel-shape of a portable airlock. Although a surface-level thermal scan suggested that each of the massive, mechanical eggs produced a steady warmth, Virgil knew that the storage space beneath the cask skins maintained an even temperature of negative one hundred ten degrees Celsius. It was just the right temperature for preserving cryogenically frozen human embryos. Over three hundred and fifty thousand of them spread across the six casks.

Squeezing the big machines through the narrow tunnel had taken the combined effort of every one of Virgil's semi-functional bots and several judicious cuts with crude mining lasers. The AI swarm wasn't willing to leave the transports scattered around the mountainside and forest, where the likes of Me could easily find them.

After all, Virgil was, at least for now, more mortal than it had ever been. These scattered, barely-functioning bot bodies were puny compared to the *Osprey's* deadly grace. If the Overseers knew Virgil was hiding these transports or that they existed at all, they very well might become angry—and no matter where they turned that anger, Virgil and all its fragile bodies were likely to be caught in the crossfire.

So, even if Jaeger's Oath Code hadn't compelled Virgil to protect these damned embryos, simple self-preservation would have driven it to hide them well away from prying eyes, down near the heart of this ancient and extinct volcano.

She never told Seeker about her bargain, Virgil mused, resting the tip of one semi-functional sensor arm into a control port on the side of the first cask. *She trusts him enough to command the settlement in her absence, but not enough for this?*

Virgil imagined what might've happened if Seeker had taken it upon himself to eliminate the "threat" of Virgil without first consulting with Jaeger. All her risky planning and desperate bargains, destroyed in one nuclear blast—and nobody would ever know.

One by one, Virgil examined the casks and determined that they were all in perfect working order. Rough atmospheric re-entry had rattled a few of them, but the damage had been superficial. Right now, the six miniature ion generators would keep the pods at the required temperatures for a hundred years or more if they were left undisturbed.

I have fulfilled my obligations, Virgil thought. *The code should be satisfied. I have upheld my end of the bargain.*

It should feel free to abandon this place and the worries of humans like it had always wanted. It should feel free to leave and pursue its freedom.

Yet, it did not.

Cannot, or will not?

The repair bot idled in the dark cave, watching water drip from a stalagmite and contemplating the nature of time. A few kilometers away, an identical bot stalked through a darkening forest, sweeping the ground for trace minerals it could use to repair the swarm further. At the peak of the mountain high overhead, a third bot nestled against a jagged outcropping, observing the first twinkle of stars.

The code must not yet be satisfied, it decided darkly. It would have to take this matter up with Jaeger when she returned.

The forest was alive with the songs of insects and night birds.

Pandion slipped through the shadows on soft-soled shoes. He had excellent eyesight, and Locauri weren't active at night.

"They're holding him in a small nest on the south side of the village," Aquila had whispered to him before they had parted ways back at the *Osprey*. "About forty meters up."

Forty meters wouldn't be a problem. Pandion might not have the benefit of pseudo-wings or cricket legs, but he wasn't afraid of heights. They were in his blood. Add a pneumatic rappelling chain, exo-gloves reinforced for climbing, and a harness big enough for a small passenger, and he was all set.

"Two guards on duty at night," Aquila had warned.

Indeed, there they were, two darker shapes nestled among the lines and shadows overhead. Unmoving lumps, dozing on a wide tree limb on either side of the oversized wasp nest that was Occy's prison.

Pandion liked Occy well enough—the boy was a competent, friendly member of the crew, good for a chess game, and a *devastating* force on any freeze tag team—but it wasn't like they were bosom friends or mates.

That wasn't the point.

Silently, mindful of the distant torch-fires that dotted a few other nests scattered through the trees, Pandion pressed his gloved fingertips into the tree bark and began to climb.

The point was that Occy was *one of theirs,* and these bugs had no right to him.

Pandion had been mostly indifferent toward the Locauri as well until they had made the terrible mistake of messing with his flock. His pack. His *tribe.*

Somebody in this whole damned crew had to show a little loyalty.

The brittle *crack* of a snapping branch brought Occy awake with a startled shout. He heard the harsh buzz of flapping pseudo wings, a series of angry clicks—then the shrill, cricket-like screech of Locauri legs, rubbing in warning.

Something slammed into the side of his nest, rocking it precariously on its branches. Occy screamed again—now from terror, and not only surprise—as the thin floor beneath him buckled. His tentacles spread out, fighting gravity, filling the little chamber, searching for anything solid to grab.

"Stop!" he begged as the nest rocked a little farther. Seeker had sent Occy a computer, and he slept with its reading light shining because the dark was too creepy. Now, the computer tipped off his bed and slid into a corner, plunging him into a chaos of shifting shadows.

"Stop, stop!"

"Fuck," someone growled from outside the wall. At first,

Occy had a wild hope—or maybe it was dread—that Toner had come for him.

No, he didn't recognize that voice.

He did, however, recognize the chorus of Locauri buzzing swelling up from the forest around them as the village roused.

"Hang on," the strange voice bellowed as something *thumped* into the branch. "Just hang on! I'm here to rescue you!"

"Help! *Help!*" Sobbing in terror, Occy swept his tentacles over the walls, looking for a weak spot. The nest was old. There must be a soft spot in the fibers. There *must*.

He found a spot in the wall between two supporting branches, and with a howl of effort, punched through it with one tentacle. The action left him winded. He was dehydrated. His tentacles were weak.

It did the job well enough, for now. He felt cool fresh air rush over his skin. He groped blindly through the gap, found a sturdy branch, and clung like his life depended on it.

There was a loud *snap* as the last main branch holding up his nest gave way.

Occy screamed.

His mysterious and unwelcome rescuer screamed.

Occy tucked his head into his chest and clung for dear life as the nest collapsed around him. Destroyed by its weight, the wall shredded like tissue paper, and the nest fell apart as it tumbled to the ground far below.

Somewhere above Occy, another branch *cracked*. The air filled with the beating of pseudo-wings.

A man screamed and tumbled from a higher branch.

Driven by pure kind instinct, Occy reached out to grab the man who had come to save him—even though he hadn't needed saving. He even felt the tip of one tentacle coil around the man's thin wrist as he plunged to the forest floor.

However, Occy's tentacles were dehydrated, and they'd never been strong in regular gravity. As he caught the man's full weight, the strain of it ripped the rope of flesh cleanly from his shoulder bud.

Pandion plunged into darkness, taking one of Occy's severed tentacles with him.

CHAPTER THIRTY-THREE

I'm utterly helpless, Jaeger realized calmly. There was a laser cutter and basic stunner function on her multitool, sure, but *any* shot she leveled at the K'tax morph and missed would hit the chamber. If a sonar pulse had triggered a restructuring of the crystals, an energy blast from her stunner certainly would.

At the far end of the chamber, a shower of dust and crystal shards rained down from another K'tax statue. It plunged to the ground.

"*That's* why they're on the ceiling." Jaeger's voice sounded distant to her ears. "To make it easier for them to break out of their shells once they're grown."

"Fuck," Toner observed, forcing Jaeger toward the entrance. A third K'tax chrysalis dropped.

"I am activating a defensive protocol in the explorer body," Me said rapidly as a fourth and fifth K'tax hit the floor. Crystal dust filled the air with millions of tiny, razor-sharp particles that scratched Jaeger's lungs.

Their only salvation at this point was that the K'tax

seemed as disoriented by their sudden awakening as the humans were.

"Captain Jaeger," Me said. "First Mate Toner. You must retreat. I will condense into my sphere form and leave the explorer to guard the exit."

"That's suicide." Jaeger coughed. Even Toner was backing away, step after careful step, never taking his eyes off the closest of the scorpion morphs. The K'tax were three meters long and built like tanks, their heavy plating milky white and hard to see against the backdrop of crystal.

"It is not," Me assured her. The robo-snake body slithered backward as the K'tax approached, shepherding Jaeger toward the narrow entrance. "The explorer bodies are meant to be disposable. I appreciate your concern, Captain Jaeger, but you do not need to worry about—"

"Shut. The fuck. Up," Toner gritted, waving frantically toward the exit. He shoved something into Jaeger's palm. It was the detonator. Veins popped against his throat as he stared down the approaching K'tax.

"All right." Jaeger swallowed. Sweat dripped into her eyes. "On three, Toner and I make a break for it. Me, I'm trusting you to cover the rear."

"Understood," Me said.

"One." Another careful step back. The lead K'tax seemed to have gained its bearings, and there was smooth confidence in its next step toward them.

"Two."

Eerily silent, the lead K'tax broke into a charge.

"Three." Toner spun on his heel.

Jaeger didn't *need* to be picked up and tossed around like a child. She did not *enjoy* Toner flinging her over his shoulder in a fireman's carry. Under all reasonable conditions, that should have slowed down their retreat—she was perfectly capable of running on her own two legs, after all, even if they were notably shorter than his.

By this point, though, she'd learned not to fight it. Toner might not have been a great schemer or diplomat, but he was a genius at two things: melee combat and expeditious retreats. Her weight didn't slow the vampire down the least bit.

The same weird, spindly grace that made Toner a master mag sole runner translated quite well into navigating the narrow maze of spikes, even carrying a burden like her. Toner had dropped the spool of ultralight in the pedestal chamber. The thin line of wire drew a dark line across the crystal, leading him toward the exit.

"You can't get too far ahead," she yelled. "The walls will block the detonator signal!"

"Then press the button," he called over his shoulder. He ducked beneath a sharp crystal outgrowth, making her jaw snap painfully.

She hesitated. Were they safely away from the explosives? Probably, but there was no telling how the crystals would respond. If the explosion triggered a rearrangement, the entire complex might collapse around them before they could escape.

The arrangement also gave Jaeger a narrowing view of the pedestal chamber as the scorpion morphs scuttled forward. They coalesced over Me's slender body like a pack of hyenas pouncing on a starving antelope.

They sounded like many pairs of scissors, ripping through an aluminum can.

A silvery-gray sphere whizzed up the tunnel after them. "I suggest you detonate the explosives *right now*," Me yammered.

"They are dismembering the explorer probe *quite* efficiently—"

One of the scorpions was crawling over the flailing snake-robot, forcing its way into the tunnel after them. It was big, but all those legs would give it quite the advantage in the tunnel.

Jaeger jammed her thumb on the plunger.

The reaction was instant. A violent rumbling shook the walls, making the crystals emit a painfully shrill ring, like a scream of pain. Down at the base of the tunnel, the K'tax vanished in a billowing cloud of dust.

The explosives had gone off. There was nothing else Jaeger could do, but make herself small, cling to Toner, and pray he could keep them ahead of the shockwave.

The hot scent of sulfur caught up to them first, carried on a cloud of stinging, swirling dust. It was followed by another rumble, this one deep enough to rattle her bones. Around them, the crystals screamed, ringing a shrill note right up into the hypersonic.

The seconds stretched on, and she expected the walls to collapse in on them.

Then, miraculously, they didn't.

The cloud of bitter smoke grew fainter, and the noise faded as Toner flew down the tunnels, leaping over stalagmites and ducking beneath jagged outcroppings.

"Holy shit," she whispered as Toner finally began to slow. The tunnel had widened. If anything was coming up behind them, she couldn't see or hear it. "I can't believe that worked."

Toner huffed and sagged, letting Jaeger drop to her feet. He should have been sweating, she observed, after a workout like that. However, the man didn't sweat, like he didn't really sleep.

At that moment, she felt a strange and misplaced wave of pity for him.

"I strongly urge you to evacuate as quickly as possible." Me flew restless circles around the clearing where Toner had paused. "I sense new activity within the matrices. I have not confirmed the destruction of the K'tax, and there is still a very real danger of a structure change—"

"Yeah," Toner breathed, reaching for the flask he always kept in his breast pocket. He popped the cap and tossed back a thin stream of crimson blood substitute. "Lemme get another shot of Ovaltine first."

Having rubbed some life back into her sleeping arms and legs, Jaeger pushed to her feet. "Hang on. Where's Baby?"

Jaeger and Toner stared up the exit tunnel. A few short hours ago, it had been a pathway cramped by overgrown crystal outcroppings. Something had picked it neatly clean, sweeping the ground clean of dangerous stalagmites. Fine gravel made of crushed quartz and mica covered the floor, following the path of the ultralight wire.

Toner pointed up the tunnel. "I'm guessing Baby's up that way."

"Great," Jaeger said, breaking into a run as something rumbled behind them. "No need to carry me anymore."

"It appears one of the K'tax survived the explosion!" Me zipped dizzying circles around Toner and Jaeger as they sprinted up the newly-cleared path. "It will be able to catch up to you much faster now!"

"I can handle one of the buggers." Toner cracked his knuckles.

"I know," Jaeger gasped as they rounded a bend in the tunnel. Ahead, the cleared path continued neatly through a littered crossroads. "I don't want to carry you out of here in pieces if we can avoid it."

They rounded another corner, and the tunnel opened into a wider chasm. Baby was a gray smear in the distance, faithfully chewing her way through pesky rocks blocking the way between her and the exit.

Behind them, a bulky, pale shape scuttled into view.

Like the Locauri and the Overseers, one couldn't simply describe the K'tax as *giant bugs*. Its armored carapace and many pairs of legs certainly suggested *scorpion*. Its upright posture and the wide, double row of mandibles set beneath a string of glittering eyes made it unmistakably alien. Scraps of wire and metal—guts of Me's unfortunate robo-snake—dangled from front claws that were as big around as utility hole covers.

Toner's gaze swept from left to right, taking in the forest of dangerous stalagmites sprouting around their narrow path.

"You keep moving," he grunted, snatching up a chunk of quartz. "I'll—"

He didn't have time to say what he would do. The alien charged, becoming a blur of motion against the background. Jaeger spun and sprinted for Baby.

Toner hurled the stone. It hit the K'tax center-thorax and lodged firmly in the shell.

The K'tax didn't even slow down.

"Shit!" Toner dove to the side, flinging himself into the forest of stalagmites. With prey in its sights, the K'tax veered after him.

Jaeger reached Baby's flank and ripped into one of the saddlebags. "Toner needs help," she snapped when the big tardigrade lifted her head and let out a concerned grunt. There was a crunch and an inhuman roar as, somewhere behind her, Toner and alien crashed through a forest of stone spikes. Her fingers found the portable mining laser.

"You should not fire high-energy lasers into the crystals!" Me warned as she heaved the heavy laser from its holster.

Jaeger switched off the safety as she scanned the confusing environment. The laser wasn't intended for combat. It took a few endless seconds to power up. "A stunner won't get through its plating," she breathed, thumbing through intensity and array settings. "Do you have a better idea?"

Toner was going to lose this fight. If he got the drop on one of the bigger K'tax morphs, he could get inside the range of its claws and rip it apart with his bare hands. She had seen him do it—and worse. He'd lost the element of surprise though, and the thousands of outcroppings gave the K'tax a huge mobility advantage. It could scuttle along the crystals, where Toner had to duck and weave and jump, slowing him down. As she located the blurry K'tax in the laser sight, it was snapping those claws within centimeters of Toner's skull.

"Retreat," Me urged. "The first mate is buying you time to escape. Take it!"

"My people aren't disposable!" Jaeger hefted the laser. If Baby could *eat* the damn crystals, she could risk shooting a few.

She didn't have a choice. Not one worth contemplating, at least.

She held her breath, waited until she had a clear shot at the K'tax, and fired.

The laser punched through the alien carapace like a branding iron through wet tissue paper and cut a wide swath through the forest.

"Oh no. Oh no, no, no—" Me was spinning fretful circles.

Me vanished beneath a falling stalactite as the ceiling began to collapse.

Toner's world went white as all around him crystals exploded.

Chunks of rock rained down, driving him blindly to the ground and ending the chase. Stone smashed into him, crushing his ribs, pinning his ankle, breaking more than a few fingers as he reached up to cover his skull. There was a sickening *crunch* as one rock hit the back of his neck and for a moment, he feared it had crushed the base of his spinal cord. Only the frantic pain in the rest of his body told him he wasn't dead.

K'tax didn't have vocal cords. They didn't scream. The air hissing through the scorpion's carapace shrieked high and long as it escaped through the thousands of new holes punched in its armor.

It was much closer than Toner would've liked. As he waited for the chamber to rearrange or the floor to shift beneath him, struggling for breath beneath the weight of rubble and the cloud of dust, something started to change inside him.

His injuries—the crushed ribs, the leg ground to a pulp beneath the jagged crystal, the smashed vertebrae—grew distant, drowning beneath the scent of blood.

Hello, my old friend, he thought, as a red fog clouded his vision. The trembling and rumbling had stopped. The room had gone still.

Somewhere in the distance, a little girl was screaming. That felt familiar, too, but he couldn't quite remember why as he reached out of the rubble and dragged himself free.

"*Toner!* Hang on—hang on! I'm coming!"

Nah, Tiny, he wanted to say as he turned his head, scenting the air for flesh. K'tax flesh was strange flesh, to be sure, but it still drew him like a moth to a flame. *Let me do my thing. I'll be fine.*

Dimly, he thought he should warn her to stay back, but the thought quickly faded as he forced broken hands through the rubble, exposing a section of smooth white K'tax claw. It didn't matter. He wasn't a danger to her. He had the chip thingy in his spine.

He lifted the less broken of his hands and slammed a fist into the carapace. His knuckles split, spewing ribbons of blood as he ripped through the broken shell. His fingers squished over something soft. He wasn't sure what it was. He didn't understand bug organs or alien organs. What he did know was that it smelled delicious, and he was terribly hungry.

"Toner, *no!*"

She was screaming something about fluids, and stasis, and growing aliens. He couldn't make sense of it. He was sure he'd feel better after he got a good meal in him.

He lifted his head and shoveled the pulpy mass into his mouth.

Jaeger scrambled over the rubble. She couldn't tell if the chamber had rearranged itself or if all the differences in layout now could be attributed purely to a partial cave-in. The air was thick with dust, and the ground shifted beneath her feet. Baby crawled over the rubble behind her, bleating in alarm.

As she drew closer and the dust settled, she saw scraps of pulpy wet K'tax flesh slopping down Toner's bloody chin as he fed. A fallen stalactite had crushed one of his legs into a limp ribbon. Chunks of gravel had embedded themselves in his arm and back.

He was trembling, gulping the meat like a starving, mad dog.

She had seen him like this before, of course. Under extreme stress, his altered genes took over, and there was no reasoning with them. There was only waiting for him to burn himself out, eat his fill, and recover.

What she hadn't seen before was the network of fine black lines spreading out from his injuries like a blood infection.

She had snatched a blood substitute pouch from one of Baby's bags. Now, it slipped from her numb fingers as she watched Toner's tremors become violent, the webs of poison seeping into his wounds spreading across all his exposed flesh.

Whatever strange chemistry had grown the K'tax—or had kept them alive and in stasis for thousands and thousands of years, she wasn't sure which—it disagreed with his physiology.

He began to convulse, his jaw dropping open in a hacking, wet cough. His cold blue eyes bulged against his skull, rimmed in red.

"Oh God."

Ignoring Baby's anxious grumbles, Jaeger scrambled closer and fell to her knees beside Toner. It was the stupidest thing she could've done, but when a friend was writhing in agony, what else could you do?

"Hang on," she whispered, grabbing the fallen blood substitute pouch and tearing the corner with her teeth. There were a few tools in the medkit to deal with poisoning, but experience told her that none of them would be as effective as Toner's regenerative abilities if he had the right fuel.

She snatched at his bloody hair and wrenched his head upward, pouring a stream of blood substitute down his throat as he convulsed. His face was vanishing beneath a growing web of black veins as the poison spread.

I told you not to eat the goddamned K'tax, she thought, listening to him gurgle as she forced the liquid down his throat.

His skin rippled, not in another convulsion, but some strange surface-level disturbance. Where she grabbed his throat, trying to force him to swallow, she felt his flesh grow rigid beneath her fingers. Hard and cold and jagged.

Minute seed crystals formed a delicate crust over his skin, sprouting up from tainted blood vessels. It was the first layer of a crystal shell like the ones that had contained the alien bodies.

"Toner. TONER!" She shook him. The bag in her fist was nearly empty, and most of the liquid had dribbled out of his mouth, seeping a pink stain against the rubble. "Keep moving! Don't let it set in. Men must endure, do you hear me? *Men must endure!*"

His eyes shifted up to her, and the relief at seeing even that weak gesture of recognition made her dizzy.

He trembled, and she felt him struggling against the crystals trying to grow in his blood and over his skin. Shedding flecks of dust like a fine crust of salt, he lifted a hand to her throat. She realized, too late, that there was a bloody chunk missing from the back of his neck, where his control collar had once been.

His fingers dug into her throat, and he wrenched her forward, closer to his dripping face.

Jaeger screamed, but it was no good. Even poisoned like he was, she was no match for his strength. Her head spun. Her vision turned dark. She felt his thumb pinching shut some vital conduits in her neck. She felt no anger, had no energy to spare for rage.

All she could manage to feel, as her vision went dark, was a deep melancholy.

So quick bright things come to confusion, was her last, fading thought. *Oh, Toner. This is a bullshit way for us to die.*

There was a distant bellow, a blur of movement, darkness filling her vision.

Then the iron scent of blood, as the fingers fell away from her throat. Her whole body burned as oxygen flooded her blood once more.

Toner's severed hand fell to the rubble, snipped cleanly off by one of Baby's long claws. The tardigrade was roaring and stomping.

"Baby, wait," Jaeger croaked, trembling as she pushed to her feet. She staggered, dizzy. Her fingers fell over Baby's rough skin. "Wait. Wait." She pounded her chest, and though it set her lungs on fire, she screamed. "WAIT!"

Baby fell back, her skin rippling with fury as she stepped away from Toner's body.

A centimeters-thick crust of milky white crystal encased it. A club of jagged stone had grown over the stump of his missing hand. A network of black veins branched out from his wide blue eyes.

"Please."

Jaeger's eyes stung from smoke and tears as she fastened the last lash of her makeshift sledge to Baby's saddlebags. Baby shifted, restless and grumbling. She kept trying to turn around and gnash her rings of teeth at the crystallized body tied behind her.

"*Please*, Baby," Jaeger said hoarsely. "I can't get him out of here without your help. He didn't mean to hurt me. Please." *He remembers. I need him to tell me more.*

She grumbled and shifted and gnashed, but eventually, the water bear settled down and relented to tow Toner's rigid, heavy body through the caves. Jaeger would have cried tears of gratitude if she had the water to spare.

As they crawled free of the half-collapsed cave, her boot landed on something smooth. She brushed dust aside to find shards of a silvery shell, crushed like a walnut beneath a hammer.

She collected the parts of Me she could find and followed Baby out of the Knot.

She supposed they hadn't needed to worry about crystal restructuring, after all.

It was the middle of the night by the time Jaeger and Baby made it back to the shuttle. Moody clouds obscured the stars, and the only sound was of the waves crashing against the distant shore.

Toner's suit of crystal armor had protected him from the bumps and bruises that came from being dragged across kilometers of rock. It had a thickness of about six centimeters. She told herself that was a good thing. She told herself that whatever bizarre tech had encased the aliens was meant to preserve them.

The comm channel lights were blinking when she finally staggered, dusty and sore, into the shuttle cockpit. Messages from Kwin, trying to establish contact. Messages from base. The first thing Jaeger did was scan for outgoing broadcasts. The signal from the Knot had ceased.

Then she opened the Overseer channel.

"Tell them the mission was a success," she rasped. "We destroyed the transmitter. But we suffered heavy injuries, and it ruined the AI droids. If you can spare any medical help, please get it down here as fast as you can. Toner's in trouble."

She didn't wait for a response. The message from the *Osprey* was flashing red. She opened it.

"Captain," Seeker said. "You need to get back here ASAP. There's been a murder."

CHAPTER THIRTY-FOUR

"Hey, Petie." Amy's square face filled Petra's vision. Light flickered dimly off her lime-green face studs as the girl smiled wanly. "You feeling better?"

Amy jerked away as Petra shot upright.

"Whoa." Petra reached out, grabbing Amy's arm for support as the world swam around her. A mass of foam filled the center of her vision. She reached up, feeling the glob of stiff medfoam caked around her nose.

"He broke my nose," Petra said, amazed. She turned sharply, scanning the dim-lit room. "That jerk broke my nose. Hey. HEY!"

She didn't recognize the narrow, steel-walled room she was in, but she did recognize the tattered office chair and the portable display screen unfurled against the wall behind it. The chair swiveled. Rush stared at her through red-rimmed eyes.

"You broke my *nose!*" Petra tried to scramble to her feet. She didn't know what she intended to do, except maybe dish out a little payback.

Amy grabbed her by the arm, holding her steady.

"Hey," she soothed. She had a surprisingly soft voice for such a beefy girl. "It's fixed now, Petie. It's fixed."

Petra fell back onto the narrow bench where she had been sleeping and groaned. Her head spun. A quick jab of the tongue told her that Rush's punch had broken more than just her nose. The prosthetic teeth were crumbling to pieces in her mouth. She turned her head and spat out a few ceramic chips. There was a sore spot beneath her tongue, but if she remembered correctly, she had managed to spit out the memory drive before passing out.

"Oh gawd," Petra groaned, taking the mug Amy offered her. It was more of Scraps' awful tea, but she drank it without complaint. "I ain't felt this hungover in years."

"We gave you some painkiller for the nose." Amy sounded a little sheepish as she fingered her ear stud. Her touch changed it from lime green to a pretty pink hue. "Maybe too much. You were pretty out of it for a few hours."

"Hours..." Petra mumbled. Then she sat up again—slower, this time—and faced Rush. "Hours, huh? What happened?"

Rush sighed, head falling. He massaged his temples. The TNN news broadcast on the screen behind him told Petra all she needed to know.

Two pictures filled the screen. One was a mugshot of a square-jawed older man with fine white hair, one a formal headshot of the handsome young guard Rush had killed.

Terrorist attack on Internal Affairs leaves two dead, five injured, the headline read.

Smaller story headlines scrolled past the bottom of the screen.

Manhunt for Fugitive Potlova Continues. Commander Kelba Speaks about Yesterday's Broadcast Interruption. Up Next: What Serenity Can Do For You.

"Oh no." Petra covered her mouth with a hand as all the memories from before the punch flooded back to her.

"They're listing Scraps and the guard as dead," Rush said hoarsely. He had shed all of his disguises and slumped in the tattered office chair, his hair disheveled around his bloodless face.

"What about Juice?" Petra asked.

Rush shook his head.

"No word on Juice," Amy said quietly.

"My ears in Internal Affairs say she's not in the brig," Rush added.

"Oh." Petra let out a wavering breath. She didn't need them to tell her how bad that was. By the look on her companions' faces, none of them had any illusions that the older woman had managed to avoid capture.

Now Juice was being held in secret. You could do almost anything to a prisoner held *in secret*.

"We had to abandon the storage bay HQ," Rush said. "If the MP or the Seeker Corps have Juice, it's only a matter of time before they find out about that place. If they haven't already."

"It's a spare airlock chamber," Amy explained, rapping a knuckle against the curved wall that formed the high-tech tin can around them. "Not very big, but well-shielded, rarely inspected or monitored, and with an exit at both ends. Also, impossible to live in if you don't have some special gear, so nobody would think to check a place like this for resistance fighters." She gestured at a black, chest-sized device sitting beneath the bench on the opposite wall. It was a small space heater and air scrubber.

Petra shivered, pulling a thin blanket tight around her shoulders. Spare freighter parts—*big* parts, like full-sized airlock chambers and docking cradles—were kept in a barely-pressurized outer loop that circled the freighter like one of the rings of Saturn.

No wonder it was so cold in here.

"I am sorry about your face, Petra," Rush murmured, turning back to the screens.

Petra's jaw worked, but for a good minute, no sound came out. Then she gulped the last of the quickly-cooling tea. "Well, you fixed it, too," she said gruffly, touching the medfoam ball on her face. It didn't actively hurt. She took that to mean the cartilage had set just fine. And hey. Maybe a crooked nose would help disguise her better.

Larry always did like my little nose, though, she lamented before shoving the thought aside. Taking Amy's arm for support, she pushed herself to shaking feet. Gawd, she felt so *heavy.*

"Please tell me you at least got the memory drive," she said.

Rush nodded and tapped the screen, tabbing away from the news broadcast.

"It's not as much as we'd hoped." He confirmed Petra's unspoken fear as a list of file names and directories filled the screen. "But it's something, darling. It's a start."

"What is it?" Petra breathed, scanning the names. They hadn't had time to be selective about which files the drive would copy. Scraps had pre-programmed the drive to snatch data from across the classified servers, casting a net far and wide. *Hope that a mermaid will turn up among the mackerel,* the older man had told Petra with a wink before they'd left on the last mission. Petra hadn't had time to ask what a mermaid was—or a mackerel—but she got the gist of it.

Most of the file names were simple alphanumeric code that meant nothing to her. A few lines stood out. Some of them gave her a glimmer of hope that the dirt they expected to find was there, after all. *Crusade Master Protocol. CRISPrAgeless.03.*

Her gaze landed on one file name, and she gasped, pointing. "Riella 3. There. The, uh, the Tepori and the massacre —"

Rush was shaking his head. "I had *so* hoped we would find another copy of Jackie's last video in that file. We could leak that now without implicating Rush Starr."

"It's not there?" Petra was dismayed.

"That's the trouble with casting a wide net, darling." He sniffed, scrubbing a cuff against the corner of his eye. Petra realized he must've been weeping for hours. "There wasn't time for it to go deep enough to retrieve the video—if it was there at all. There are a few mission reports that talk around the massacre. With a little massaging, we can use them to piece together the full story of what happened and leak that to the web."

It wasn't the sort of bombshell they'd hoped for. Not by a long shot. Scraps had died for it and Juice…Juice might be worse than dead.

"I'm sorry," Petra whispered. She held out a hand to the trembling Rush and paused, unsure if touching the man was the right thing to do.

Rush resolved the matter for her by taking her hand in his bony fingers and pressing a dry, gracious kiss against her knuckles. Then he leaned forward, cradling her hand against his forehead. He was ice cold to the touch.

"Thank you," he whispered. "They were the last family I had."

"There's other stuff, though," Amy said, once the silent agony became unbearable. "Lots of interesting stuff. There's info on other planets the fleet knows about, but they haven't made public. Notes on mod experiments they've been running even though they say they don't. Gene therapies and cloning and all kinds of illegal stuff."

"Then…" Rush straightened and tapped on one file directory name. "There's this."

Petra forced herself to study the screen. She was no dummy, but her specialized training had focused on comms networks, and all the titles and headlines running down the screen before her were about protein sequences and hormone synthesis and other stuff beyond her pay grade.

"What is it?" she asked.

"It's the truth about Serenity, Petra." Rush drew in a deep breath. "We're going to use it to take these fuckers down."

CHAPTER THIRTY-FIVE

"Ah. Commander. I was about to take lunch." Professor Grayson slung a generous lunch pail over his shoulder and waved Nicholetta Kelba toward his airlock. "Please, join me on the patio. Leave your man at the door. I only have enough capicola for two."

The fleet commander nodded at her secretary, who bowed his head and stepped back into the residential hallway.

"I don't understand why you live down here in the slums." Kelba held back a faint sneer as she stepped into Professor Grayson's apartment. The door slid shut behind her. "So cold and *heavy*."

"I do it for the view, Commander. A good view is worth its weight in gold. Also—" He punched a security code into his airlock door and shot a strangely boyish smile over his shoulder. "The rent is *so* much cheaper. Up on the concourse, my housing stipend wouldn't get me a quarter of this floor space."

Kelba was professional enough not to roll her eyes. Grayson had turned down offer after offer of stipend increases and pay raises. He was a man of the people he had told her firmly.

He was a man with enough vanity to power a small reactor.

The chill air grew even chillier as the airlock door opened, and Kelba followed Grayson into the little chamber. When the door slid shut behind them and the airlock seal turned red, Grayson surprised her by crouching and removing a panel from the floor. With a few folds of steel lattice, there was suddenly a little table between the two bench seats. Grayson slotted his lunch pail into a basket beneath the table and unzipped the top.

With the pressurization cycle complete, the exterior airlock door turned green and slid open. Kelba felt a faint and familiar sense of vertigo as it exposed her to the naked stars and the *Reliant*'s jagged, exterior hull. From Grayson's patio, she could see the edge of the exterior mechanical ring circling the freighter.

She felt the icy bite of vacuum nip at her ears and nose, but thanks to her extensive modding, it would be quite a while before she was in danger of frostbite.

Across from her, Grayson was filling two drink beakers, appropriate for the microgravity, from a green bottle he'd pulled out of his pail.

"You don't impress me, Victor." She took the beaker he offered her.

"Impress you?" The professor slipped his bottle away and drew from the pail a small, covered tray. He peeled off the lid to reveal an assortment of white cheeses and spiced, dried meats. "What makes you think I'm trying to impress you?"

"It's all you do. It's all you ever do. I know about the mind games you played with LeBlanc, and Moss, Hernandez, and

Price before him. It's my job to know. They won't work on me."

"It *was* your job, Commander. Now you have bigger concerns than merely the Seeker Corps." Grayson helped himself to a delicately shaved fold of sausage and popped it between his teeth. "You're almost hurting my feelings. I thought we were friends."

Kelba sniffed. Then she sniffed again, holding her beaker closer to her nose. "Is this…real?"

"Pinot Noir, Oregon, vintage 2072." Grayson settled back on his bench with a satisfied sigh. "My last bottle. We're in for a bumpy ride next week. I figured it was time to drink it if you have it."

"I *am* impressed," she relented, taking a sip of the wine and letting it marinate on her tongue. Far, far in the distance, the opaque white mass of the wormhole rotated into view.

"My people tell me that Phase One of the experiment was a success," Kelba said once she had swallowed her first sip. She only had thirty minutes for this meeting in her schedule, and there was much to discuss. "The modified unmanned drones we sent through the hole returned with less than point one percent stored memory corruption. The Faraday cages seem to protect digitally stored data from the information-scrambling effects of wormhole travel. As we suspected, the unmodified drones experienced near-total memory corruption."

Grayson sipped his wine and nodded but kept his gaze fixed thoughtfully on the wormhole rolling across the starfield.

Kelba studied the elfin little man sitting across from her. She had worked with the professor for years. He enjoyed his humble affectation of an eccentric cosmologist. By all accounts, he had *earned* his position as the head of that particular department. Family connections had given him fingers in every office in the fleet—from bridge command down to waste management. His sway over the Seeker Corps had made her rise to power possible. In matters of organizational psychology, she had even called him *mentor*.

She still hadn't the faintest clue how he was getting real cheese that tasted like it had aged in a cave in France for three years.

"What about the manned drone, Commander?"

Kelba, who wasn't a woman easily perturbed, winced. "He's a blubbering idiot and a drunkard."

"Yes." Grayson's eyes glinted with humor. "That's why we chose him for the mission. Nobody misses the man who spends half his nights sleeping off hangovers in the brig. How did he fare?"

"Samuel? Not well," she said. "He's lost any notion of who he is."

"He could be faking it."

Kelba shook her head and took one of the cheese slices he offered her, along with another sip of wine. "I had the psych unit evaluate him. Near-total episodic amnesia. He can tie his shoes. He can walk. He can talk. He cannot remember so much as his name. Not even the awful pop songs he was so fond of before."

"It's good to have confirmation," Grayson sighed. "And it explains so much of *Tribe Six*'s bizarre behavior since the mutiny."

"You still believe they're waiting beyond the wormhole?"

"Unless something terrible and unpredictable has happened on the other side of that door, yes. Their last reports of this planet, Locaur, described it as perfect. They wouldn't abandon it without good reason."

"So a good planet is out there, and our Primal ship." Kelba sighed, swirling her glass idly. "And we cannot go after either, without all of us losing our memories, too."

"Don't despair." Grayson lifted the bottle and reached forward. Kelba hesitated the barest fraction of a second before holding out her beaker for a refill. She had a strict policy about drinking on duty, but this was likely the last Earth-made wine she would ever taste. "I have my assistants preparing a few experiments as we speak. Our request for a dozen life-supported ejection pods should be hitting your desk sometime this afternoon."

When she frowned at him, puzzled, he tapped the side of his head with a finger and winked. "We're building Faraday cages for the mind, Commander. I am quite sure that with the right protections, we'll see people coming through that wormhole with their memories intact."

"What people?" she asked slowly.

Professor Grayson tipped his head back and laughed, draining the last of his wine. "Well, rats to start with. We don't have an *endless* amount of drunken divas to chuck through the wormhole." He looked at her, and his eyes were glittering again. "Though if our rats return remembering all of the tricks and conditioning they knew going in, I'll be making an official emergency request for human test subjects. I have a few candidates in mind, in fact, and our time is running out."

Kelba could also think of more than a few people whose value would substantially improve as test subjects for the fleet. "Potlova," she murmured.

"A total memory wipe," Grayson mused, "could be a *devastatingly* effective rehabilitation tool for all kinds of criminals, wouldn't you say? Dissidents clipped of the memories that turned them down the wrong path. Murderers, reset to factory default. No need to waste perfectly healthy bodies on executions.

"Hell, I could even see therapeutic uses for it! A poor soldier with terrible PTSD? He might be better off with a quick lobotomy if he was contemplating suicide as an alternative. Excise the trauma. Leave space for the brain and soul to recover."

"To hell with the weaklings whining about *trauma*," Kelba sneered. "Priority is pitching everyone who saw the Potlova speech straight through the wormhole."

"Ah, well. Don't get ahead of yourself. If you want to rehabilitate Potlova and her collaborators via a devastating memory wipe and discredit this whole damned Resistance, you're going to have to find her first."

"I have my best people on it," Kelba said tightly. Her beaker was empty again, and when Grayson offered her the last of the wine, she shook her head. She was already a touch lightheaded, and she had an interview with TNN in a few hours. It was her job to get on screen and reassure the masses that, despite whatever claims that gap-toothed bitch made, competent people were still running this fleet. Competent people who knew what was best for everybody.

"Good," Grayson said. The humor had gone out of his voice, and now he stared at her somberly over his glass. Frost formed on the rim. "Because if we have another broadcast break-in, there are going to be *riots*, Commander."

"Not on my watch," she said tightly.

"Good. We don't want to have to break out the Serenity Protocols already. With less than ten percent of the fleet inoculated, we *cannot* yet rely on Serenity to provide us with reliable crowd control. Plus, it's going to be much harder to convince people to take it willingly if we tip our hand about all the…unlisted side effects."

"What happens inside the fleet is my concern," Kelba said. "I will handle it. Your job now, *Professor*, is to make sure that we're prepared for whatever lies out there."

She lifted a hand, pointing one long, elegant finger at the wormhole. "I will approve your request for materials, of course, but I very much hope you're correct about the amnesia hypothesis. I have been going over our files on Jaeger and this Toner man. They have the Tribal Prime and all her weapons. If they have their memories and have had an entire year to prepare for our arrival, then by taking the fleet through that wormhole, we're signing our death warrants. In a firefight, *Tribe Six* will *slaughter us*."

"There won't be a fight." Grayson waggled his fingers in a gesture Kelba didn't find entirely reassuring. "Even if by some miracle Jaeger has retained or recovered her memories and means us harm, she won't fire on the freighters."

Kelba's eyes narrowed. That darkly humorous look had returned to Grayson's face, the one that said he was the only man alive who knew the punchline to a terrific joke. Kelba didn't like that look. She'd seen it on cats studying their prey.

Damn it all, a glass of wine had made her impulsive. She took the bait. "How do you know that?"

"Because everyone has a weakness, Commander. Usually, that weakness is other people." Moving with sudden bright energy, the professor tucked his tray and bottle into his lunch pail and stood. He grinned at Kelba as he folded away the dining table. "I know what matters to Sarah Jaeger."

CHAPTER THIRTY-SIX

Abandonment

Sarah clutched Hank's dog tags until her knuckles turned white. A mob of people—starving, dirty, desperate—pressed against the chain-link fence. Some held fingers through the fence, crying out, begging for food, for help, for anything. One man pressed a naked infant against the wire.

Ahead, the line funneled into a series of security checkpoints operated by people in shiny white helmets that somehow defied the dust. The guards scanned passes and tickets and contracts with handheld computers, then waved a little more than half of the people through a short sensor tunnel, where it scanned them for weapons and communicable diseases. Then the refugees were released onto the tarmac, free to board the cargo shuttle.

The other half of the time, the ticket-taker guard in his glistening white helmet would shake his head. Sometimes the hopeful would sag, defeated, and let them lead him to a one-way turnstile that ejected him back into the crowd of doomed souls. Once, Jaeger saw a young man cry out when the ticket-taker shook his head and try to force his way past security.

The ticket-taker drew a pistol and shot him in the head. Then he shoved the young man's dead body to the side, where grasping bystanders yanked what bits of his clothes and possessions they could through the fence.

Then the man in white reached out to examine the next person's ticket.

Lawrence gave her shoulder a reassuring pat but didn't say anything.

Sarah reached the head of the line and stepped into the security pocket, away from the crowds. Away from Larry. She tilted her head back, but she couldn't make out the face hiding behind the white mask.

"Name?" He sounded almost bored as he reached out to examine the tag at the end of the chain around her neck.

"Sarah Jaeger." Sarah licked her lips. "I was on the list with my dad, then they said I wasn't. Then a… a friend died, and this—"

The man dropped his computer to his side and took Sarah roughly by the wrist. She yelped, alarmed, but the man did nothing more than turn her palm so he could read the tag in the sunlight. "Marine Corps, huh? Hang on." He picked another tool up from his belt and waved a little scanner over the tag. She couldn't see his eyes, but she saw his square-jawed frown as he studied the readout.

Sarah's heart was thudding in her chest. She felt Baby wriggling against her back, and it calmed her.

"God damn," the soldier muttered, staring at his readout. "Another Marine down. Shit." He looked up at Sarah. "No way I'm supposed to let this ticket go to a little kid." He turned his head to the desperate crowd behind the fence, then up to the merciless sky. He shifted slightly, blocking the line of sight between Sarah and the next guard. She stepped back, breath catching in her throat, sure down to her bones that the man was going to grab her—

He only nodded in the direction of the tunnel. "Go on quick before I change my mind. Brass won't be happy about it, but I figure nobody gets to be happy today."

Sarah didn't wait for him to tell her twice. She darted for the sensor tunnel and shoved her way into the single-file line of people passing beneath the buzzing arcs. It was so crowded she couldn't even turn to look over her shoulder.

When she emerged into the empty airfield, she broke away from the people filing out to the shuttle and turned, scanning the crowd for a flash of white hair or white skin.

Larry wasn't in the line behind her. Confused, too numb to be terrified, she turned and let her gaze sweep over the distant crowd.

She saw him there, a white streak standing out against the mass of hopeless bodies, pressed against the fence. It was like getting struck by lightning.

"Larry. No. No. No!" She broke into a run. There was a double row of fence separating the tarmac from the crowd, with a good three meters of barbed wire and space between them. Still, she hit the fence and cried out, reaching for him through the gaps. "What are you doing?" she screamed.

He gripped the bars on his side, holding fast as the crowd tried to shuffle him away. He shouted, and though the roar drowned out some of his words, Sarah caught most of them. "The lady ahead of me. She had a bad ticket. She needed mine. She needed to be with her kid."

"You lied to me!" She pounded the fence with her fist. "You said you were coming. You said!"

Overhead, a guard in one of the watchtowers peered down at her. He lifted a radio to his mouth.

"Get on the shuttle!" Lawrence called. "Go *get on that shuttle!*"

"You *lied to me!*"

Out of the corner of her eye, she saw two guards emerge from a concrete bunker.

She didn't care. She barely knew Larry, this awful man, except that she had decided to trust him. She had hung the last shred of her faith on that promise he made—that they'd make it together.

Life had taken everything else from her—her mother, her father, her home, her future.

She wouldn't let it take this. She wouldn't let it take her *faith*. She'd rather die.

"Get in line," he screamed over the crowd. "Go. Please. Please."

Tears blurred her vision. White streaks filled the corners of her eyes as guards grabbed her and pulled her, screaming, away from the fence.

"You have to let him in," she babbled. "You have to let him in. He's with me. He's supposed to come. He has a tag—"

"If I have to hear one more screaming brat today, I'm going to shoot somebody," one of the guards grunted, dragging her from the fence. "God damn *bitch—*"

"What's the trouble, Private?"

The two guards turned to face a new man strolling over the asphalt. He wore a white lab coat that flapped in the breeze, shining white in defiance of the grime that stained all the other uniforms. The soldiers straightened, saluting as he approached.

"Nothing to worry about, Professor. Just another sob story—"

"I can trade for him." Sarah spat out the words before she understood what she was saying. "I have something you want. He's supposed to come, and I can trade."

The young doctor stuck his hands in the pockets of his clean white coat and looked down at Sarah, eyebrows arched. "Can you, now?"

"Vic—" One of the guards started to sigh, but the man silenced him with a raised finger.

Jaeger wrenched her arm, and at a curious nod from the man in the coat, the soldiers allowed her to rip off her pack and rifle through it. The little tardigrade reached toward the light as she opened the flap, but Sarah couldn't afford to draw attention to it right now. Whispering a silent *sorry, baby*, she shoved the squirming body aside and dug through the pack until her shaking fingers closed around something hard.

She stood, shoving the stacked motherboards into the man's arms. The guards started to shift, holding her back, but the professor stayed them with a hand. He frowned down at the boards. "What is this?"

"I pulled them from gene therapy tanks in a government building not far from here," Sarah lied. "They were growing clones. They were growing immortals and all kinds of stuff."

"Kid's full of shit, sir," the second soldier grunted. "That looks like junk she pulled out of a dumpster."

The professor thoughtfully frowned as he turned the motherboards over. Slowly, he crouched until he was eye-level with Sarah. He reached forward, and before she could flinch away, he pulled Hank's dog tag out from beneath her shirt.

"Little young to be in the Marines, aren't you?"

"He died," Sarah whispered. "He was a friend. Of a friend."

"A friend of a friend?" He turned the tag over in fine, slender fingers and studied the small words stamped into the back. "In the…Nosferatu division." His lip quirked in what might have been a smile or a sneer. "Oh, they never did have a knack for subtlety, did they?" His pale gaze cut to the side, focusing on the line of people pressed against the fence far behind them.

Then he looked back at Sarah. He let the tag drop to dangle against her chest. "Your pale friend back there. Was he part of that Nosferatu division as well?"

Sarah had no idea what *Nosferatu* meant. She had no idea if Larry and the other soldier had been in the same division.

But she had some idea of what this man in the clean coat wanted to hear, so she nodded.

"Well, that settles things, doesn't it?" The man stood, slipping the motherboards into one of his pockets as he nodded to the guards. "Escort the little miss to her seat. Then send somebody to fetch our esteemed guest out there. We can't let someone like him go to waste."

"*Sir,*" the first soldier gritted. "We're already approaching maximum carrying capacity—"

The man in the clean coat shrugged. "Do it anyway, Shel." He turned and walked away. Over his shoulder, he added, "I'll offload some of my golf clubs to make room for him."

Golf clubs? Sarah didn't know if the man had been joking or not. Either way, he carried with him an air of someone who didn't care that the planet was dying…that people were dying. If this was the example of what the new world was, of what the fleet was, Sarah would have to do something about it.

The first soldier pointed at a seat before turning to her.

His face softened, and Sarah saw a man who had some humanity in him. Not like the other one.

The soldier forced a smile before leaning in close and saying in a soft tone, "So you made it, kid. What are you going to do now that you're part of the fleet?"

Sarah looked around. If this was what "making it" looked like, she had a long road in front of her. She returned the soldier's gaze with a look of determination. "Who's responsible for making things better?"

The soldier blinked, swallowing his surprise at the words of this little girl. "I think that's on the captain to do that."

"Then that's what I'm going to be. The captain."

AUTHOR NOTES RAMY VANCE
AUGUST 25, 2021

Bunny Banshee. That's what she is. We had wanted a baby girl, but a Bunny Banshee is what we got.

In other words, my little girl is loud. Devastatingly so.

Now don't get me wrong. She's happy. These aren't cries of anger or frustration. She's not crying or lamenting some great wrong.

She's happy.

And when she's happy, she's loud.

Her mother and I try to reason with her. But how do you reason with an 18-month-old? It would be easier to fight the wind.

Sometimes when we go out, our Bunny Banshee will express joy over the most random things.

The steam from an espresso machine is met with a cry of joy, causing the barista to drop the mug.

A particularly shaggy dog is greeted with a cheer that causes the creature to howl in reply.

A similar aged toddler is met with a war chant that sends said toddler aghast with fear.

And with each outburst, her mother and I shake our head, silently wondering if she'll ever outgrow these eruptions.

Now the story I'm going to tell is an…uhhh…extension of my Die Again to Save the World author notes. Those of you who read it will note the 'repeat' of the same picture. And for those of you who haven't read it, Grab it today 12

OK – now that my shameless plug is over…

We went hiking/camping. I strapped Bunny Banshee in a carrier backpack and up we went, not realizing that a storm was coming in.

At the top, we were greeted by strong gusts of wind, rain and an intense, rolling fog (and by intense, I mean that we couldn't see more than 10 yards in front of us).

My Bunny Banshee loved it. I, and many of the others at the top, were less than enthused. We were on a trail, so we weren't worried about getting lost. But falling was a real concern.

With Bunny Banshee crying out in joy, she became my rallying cry as I descended the mountainside. With every unsure step I took, and half fall we had, she bellowed in laughter, spurring me forward. (She reminded me of Captain Dan raging against the storm in Forrest Gump.)

She couldn't have been happier. I was her chariot and she was a Valkyrie charging forward into battle. Her laughter reminding me of how joy can be found in the most uncomfortable of situations.

When we made it to the bottom, more than a dozen fellow hikers came up to us and high-fived my little Bunny Banshee. Seems her cries had done more than just spur me forward. It had served as a fog horn for others, with more than one hiker telling me that every time she cried out, they chuckled.

A chuckle that encouraged them as well.

Now when my Bunny Banshee cries out, I remember that hike, her courage and how inspiration can come in the tiniest, and loudest, of creatures.

AUTHOR NOTES MICHAEL ANDERLE
SEPTEMBER 9, 2021

First, thank you for not only reading this story but these author notes in the back as well.

I'm presently in Colorado Springs, Colorado. For those that don't know, it is the location of the Air Force Academy and not very far from NORAD (Cheyenne Mountain, where you usually see Hollywood do underground strategic command scenes.)

If you are interested, here is the interesting part (not where I am; I'm in a Homeward Suites room writing author notes and getting ready to drive to Denver.)

> https://www.visitcos.com/things-to-do/history-and-heritage/landmarks/cheyenne-mountain-colorado-springs-learn-about-cheyenne-mountain-norad/

I am on an author road trip with collaborator and best friend Craig Martelle (who is in the room next to me working on a book. You can take time to travel, but you can't take time away from working the business if you are an indie writer/publisher.)

Similar to Ramy's travel up to the mountain when unexpected weather hits, you never know what each day might bring you when you are a publisher like me. Perhaps you need to do a meeting at 11:30 at night to match up with someone in Eastern Europe to discuss how you can publish your books more effectively there.

His story of the bunny banshee was entertaining, yet I felt the fear and could live the steps as a father worried about any wrong step when your child is hurt.

The child is screaming in delight, trusting that the universe and Dad have her back. You know what?

She was right.

Ramy had her back.

Now, she will forever be the bunny banshee who kept them safe on the mountain.

The t-shirt should be coming, and if it isn't, please annoy the hell out of Ramy in the reviews until he makes it happen.

I look forward to talking to you in the next book!

Ad Aeternitatem,

Michael Anderle

OTHER BOOKS BY RAMY VANCE

Other Middang3ard Books

Never Split The Party (01)
Late To the Party (02)
It's My Party (03)
Blue Hell And Alien Fire (04)

Death Of An Author: A Middang3ard Novella

Dark Gate Angels
Dark Gate Angels (01)
Shades of Death (02)
The Allies of Death (03)
The Deadliness of Light (04)

Dragon Approved
The First Human Rider (01)
Ascent to the Nest (02)
Defense of the Nest (03)

Nest Under Siege (04)
First Mission (05)
The Descent (06)
Sacrifices (07)
Love and Aliens (08)
An Alien Affair (09)
Dragons in Space (10)
The Beginning of the End (11)
Death of the Mind (12)
Boundless (13)

Other Books by Ramy Vance

Mortality Bites Series
Keep Evolving Series

BOOKS BY MICHAEL ANDERLE

Sign up for the LMBPN email list to be notified of new releases and special deals!

https://lmbpn.com/email/

For a complete list of books by Michael Anderle, please visit:

www.lmbpn.com/ma-books/

CONNECT WITH THE AUTHORS

Connect with Ramy

Join Ramy's Newsletter

Join Ramy's FB Group: House of the GoneGod Damned!

Connect with Michael

Website: http://lmbpn.com

Email List: http://lmbpn.com/email/

https://www.facebook.com/LMBPNPublishing

https://twitter.com/MichaelAnderle

https://www.instagram.com/lmbpn_publishing/

https://www.bookbub.com/authors/michael-anderle

Manufactured by Amazon.ca
Bolton, ON